Hope you all have a really enjoyable Read!

ARTHUR'S ARK

Marion Athorne

2011

MARION ATHORNE AND OSBERT NORMAN-WALTER

Other titles in the Merlyn's Legacy Trilogy

Book 1: Wizard's Woe
Book 2: Merlyn's Heir
Book 3: Arthur's Ark

Also by Marion Athorne
The Glass Slipper

Published by Green Dragon Books

ISBN 978-0-9565563-2-5

Cover illustration by Imogen Hallam

Prepared and printed by:

York Publishing Services Ltd
64 Hallfield Road
Layerthorpe
York YO31 7ZQ
Tel: 01904 431213

Website: www.yps-publishing.co.uk

To my father
The greatest weaver of tales I ever knew

ACKNOWLEDGEMENTS

There are a number of people whose help and encouragement I would like to acknowledge, but especially my sister Sheila, whose unfailing enthusiasm nerved me to take the apparently presumptuous step of rewriting someone else's story. I would also like to thank my Wise Readers: grandson Edward, friends Alan, Peggy and Susan with the initial efforts, and pay tribute to all my family's patience. Also to Shirley Hamilton and to Editor Sheila MacKenzie for their insights, suggestions and plain hard work needed for proof-reading. And pay tribute to Carole Millin, Class Leader for Sutton Coldfield's U3A (University of the Third Age) Creative Writing Group for her enthusiasm and inspiration which has taught me so much, and to the expert and professional help of Cathi Poole and Clare Brayshaw of York Publishing Services team. Finally, and not least, my thanks to Imogen Hallam, artist and illustrator, who created such a fantastic cover.

ABOUT THE AUTHORS

Osbert Norman-Walter, born January 23rd 1900 in Lewisham, London, was the son of an actor Thomas Walter, (who toured with one of seven theatre companies in the late 1800's playing the title role of *Charlie's Aunt* by Brandon Thomas). Osbert, the youngest of four children, grew up an idealist who shared the concept of the *Woodcraft Folk* with its founder Leslie Paul. He went on to become a writer, playwright, journalist, and Astrological Consultant *Seginus* of the *News of the World* (1937 – 39)

Osbert conceived the first part of a fantasy romance *Wizard's Woe* in his early twenties but could find no publisher. The next two parts were not attempted until over thirty years later, but reflect the maturity, sophistication and humour gained over the intervening years. On his death in 1974, he left his daughter an unfinished manuscript of over a million words which she re-edited, cut, and revised, and subsequently published the first book of the trilogy (84,000 words) in 2009 with *ideas for writers*, Dave Haslet. The second book, *Merlyn's Heir* (94,000 words) was published by Green Dragon Books, August 2010, and now the last *Arthur's Ark* (85,000 words) in 2011. The whole trilogy of *Merlyn's Legacy* preceded Tolkien's *Lord of the Rings,* and is a story that finds rapport with teenagers to nonagenarians.

CONTENTS

PROLOGUE

When Diana We'ard became conscious, she knew something terrible had happened but couldn't think what – only that it had blown her whole world apart. Yet she lived; although frightened at being unable to account for finding herself in a giant-sized car with the huge body of a man on her right slumped over the restraint of a seat belt. She, herself, lay sprawled across the lap of a woman as enormous as the man. Splashes of blood and the pebble-like glass of a shattered windscreen lay everywhere, whilst a continuous note blared with deafening urgency from somewhere nearby. She scrambled to her feet clinging to the bloodied material of the woman's dress, as she sought a way of escape from the nightmare.

Above her, and somehow even above the noise, a light voice called: 'It's alright, darling, we can get out this way.'

She looked up. Someone, slim, golden skinned, distinctly feminine, and only nine-inches long and naked, lay along the top of the dashboard,.

Diana stood, tiptoe, to reach the slender hand that stretched down her. 'I can't,' she said.

'Try jumping.'

'But I'm standing on someone!' she said, shocked.

'They won't feel a thing. Try.'

To Diana's surprise, she found the jump effortless. She had no need of the other's help either, but nevertheless discovered her hand held fast with the other getting to their feet.

'I can still remember *who* I am, and it wasn't either of them,' her helper said in a voice tinged with wonder and pointing to the two bodies. 'Nor was it the other driver–'

Diana tugged at her hand. 'It's coming back to me. I was – I *am* her! And that's – that's my husband Humphrey. Please, *please,* let go – I can't stay here!'

The clasp tightened. 'Diana dear, of course you can't! Come – we'll go together.' Suiting action to words, and still keeping a firm hold, her companion leapt from the empty windscreen to the ground taking Diana with her.

Like the graceful, effortless jump, Diana's sprint to put the scene out of sight behind them seemed to skim the ground and, calmed now by the other's self-possession, she began to realise how alive she felt and to marvel at the world in which she now found herself; trees and plants glowing with life and vibrant colour and glistening with jewel-like drops of recent rain. Snowberry that had escaped into the wild had formed thickets in which their small bell shaped pink flowers chimed in the slow movement of a faint breeze.

Diana pulled her companion to an abrupt halt, pushing aside a strand of golden hair that fell across her face as the rest flowed and settled around her like a mantle. She had brought them to a halt beneath a Cherry plum. Sunbeams slanting through the branches burned its scarlet fruit to brilliant gems that spangled the open crown of the tree's head and gesturing limbs like some elderly smiling giant.

'Everything's so beautiful!' she exclaimed in an awed whisper.

'It's *real* real,' the other assured her. 'This is what we can't see as mortals.'

Waves of exquisite joy thrilled through Diana's being and a new wonder struck her. 'I'm not even out of breath with all that running!' she said. 'In fact, am I breathing at all

– or is it just my imagination?' Then a more urgent question compelled her eyes to seek those of her companion. 'Who are you? What's your name?'

The other stood silent a moment before saying in a quiet voice: 'I was – I am Ann – Ann Singlewood – and I *shouldn't* remember that–'

Diana seized on her name. 'Ann, are we breathing?'

She laughed. 'Dear one, we don't *need* to!'

'Am I dead?'

'Do you feel dead?'

'I've never felt more alive in my life before–!' Diana broke off to stare at her companion with a sudden realisation of how she had identified herself. 'You said "Ann Singlewood" – but that's White Wand's name!'

Ann's eyes widened. 'How would you know that?'

'Myrddin Black wrote all about her in *Wizard's Woe* and *Merlyn's Heir*.'

It appeared that Ann had had never heard of Myrddin Black: '…I remember *Wizard's Woe*, because August left it to me to read before he died in mortality and came back here as Black Wand,' she said.

When Diana explained that Humphrey had told her all about his meeting with Myrddin Black, she saw light dawn in Ann's eyes.

'I never knew,' she said, looking wistful as she added: 'There was *so* much my partner Wand never told me. I wonder if I shall ever see him again.'

'We should.' Diana could be definite on that point. 'He didn't go to Dragga. He's still out here *somewhere*.'

'But that would have dishonoured the pact with Dragga – and that could be why I can't I remember any life as a mortal.' Her voice had taken on a slight tinge of concern. 'I took the bane. I *should* have forgotten that I was Ann *or* White Wand. I should be remembering the mortal I must have become *and* my new name – the same way you do.'

'Well, you're here with me now after the crash,' said Diana. 'And if you know you weren't the other driver, it could mean you might have been incarnating in the baby I was expecting?' Her words began to quicken again in almost disjointed sentences: 'If it – the baby – were a girl, we were going to call it – you – Lindsey. Humphrey was rushing me to hospital with a threatened miscarriage–'

'That's a relief!'

But Diana hurried on: '–What a mercy we left the other two children at home! That oncoming car came round the bend on the wrong side of the road. I wonder if Humphrey *is* still alive. He'd be with us, otherwise, wouldn't he? But no, I remember – when you were White Wand, you said–'

A little furrow had formed between Ann's eyes: 'Come,' she said cutting her short. 'We must to get to the forest–'

'We can't!' Diana stopped, drawing her back. 'I forgot,' she said, with memories now crowding in on her that also threatened to drain again with the rapidity of any mortal dream while she strove to hold the fading images. 'Fire!' She shivered. 'The most awful fire. It destroyed *everything*. The forest is a wasteland. The Weirds flooded!'

Ann shook her head in dismay: 'Oh no, that can't be. We'll have nowhere to go. No one to meet us ...'

*

Even before the pair reached Wychies' Lane, the jagged, blackened trees ahead were plain to view spiking the sky line from a cold desolation of burnt earth and vegetation beneath.

Ann had taken charge in a firm lead though what seemed an endless wreck of wet devastation with a reluctant, almost sobbing Diana trailing behind until they came to where the ruined trees fell away on either side to leave the pair standing over an almost vertical drop that rushed headlong to the water below.

Wychies' Weird and King's, were now joined as one vast stretch of water while, on what still remained of The Wandle itself, lay all the debris and chaos collected and left by a flood.

Ann gazed in distress at the broken bits of blackened branches, empty tins and bottles washed down by the river, all of it covered with what looked like virulent looking grated green ribbon until she realised they were all that remained of 'Dragga's Teeth'. The once deadly reeds that had sliced mortal – and immortal – bodies to shreds also hung in dank looking strips from the lower branches of the fir trees, their trunks coated a dirty grey where the water had risen two feet above normal. Below them on the cliff-side ran a similar demarcation line.

They'll all have been drowned!' she thought, her imagination aghast at images of helpless wiccas and wiccies bobbing and struggling in the rising waters that would have swept them off their feet. She shook the vision away. *Don't be silly,* she told herself. *Fae can't drown.* But reason argued back: *They would have been terribly frightened and disorientated, all the same.* Then allowed herself a wan smile as she remembered how easy it would have been to help the little people laugh and enjoy the novel fun of finding they could catch and ride the sticks and branches that would have been floating by. ... *Wych and Wychy would have rescued and guided them,* she assured herself. *But where had they gone? What had been the words of prophecy?* She searched her memory, taking comfort again just as she had when she first heard the soundless voice. She repeated the prophecy now, her voice soft: 'Behold Merlyn's Heir and Mergyn's daughter and Dragga also. Before Mona's light thrice more has waned, there shall be a passing and a coming, and a desolation within your lands unknown since their beginnings, and Wands all three divided one-and-one-and-one, and Dragga, too, undone, until the One who comes is seen and known by all ...' *The One who comes!* she thought. *That had been Arthur.* And then assured herself: *and that means that wherever he is now, the fae are there safe with him. It can't be anything else. As for Dragga ...* She remembered what her partner had written of his Wych's words after the Wreak had overwhelmed the Wandle. Hadn't he marvelled that The Wandle wasn't still saturated with its presence: 'Perchance it is,' his Wych at the time had answered. 'It had existence over all, did it not?' *How truly she had spoken ...*

Ann looked aside at her companion. Tears streaked Diana's face. The poignancy of the moment for both of them threatened to become intolerable. Remembering her first duty as the Wand she had been, Ann took the fay in her arms, stroking her hair and soothing her. 'All will be well, little one,' she said, although more in faith than with good reason. An idea occurring to her, she led the way along the top of the cliff towards the Spinney. A bridging tree could be seen lying across Wychies Weird to the Wynn and gladness overwhelmed her: *That had to be the way they had escaped!* Amyas would have had felled the tree with *Moldwarp..* She turned as another memory came to mind. *Queen's Glade!* The Bower had been built underground. Dare she *hope* it might have survived ...?

It had. Although burnt to a crisp like a cinder on the outside, the inside lay untouched by the holocaust, and she recognised Nyzor's cabinet with relief. The Royal Vintner's labelled, silver topped, nectars and ambrosias were all of them intact, while beneath them lay several silver bound barrels. It was a wonderful find and Ann took immediate advantage of Nyzor's skills towards restoring Diana's spirits and her own.

With each of them carrying a tiny goblet, she led the way down the spiral staircase to the room below. There they found another great and necessary blessing. A number of faerie robes and cloaks still hung in the Queen's wardrobe with shoes for them both.

To have clothes and the mercy of the Vintner's own specifics lifting them out of the black despair that had threatened to engulf them both; Ann could hardly believe it.

As they sat on the bed together dressing each other's hair with the jewels and tiaras that wiccies loved to wear, they discussed their next step.

'We *can't* be the only ones who have come back since the fire,' Diana said. 'And I remember from what Myrddin wrote in his last book, the sort of thing we have to face outside the forest.'

'I think you may have a clearer memory of that than I have, darling,' Ann said, her eyes wistful. 'My memory *is* still hazy. But we were trying to rescue the incarnated fae. And I remember wolves, too,' she added with a sudden shudder: 'And a war.' She sipped again from the tiny goblet she held in a suddenly trembling hand.

Diana smiled in reminiscence. 'It's funny, I remember the books in detail – but you knew exactly where to find this place. I wouldn't have known where to look. I wonder if all this was left for returning fae like us. Maybe there's even someone who will come to check, and take us to wherever the Weirdfolk have gone. What do you think?'

Ann looked around the room with doubt: 'There's nothing in the way of clothing for wiccas,' she said, adding: 'But I remember Arthur being born here – we could go and look for him?'

Diana jumped up with a little cry of excitement, clapping her hands. 'That *would* be an adventure!'

Ann agreed, but advised that each should look for a pouch to hang on their belts to take small phials of Nyzor's distillations with them.

*

Standing once more outside the mound, they were startled by a sudden rush of wings overhead and looked up to see a mortal sized white owl circling above them. It landed a few feet away, and transformed into a fae sized knight. Distinctively armoured in green, with a breastplate emblazoned with a red dragon, his shield bore the device of a white owl crowned in silver.

The raised visor revealed a face beaming with hearty good humour. 'Hael and Wynn, fair wiccies of the Weird. Behold Gwyn ap Gwyn ap Nudd, Lord of the People of Beauty. I like to think I have happened upon a most opportune moment to be of service …?'

CHAPTER 1

A NEW LEASE

When his Wand of Office refused to return to his hand, Myrddin Black had had to accept that it had cast him away. The rejection still rankled after a timeless interval that had turned out to have been eighteen mortal years as an elfin guardian of a faerie kingdom in the Sussex Forest of Weir. He soon realised, however, that he had been given a new lease of life just when the need had become vital. Unlike his predecessor and those before who had gone to pay their debt to Dragga when the term of their Office had ended, Myrddin had not. He had saved Dragga's roots from destruction before they were swept away by flood, and so freed himself to take on a new role. And his destiny now? He had to find and save the true infant Arthur before Mortleroy, the 'Herod' of Faedom, found the young king first and destroyed him. As for the young 'Arthur' whom he had left lording it over the little kingdom in the forest, he had to be prevented from misleading the fae that he was their true King. It would be disastrous to have *him* declaring himself to be the Saviour of all Faedom!

*

He set off towards Weir Court, his stride quick and purposeful. The full moon's brilliance cast a sharp-edged, ink black shadow before him of the gaunt humanoid form that Myrddin had inherited from Merlyn. The blinding sweep of a car's headlights from a bend in the lane ahead made him step to one side, but not the rabbit that had started to cross. It froze, mesmerised – the next moment flattened. Regrettably unpreventable. But did the driver even care? The white gleam of entrails spilling out against the dark fur and the leak of blood widening into a small pool of shining black both reproached and angered him. He gave the twitching animal the quietus of the magic disguised in his staff, and moved the stilled body to the grass verge. He reflected a moment on the small mortal form that needed blood to live, while his immortal being – and even Merlyn's frame – survived without.

*

The arrangement with the now deceased baronet, Sir Edward We'ard allowed the enchanter the use of a small outhouse in the grounds of the house for privacy to change out of his medieval beggar's robe into a modern sports shirt and trousers that were kept there in a small suitcase. A key to the back-door also lay beneath a loose floorboard.

Once inside the hut, he looked about him for a safe place to leave something small, valuable and invisible. The density of Merlyn's form made the wearer blind to astral objects so Myrddin had no way of seeing or feeling the six-inch long bundle that he nevertheless knew that he carried in his left hand. He needed to leave it somewhere unlikely to be disturbed. Spotting a corner with some old pots robed in moonlit cobwebs promised the short-term hiding place he looked for …

*

He had been typing half an hour or more at his usual frenetic speed when the study door burst open, to frame a middle-aged man in pyjamas and dressing gown who stood looking him up and down with an expression of outraged disbelief.

'And just who the hell do you think you are, making yourself at home in *my* clothes and using *my* typewriter?' he spluttered.

The greeting identified him at once to Myrddin as the new Weir Lord, Sir Humphrey We'ard, Bart., son of the late Sir Edward We'ard.

The wizard rose, with a smile and held out his hand. 'Myrddin Black,' he said. 'And delighted to meet *you*, Sir Humphrey!'

The Baronet's expression turned to one of acute embarrassment. 'Hell – sorry! The old man left a note … I expected – well, I don't know what I expected. He said nothing about your "dropping in" at two in the morning! When do you sleep, in God's name?'

Myrddin apologised. 'Forgive me, your father loaned me the clothes and I forget the mortal need for sleep. My work never seemed to disturb him.'

'I don't mean to sound rude, but knowing my father, he would never have dreamed of saying so if it had!'

'Touché,' said Myrddin said with a wry smile. 'But look, I've more freedom now than when your father and I came to that arrangement. I could limit my visits to when you're not here …?'

A reluctant curiosity seemed to get the better of Humphrey. 'What are you writing?'

'How much do you know of your Wardenship of Weir Forest?' Myrddin asked.

'That it's a prize headache I've inherited from the old man.'

'Well you won't have to worry about it for much longer,' Myrddin replied.

'Oh – why?'

'Because Weir Forest will be gone before the next new moon.'

'Gone?' Humphrey's tone sounded testy. 'What do you mean, gone? You don't *look* as if you're from the Ministry. You know something I don't?'

'Actually, when I asked what you knew of your Wardenship, I meant in terms of the forest's inhabitants …?'

'The legendary little kingdom, you mean? Well, of course I know the myths and legends bit and that the old man took the whole thing really seriously – really did believe that a whole race of little people lived there.'

'But you don't?'

The Weir Lord shifted, looking uncomfortable. 'I'm prepared to carry on the old man's fight for the forest. But that doesn't mean I have to believe there really are fairies at the bottom of the garden, does it?'

'Of course not,' Myrddin reassured him. 'But wouldn't you agree that under the terms of the charter and your inherited title, the little kingdom has a right to expect help from you, its purported guardian? Provided of course that it can communicate that need to you.'

Humphrey waved a hand in agreement. 'Put like that – and *if*, as you say, there were some communication to that effect – then yes, I suppose so. But damn it, man, how do you prove such a thing?'

Myrddin held out his left hand, showing a thumb encircled by a thick gold ring set with an amethyst inscribed with small wedge-shaped characters. Humphrey switched on the main light to observe it more closely.

'If I take the ring off,' Myrddin said, 'I shall disappear. These clothes will be a heap on the floor and the ring will be beside them. You can pick them up, examine them, look at the ring … then, when you put it down again, just say the word and I shall come back into this shape *through* the ring. You will have to excuse me, though, I shall be naked. Merlyn's usual apparel in his human form is in your outhouse. It's rather ancient which is why your father loaned me your clothes, so I could look more … normal.'

Humphrey stared at him for a moment, and then gave a resigned sigh. 'All right, I believe you … not that I want to,' he added. 'I've struggled against it all my life, but there comes a time I suppose when one can't go on denying something that's been ingrained in the family for so long. Pity really,' he went on, sounding regretful. 'I quite enjoyed believing it was our particular brand of upper class lunacy.' He moved to the drinks cabinet, opened it, and peered in.

'What's yours?' he asked.

'Brandy?'

'Cognac all right?'

'Thanks.'

Humphrey chose a stiff whisky for himself. 'How do you do it then … this thing with the ring?' he asked, handing his guest the liqueur. 'Where are you when you're not "in the flesh" so to speak?'

'Invisible and rather small, Sir Humphrey. Just a nine-inch-tall elf magician rejoicing in the title of Merlyn's Heir.'

'And your writing?' prompted Humphrey. 'You still haven't told me.'

'Ah, my writing is a record of the little kingdom of the Forest of Three Weirs, for whom your family has been responsible; keeping it safe from incursion for hundreds of years. I hope to leave the record with your family as a token of what the Weir Lord's guardianship has meant to us while we were there – rather like the *Book of Amaranthus* the Marquis of Rules sent your father.'

'Ah, yes. He left a note telling me I should read the thing before returning it. He also left a ton of other stuff that I haven't even begun to sort yet.' His expression became quizzical. 'You say the little people are leaving?'

'Inevitably, Sir Humphrey. The forest is doomed and I have to find a new home for them where they will be safe once again. And not just them; there are others who need rescuing too.'

'So how can I help?'

Myrddin shrugged, saying: 'Quite frankly, I have no idea as yet. The whole thing seems a bit like transplanting a cobweb – make a frame, I suppose, and attach it point by point ...'

'Then let's be practical,' said Humphrey, his tone brisk. 'My wife and I live in London and the gardener will be keeping an eye on this place while we're not here. I'll leave instructions that it's "open house" to you at any time. Then, when you need to get in touch with me, you can use the phone; I'll leave a number where I can be contacted. Diana and the children will be arriving shortly for father's funeral tomorrow. They'll be staying on until Sunday, but I have to leave straight after the service.' He fell silent a moment, then nodded towards the manuscript piled on the desk. 'Is that it? Can I read it?'

'I would be delighted if you did, Sir Humphrey. It's only the first section of the whole story, but complete in itself. It is for you and yours ...' He got to his feet to look around the room. 'And if I might have another look at the Book of Amaranthus, please?'

'Certainly, should be around here somewhere ...'

With the Weir Lord's departure, Myrddin completed the manuscript for *Merlyn's Heir*, leaving it in a neat pile on the desk for his host to read, and took up the Treatise on the Faerie Realm that Humphrey had found for him. He leafed it through until he found the heading *On Faerie Pathways*. He had noted the chapter when he first read the book, but had no time then to read it; having to concentrate on a description of Faerie kins he had never heard of that lived beyond the Forest of Weir. Now that he was thinking of travelling through their realms, it seemed advisable to read whatever Amaranthus had to say on the subject. The monk had been right about everything else he had written.

Writing from a mortal point of view, the discourse began by saying that faerie paths were best avoided; that wherever they were detected they should never be obstructed by any building – even the corner of a house cutting into or across one could result in huge misfortune for the owner until he either cut off the offending part or pulled his house down. When Amaranthus then went on to explain that such 'paths' were all part of a fast-track faerie travel system, Myrddin supposed it made sense. As a fay himself, he didn't go through solid objects, but rather around them. He could imagine that finding one's high speed route with an unexpected block could be frustrating at best and quite dangerous at worse. But how to identify these 'pathways'? From the monk's account a man should signify where the four corners of his intended building would lie by marking each with a small stone on top of a large one and then, if nothing got disturbed or thrown aside in the night, it was safe to go ahead with the structure. Either that or, if you were suffering severe bad luck, you consulted a wise-woman who might advise which corner of your structure needed demolishing. It made Myrddin think of all the road and building programs embarked on by the Ministry of Town and Country Planning that had become accident 'black-spots'. Yet nowadays, who would seriously consider the possibility that their proposal might bisect a faerie pathway running between two ancient sites and thereby invite calamity?

So how could he identify possible pathways himself? He looked for the ordnance survey map which he knew Sir Edward always kept in his study, and found two small red-bound inch-to-a-mile sheets folded in a drawer of the desk. Both were contoured historical maps of East Sussex: one covering the district around Corsham, the other the district of Lewes. Printed in 1898 they showed every church, village, farm, road, lane, pathway and track. There were no straight lines, but then he hadn't expected any. He had to look for a high point, and the highest was Caburn Hill on the Lewes Downs. He wanted a commanding view of the surrounding countryside, and Caburn appeared a good one.

He folded the maps and, about to close the Treatise, paused. Had he checked that he hadn't missed anything in his excitement over the trackways? He had. The next sentence leapt out at him: ... *it is also recognised among these races of the faerie kin that they may also be known to each other through the eye of the horse* ...

The eye of a horse! The sentence sparked a vivid memory for Myrddin. In his mortal life, he had once seen a boy left in charge of a horse. A farmer had ridden into to the village and had given the reins to the boy to hold while he attended his errand. Myrddin remembered how the boy had eyes only for the horse and had stood rapt in silent worship for the great animal, gazing up at its powerful outline lit by the sun's brilliance behind it – until a car had backfired. He remembered how the horse had thrown up its head in terror, its eyes brown and wide showing their whites, and the boy's hand reaching up lovingly, stroking the animal's nose and the horse calming, lowering its head to the boy's unconscious but masterful touch.

Myrddin shook his head dismissing it as an association of ideas; a Celtic memory, the ancient dependence on the strength, power and endurance of a horse. *And something else* –whispered a voice within him: *their likeness to dragons ...!*

Returning to the outhouse, he stripped off, packing Humphrey's shirt and trousers into the small suitcase, re-clothed himself with Merlyn's brown habit, and removed the thumb ring. To all intents and purposes any observer might then think he had vanished into thin air.

Resuming his mortally invisible elf form always gave Myrddin a welcome return to a dimension in which the circle of the moon became an enormous blazing likeness to a summer's sun filling him with warmth and elemental joy. Through the open door, the blossom of a tall Mock Orange shrub shone like star-bright Chinese lanterns; the surrounding plants glowing equally with vibrant colour.

Back in a dimension in which he lived and moved at lightning speed, however, he had a lot to do. Ever since he had found and put on Merlyn's ring, living between two time-frames had become an uncomfortable paradox. Mortals might appear to move with ponderous slowness to him but, when he had no connection to it, their time flew with the speed of an express train. It left him with a sense of forever playing 'catch-up' – and that sense of urgency spurred him now.

He had invented a new persona when he left the forest and decided his nine-inch guise should have an eastern flavour. He had therefore changed his previous dove-grey hose and jerkin into a man's pair of loose white salwar trousers; embroidered slippers and a long embroidered tunic; crowning the outfit with an impressively jewelled turban.

Now he had to find a base for operations somewhere near the Forest which posed the question of what form of travel he should use. He could fashion a horse from plasma and ride in search of a place at ground level, or turn himself into a black falcon and look for it in flight. In a faerie world at war, flight appeared the wisest option, and a black falcon the best choice of bird. Who would interfere with a bird as recognisable as a Royal Falcon except Mortleroy's enemies? A horse and rider on the other hand could attract unwelcome attention. It meant leaving his few possessions behind in the outhouse for the moment, but they were retrievable.

He picked up the now visible bundle he had so carefully hidden behind the cobwebbed pots. It held a six-inch-long-sword in a jewelled scabbard – which he believed to be a fake Excalibur – a pair of elfin wrap-a-round shades made of black crystal; a two-inch long tube of scrolls containing all that he had been able to salvage of Merlyn's magic lore, and a small pot. Removing the latter, he retied the bundle and placed it with care back behind the cobwebs, together with the ring, before returning his attention to the pot.

It contained human ectoplasm; its elastic properties would allow him to fashion a black falcon small enough to take into himself, but able to expand to its correct mortal size when he projected it outwards to become the bird. Halfway through the job, however, he changed his mind. *It should really be a golden eagle!* he thought. A daredevil thing to do; he had been shot down the last time he had chosen that particular form. Nevertheless, a certain obstinate audacity to stage a comeback took hold of him. After all, the enemy had seen the eagle torn to pieces by their wolves and wouldn't be on the lookout for it again. And apart from which, an eagle had the keen sight he needed to spot what he wanted.

The moon still blazed in a dawn-brightening sky when he took off and winged his way high over the Sussex countryside towards Caburn.

CHAPTER 2

THE MUNG

Just before Lewes, around twenty miles from the forest as the crow flies, he came across a sight so strange he would have rubbed his eyes in disbelief if he had had hands and not talons: a group of three small ape-like beings racing along the tightrope of a telegraph wire!

Although bigger and bulkier than the nine-inch high Weirdfolk, seeing them from the air put them into greater perspective. Covered in shaggy hair, the apparitions were moving their round-shouldered and lumbering-looking bodies with incredible speed along the topmost of the wires running beside a secondary road from Lewes to Hurstpierpoint. More than his amazement, however, alarm bells rang at seeing the foremost carrying the naked wraith of a half born fay under one muscular arm while on the road below a pack of voracious-looking grey wolves were racing along the grass verge to overtake them. The fact that the wolves were astral yet of mortal size, did not surprise him. He knew how to make his own creations increase or decrease in size depending on what he wanted of them. These were terrifying the monstrosities on the wires above them as much as Myrddin's own appearance.

With his first thought to rescue the fay, he swooped; talons spread for murder, only to check in mid-flight when he realised the frightened waif already lay between the devil and a very long drop. If the ape-thing let its burden fall under his attack the wolves would have it.

The 'apes' looked up at his downward plunge and put on an even greater spurt. He hovered above them, consumed with frustration, wondering how he could affect a rescue. If he could only get rid of the wolves for a few minutes, he might be able to snatch the half born.

He made another swoop, but this time diving under the telephone wires to hover a few feet above the animals on the ground. They leapt for him at once, snarling and snapping at each other, eager to be first to catch him. He flew in tight circles above them just out of reach until, in a moment, they were scattered all over the road. As the sole object of their attention, he led them further and further away from their first quarry. Simple then to hop over a hedge into a field knowing they would break through after him. With plenty of room to manoeuvre, he soon had them spread in all directions, although he almost lost a couple of his longest wing-feathers to a pair of snapping jaws whose distance he misjudged.

The brutes were swift and quick, and he found that trying to separate one out from the rest more difficult than he imagined. In the end, he dizzied them to the extent that when he shot into the air, they all came to a halt where they were just to stare up at him.

He dived again straight on to the back of a single member. At lightning speed his hooked beak removed the beast's eyes with two strikes and he flew free before the rest closed in. They tore the eyeless one to pieces between them and feasted.

Knowing it wouldn't take them long to finish their meal, Myrddin streaked aloft again to look for the ape-things – and found them half a mile ahead standing motionless on the telegraph wires looking back.

It seemed a silly thing to do, wasting valuable time. *Still, their funeral,* he thought. In majestic flight, he sailed towards them and saw too late the method in their madness. They had stopped beside a farm, the nearest building of which still lay quite a way from the wires – but Myrddin miscalculated. Just because there seemed no way that such cumbersome creatures could make it from the wires to the roof and possible shelter during his dive, did not mean they couldn't – and they did with a leap and a bound – and moments to spare and scrambled from the rooftop to the ledge of a small high window to squeeze in to the room beyond through a broken corner of its glass pane.

The hole being too small for him, he flew around the building looking for another entrance and found none. It presented a small, disused stable with both half-doors at one end closed and barred, and the only other window intact and shut. It seemed clear his quarry had reconnoitred the place even before he came in sight and were now snug in its hayloft.

Perched on the roof ridge, he began to feel some respect for the grotesque creatures. Seeing that they were so at home above ground, it appeared probable they been more worried about him than they were about the wolves. However, that didn't explain them, or the chasing wolves, and he had to move before the wolves saw him. It seemed tricky but, shrinking himself to a fae-sized bird before flying off a little way, he made a swoop at the window with sufficient speed to throw him onto the windowsill so that he stood upright at the moment of his transformation. He had to catch hold of the broken pane for balance, however, and two terrified eyes in a now large hairy face flicked away from its other side. Crawling through, he saw the owner's bulky form dwarfed as it scuttled for cover behind a mortal sized bale of hay in a far corner.

He jumped to the dusty floor, stayed still and thought. If he went for their hiding place, their incredible agility might well enable them to escape and be out through the window again before he could stop them. So he stayed silent and unmoving, waging a war of nerves instead although not for long.

'Stop breathing down my neck, you blasted orang-utan,' came a voice, sharp with fear and irritation 'God knows, I'm scared enough of you lot, but this hole and corner existence is getting on my wick. God, what a nightmare! Why don't I wake up and be shot of the lot of you?'

It sounded promising. The half born still had his mortal memory. From among the guttural whisperings, the fay's voice went on: 'Stop tickling my ear, Frankenstein. If you've got something to say, say it intelligently. What …? You're joking. There's never anybody out there like me. And you want me to call out to this person that I'm a what …? One of the Weirdfolk? Well, I'm certainly *feeling* weird, all right. Wait till I tell the family in the morning – what a nightmare! What's that …? Oh, come off it, why should I play your silly games? Why don't *you* talk to him yourself if it's so important? Me – I'm getting out of here with a header out of that window – that should wake me up.'

'It won't, you know, little brother,' Myrddin called out at once to overcome the scuffling he could hear going on behind the hay.

'Who said that?'

'Merlyn's Heir. Tell your friends that I am the ever-living wizard of the Forest of Weir which Merlyn made. Tell them that I do not destroy needlessly. Remind them that it was I with my magic who saved you all from the wolves.' He smiled at the suddenly excited but indistinguishable whispers that greeted this, then called sternly: 'Come out, each one of you children of hair and hide. Deliver to me the one who is of my kind, unharmed, and no harm shall come to you. This I promise in Mona's name and upon the Sceptre of Merlyn which I bear.'

After a few moments they came, the astonished half born first and the three ape-like creatures cowering behind him. All four froze, however, as the sound of the wolf pack drew near and raced by outside. No sooner had it begun to die away, however, than it returned to investigate the farmyard. No one moved as the frightful howling came closer to the stable and encircled it before moving away as if to examine the other buildings. Minutes passed before the noise returned for a brief moment and then retreated, dying away to the north.

During the wait, Myrddin's careful estimation of the terrified creatures before him told him they were not plasma creations like the wolves, but innate and intelligent beings and, hard to believe, of faerie origin. He beckoned the half born to him. The fay responded tentatively and in obvious awe, to find himself enveloped by the wizard's embrace and with healing words sounding in his ears.

'Hael and Wyn, little brother. Be at peace, the nightmare is at an end ...' Touching him with his sceptre, Myrddin lowered the then unconscious elf gently to the floor, before he addressed the others kindly: 'Hael and wyn, strangers. Do not be frightened. Come, be seated here before me.' But they shrank back, huddled together at the far end of the loft, their fingers in their mouths, trembling. Myrddin made no effort to insist, but went on to ask them who they were and why they were so afraid of him.

After a moment, one took his fingers from his mouth: 'They call us Mung, lord,' he quavered, his voice hoarse and rasping. 'But we are High Travellers. We dare not come near you because it is against the law. Your beauty and your magic are too terrible to be approached by such lowly as we.'

'Where do you live?'

'We live everywhere and nowhere, lord wizard, because of the curse that made us what we are. We dare not rest for more than a little in one place.'

Myrddin sat down crossed legged on the floor. 'Be seated, High Travellers,' he invited. They hesitated then sidled forward to squat at what they appeared to think a safe distance but still nervous and shifting about.

Intense curiosity made Myrddin frame his questions with care: 'What is your tradition? Who cursed you?'

The trio looked at each other, making signs between them with their hands until two of them gave vigorous nods and the first speaker answered in a low whisper: 'O lord and mighty wizard, we are the elders of our tribe and we alone are told this ... 'Tis said ...' And the speaker lowered his voice still further; ''Tis said ...' there again he paused as if doubting the wisdom of saying anything more at all, then crawled forward before crouching midway and faltering in an even fainter voice that Myrddin had to strain to hear: '...'Tis said that ... that once we Mung were not Mung ... that we ...' he broke off, shrinking back, his eyes going from side to side, looking terrified he had said too much already.

'I believe what you say – that you were not always Mung,' Myrddin said. 'Do not be afraid, friend Traveller. Your secret will not escape these walls. Speak on.'

'It is said even ...' continued the grotesque figure, shielding his face behind his hand, 'that once, long, long ago we were even like – oh forgive me, Great One, I hardly dare say it ...'

'That you were once in form and feature even like me?' Myrddin asked, hazarding an educated guess.

'You *know*, O Great One?' The hand fell away showing the simian mouth gaping in relief and bewilderment. 'You *know* this is true?'

'I may even be able to prove it,' Myrddin answered, an idea occurring to him. 'But first you must tell me, why you were cursed, and who cursed you?'

This opened the floodgates. The ungainly creatures told him how once, long, long ago the race of Mung were not known as Mung but Mabyn, a very old and pure race who had once ruled over all Brython – this Myrddin knew to be the old name for Britain. But new races had come, they said, and the Mabyn retreated to under-earth strongholds because they did not want to fight against their own kind in defence of their possessions. Then a Great King had come who promised to restore their ancient freedoms in return for their fealty, and that had been a golden age but did not last. Enemies had conspired against the Great King who had died in a terrible battle, and after it another king had come, an evil king who swore vengeance on all who had fought on the side of the Great King. By treachery and magic, he had hurled all their Dragons to the ground, save one, the Great Green Dragon of the South whom Great Merlyn had made to vanish into safety with the Weirdfolk. The rest of Faedom enslaved, and tortured into horrible and pitiable appearance, were beset with wolves and hawks so that they were separated from their other kins and kinds. The Mung had taken to the trees and, later, to the high wire-roads to evade their enemies and could travel further than they had ever done before, although unable to rest for long for fear of the wolves finding them. When this evil king now styling himself King of all Brython, had discovered how the High Travellers were escaping him, he had set evil birds of prey above to seek them out and destroy them.

'Hawks and black falcons?' Myrddin asked, inwardly horrified as well as thankful he had discarded his first choice of flying form.

The old mung shuddered. 'Indeed, lord wizard. It is a terrible fate to find yourself between the tooth below and the talon above. That is why we fled from you, not knowing that you were the very person we were on our way to find.'

'To find *me*!'

'Ah yes, lord wizard. A dove came with tidings from the Queen of the Weirdfolk to all the races of the Faerie Kin that

Great Arthur would be born again. So when we chanced on your half born, we took him, thinking we could ask him to bear our humble plea to yourself, lord wizard of the Weirdfolk.'

'But didn't the bird say that the Weirdfolk were doomed themselves?' asked the Wychy, realising Mergyn must have instigated the messenger when she had possessed Queen Gwen. He hadn't programmed his own dove messengers to say anything about Arthur.

'It did, lord wizard, but what can we do? You see how we are and so we humbly beg that we might see Great Arthur when he is born?'

And much good could that'll do you, thought Myrddin, knowing that his own fabrication of the child Arthur could never come up to scratch for these poor wretches. He led the conversation away from the subject by asking who the evil king was.

But they didn't know. They could only repeat their tradition. It said this; it said that. And everywhere the king's emissaries were pinning down the elfin communities into restricted reservations; preventing them from ever communicating with one another. Of such were the timid Wellsprite, a thin spidery and sharp faced people with claw-like hands and webbed feet – without even hair to cover them! And the troll-like dwellers in caves who looked more brutish even than Mung. They drew a picture of endless misery and fear for every fay throughout the land outside Weir Forest. All of them living in the same hope that had inspired the Mung: that one day the Great King would come again and restore the oppressed to all their lost freedoms and perfections.

He found it almost unbelievable and certainly depressing to learn that while the Weirdfolk had been living in sheltered bliss, the rest of Faedom had suffered like this. Now that he knew the situation, he could not ignore it. The Weirdfolk owed it to the Mung, and the rest of their kind; the Wellsprite, Cave-wight and Troll.

He said at last, 'I must return to my forest with my half born, High Travellers. But I will be back. Please remain hidden here and wait for me–'

'But, lord ...' they faltered, clinging to each other in panic, and Myrddin remembered their fear of staying for any length of time in one place.

'Why be afraid?' he asked. 'If you speak the truth, then the ordeal of waiting will be nothing compared to seeing your truth revealed. I will return as quickly as I can ...'

He wished he felt as assured of fulfilling the promise as he had sounded. He now had to somehow beg, borrow or steal the Wealspring Cup from the forest and could not imagine its guardians ever allowing their most holy of holies out of their sight. In the same position, he'd never tolerate its removal himself.

CHAPTER 3

GAWAIN

Landing his eagle form just outside the Forest of Weir, Myrddin laid the still unconscious fay on the ground before morphing back to his newly acquired eastern appearance. He hadn't expected the need to return to the forest so soon and had to improvise a further disguise. With no time to reinvent his clothing, he seized some plant plasma, layered his chin and forehead then combed it through with fingers and sceptre into a flowing white beard and bushy overhanging eyebrows. At least it would provide a focal point and seal the magical impression he wanted …

Sure enough, as soon as he broke through the Veil of Invisibility that surrounded the forest, the web of telepathic communication that bound the fae together rang with an elated note of astonished recognition.

'Am-mar-el-lyn! Am-mar-el-lyn walks the Weal!'

The fae accepted his appearance as the legendary wizard that the Black Wand-that-had-been had once told them about in a story that had come true.

In no time at all he had a bright coloured escort of laughing, dancing wiccas and wiccies with others following in his wake, clapping their hands and singing out the wonderful news.

'Hael and wyn! Hael and wyn! Am-mar-el-lyn has come to visit us. Hael and wyn, Am-mar-el-lyn! Hael and wyn!

Surely he comes with news of King Nebuchadnezzar, and his Queen Aíssa and their baby prince.'

Dreadful wasn't fooled, though. He came charging down the track like an excited puppy greeting its master, which amazed no one. After all, it had been Am-mar-el-lyn who had made him in the first place, and it gave Myrddin a pleasant surprise to find the beast seemed pleased to see him all memory of past affronts apparently forgiven and forgotten.

Then a new cry thrummed over the Forest network: '*Black Wand! Black Wand walks the Weal!*'

The news drew the multi-coloured crowd away from Myrddin to flow towards and around the sudden appearance of a scintillating pillar of forbidding black, before dispersing in all directions to leave their Wychy alone with the wizard. Myrddin knew that Redweird had simply 'wandled' the fae's easily distracted attention away from their visitor to other pursuits, effectively erasing him from their sight and memory. Myrddin had done it many times himself when he had worn that same mantle which, at this moment, betrayed nothing of its new owner's thoughts or feelings being wrapped about him by his crossed arms.

Myrddin wanted to say 'Well done, little brother.' But Redweird was no longer a 'little brother'. As the chosen recipient of the Black Wand of Power, he wore a tall jet crown and a scintillating black cloak known as a Weird, that had acquired a curious red sheen; a glitter that danced in its jet symbols like pin-pricks of fire.

'Hael and wyn, Am-mar-el-lyn ...?' the Wychy said, his tone stern, askance and reserved. 'My people appear to know you well, but that was before my time. I see you come bearing one of ours ...?'

'Hael and wyn, Black Wand,' Myrddin returned courteously. 'I know it is customary for your people to return here of their own accord, but this little brother had been taken prisoner and was in such a state of terror it seemed better I render him unconscious when I rescued him.'

'Then my Wych and I are greatly indebted to you, Am-mar-el-lyn,' returned the Wychy, allowing his Weird to fall free as he took the unconscious fae from him. 'It would be helpful to know what happened. We have only recently learned of the kind of dangers that lie beyond our forest.'

'Willingly, Black One. But I have an urgent mission which I must attend first. You have a cup – the Wealspring cup which heals all who drink from it–?'

'You need the cup?'

The directness of the question took Myrddin aback. 'I do,' he said.

'Then you must come with me to ask of our young King. It is ...' The Wychy's words tailed off as he became abruptly attentive to something that only he could hear. It caused him to listen with a slightly astonished expression before he incline his head with a nod of dutiful acknowledgement and a murmured: 'Yes, my Liege.' His gaze returned to Myrddin. 'I am told you are to be given the cup with all speed.'

It was Myrddin's turn to be surprised, his mind filling with half-formed questions. *How had 'Arthur' known ...? Who might have told ...? Why was he allowing ...?* Then recognised the question that really concerned him: *How is it possible that this creation of mine – my own fabrication – has grown into something so omniscient?* What had happened? It seemed as if someone had swapped *his* creature for a changeling with a mind of its own. And that worried him ... It seemed evil – malignant. He decided it had to be Nemway. He had not been blind to the way she had worked to gain Ann's confidence. *She's behind this manipulation of 'Arthur'. She's turning my puppet to her own use! She's advising him to give me the Cup. She knows the whereabouts of the true Excalibur and will give it to Mortleroy when she exposes 'Arthur' with Omric's sword.* The hurried arrival of a wicca interrupted his train of thought and brought his attention back to the present.

He recognised Honeyball bearing the plain gold cup of the Wealspring which he gave to the Wychy with a bow and traditional greeting: 'Hael and wyn, Black Wand.'

'Hael and wyn, Honeyball.' returned the Wychy, who still had his arms full with the rescued fae. 'You may give the cup to Am-Mer-El-Lyn …'

The ease with which he had gained the cup did not make Myrddin feel particularly grateful. He decided instead that the royal upstart was showing off his ability to make lordly gestures and that all went to prove that he, Myrddin, was the better guardian of the holy thing because *he* would never have permitted it to leave the forest …!

*

Outside the veil of invisibility, he took to the air again as the golden eagle and flew north before any wolves could spot him around the village of Three Weirs. It meant quite a detour before he felt it safe enough to fly south again to where he had left the Mung. All he needed then was water with which to fill the cup. There was a horse trough in the yard, though. He overcame the awkwardness of then having to fly with the filled cup to the windowsill by levitating the cup to it first, flying after it, and then morphing into his own form before crawling in with it through the broken window.

Considering all the effort and risks he had taken, he found it annoying to see the immensity of the hayloft empty until, when he called softly, the three mungs crawled out from their hiding place in the hay and welcomed him humbly.

'Hael and wyn, High Travellers,' he greeted them with relief. 'You have done well to wait for me. You remember what I said about being able to prove your tradition?'

They nodded a mute acknowledgement.

'In the Forest of the Weirdfolk is a spring whose magic waters have the power of granting wishes,' he said, not wanting to share the secret that it was the Chalice itself that healed. 'One of you must take this cup and drink of it, being sure that you desire and wish the thing that is the dearest longing of your heart.'

They huddled together, nervous and undecided as to which of them should dare the honour, so that Myrddin had to choose for them and beckoned their spokesman towards him.

The old mung crept forward and on his knees, holding out a trembling paw. Myrddin had to hold the cup for fear the shaking creature would spill the contents trying to do it himself, so held the paw steady as the contents poured down its owner's gaping mouth.

With a long, long sigh, the mung started to sway on his haunches as if intoxicated and then, before the bolting eyes of his companions, began to shrink and as he shrank, he changed. The hairy hide thinned to nothing and in its place, a new lithe and glowing outline appeared. There still remained an impression of sturdiness not unlike the Gnomes in strength. The head and face, although longer than before but still rather rounded and pleasant to see, reminding Myrddin of Gareth and the flowery description given of the Mabyn in the book of Amaranthus:

Not tall are these Mabyn, but in presence are powerful and agile, and in their countenance is to be seen the quintessence of integrity. These are sober spirits not given to fractious humours or teasing pranks, for builders they are and wondrous architects ...

'Arise, little brother.' Myrddin held out his hand, helping him to stand, and going on to address his bemused companions. 'High Travellers, you see your tradition is true, and I promise that you too will be freed, but not yet. I need you as you are to take your newborn brother back to your kind and to tell them what has happened, for they will not believe it otherwise.' Then he spoke to the mabyn. 'Do you remember your name, little brother?'

'My name?' He frowned a moment, then light dawned in his eyes. 'Yes, I remember!' he cried excitedly. 'I am Gawain! My name is Gawain!'

'Good! Now I would like you, Gawain to show yourself to your brethren secretly. Then go to Weir Forest where you will find Amyas, your King. And you two,' he addressed the mungs, 'you must bring your brethren to the woods of Cyngsfold which are near Weir Forest. Be speedy, speak wisely. Gather and bring news of all contrary marauders and happenings for me to hear when I come. Can you …?' His eyes took in all three of them, ' … will you, do this?'

'We can, and we will, lord wizard.'

'And you know the way?' he asked. 'It's quite a distance.'

'Have no fear for us, lord wizard. We have had need to travel much. We know these places.'

His mind set at rest, Myrddin went to climb out of the window and drew back. Several wolves prowled in the yard below. The watchful mabyn and two fearful mungs guessed a situation that they knew only too well; even when Myrddin explained the care he had taken to avoid it: '… and I saw no wolves,' he ended.

Gawain nodded. 'Even so, lord wizard,' he said, spreading his hands in a resigned manner. 'But who knows what innocent looking crow; hawk or pigeon might be a spy for the usurper? It is the way Mung are hunted by this usurper's people for sport, and you coming here twice in one day …?'

Myrddin took the point. 'I have made the place dangerous for you,' he said with a sigh, then added slowly as an idea came to him. 'There is something I can do about it though, and I don't want you to be afraid.'

Gawain became practical: 'Lord wizard, tell us what it is you will do, then we shall be prepared.'

'Very well, you will see me change into a black falcon–' Hearing this, the two mungs started to shrink away but Gawain, showing new found courage, held them firm and Myrddin continued. 'Hopefully, the wolves will think that Mortleroy has sent his own "eyes and ears" to investigate for himself, and they will go away.'

None of them looked convinced by this, although whether they doubted his magical ability, or its required effect on the wolves, he had no idea. He ejected the shrunken golden eagle, reduced it to formless plasma and as quickly reshaped it with deft fingers into an equally small black falcon. When he saw their expressions alter to watch the process with a kind of horrified fascination, he took care to make it even smaller to ingest. It seemed the only way of stopping them running away to hide.

'Look,' he said when he finished. 'I have put a grey feather here on its breast so in future you will know this one is me.'

CHAPTER 4

THE CHAPEL OF BLUE FOUNTAINS

The way the wolves cringed when he launched himself from outside the window as a full sized mortal black falcon satisfied him greatly. They cowered down, whining and fawning, their bellies to the ground and, seeming to expect some command, he gave it mentally and at full blast: 'GO!' And they fled.

Gawain and the mungs must have been watching to see what would happen for, as soon as the wolves had vanished, they emerged and leapt across to the telephone wires.

Myrddin soared above them, bearing the tiny half-inch size gold cup in one of his talons, until they reached Cyngsfold woods and got lost to sight among its leaves. Flying off to continue his aerial survey for a base, he caught sight of a small white fae-sized hare racing through the grass away from the woods where he had just left the Mung.

Curiosity getting the better of him, he dived and swept the little thing up in mid-bound with his free claw then landed carefully, and morphed back to his elfin shape. As soon as he took the petrified entity out from under his foot to sooth its quivering, he divined a messenger from Nemway – which made the message itself a rather strange one:

'O Mighty Amyas, hero from of old, hear me, Mildgyth, who waits for you at the Chapel of the Blue Fountains. Hear me and none other until I send word again.'

Nemway had a brother called Amyas. *So why is she posing as someone called Mildgyth?* He had no love for the witch, nor did he trust her. Amyas, King of the Mabyn and a friend who had saved his life, made it a matter to investigate, although he felt sure that the so-called 'Chapel of the Blue Fountains' didn't exist, curiosity led him to see where the creature had come from. He therefore set the hare free with instructions to return the way it had come before resuming his falcon shape.

For a moment, it crouched frozen, then turned and bounded off back into the woods. He followed only to see it vanish as quickly as if it had gone down a rabbit hole.

Only hares don't live in rabbit holes! he thought with annoyance. Flying back to where he had seen it disappear, he blinked in amazement at what he saw between the roots of an old oak, thinking: *It isn't possible!* To a mortal it would have seemed just a hole in the roots – if the tree even still existed in that world frame; like many things shattered and ruined by mortals, the original astral counterpart could still exist, unless something destroyed that also. In this case, however, hidden within the great roots, a soft inner radiance outlined a porch carved in early Saxon design with a graceful plume of blue water rising and falling on either side.

Changing back to himself, Myrddin shook out his tunic, adjusted his turban and, after a searching glance all around, entered.

'Dear Lord, save me!' The horrified speaker, who had crossed herself at the sight of him, wore a plain grey gown secured with a white girdle from which hung a rosary, her only adornment. A white wimple enhanced the beauty of slender features and clear amber eyes.

'Hail and wyn ... Mildgyth?' he guessed, and offered courteously: 'Allow me to introduce myself: I am Myrddin, Merlyn's Heir, otherwise known as Am-mar-el-lyn, and Prince of Damascus.'

'A wizard!' she cried, clasping her rosary. 'What have you and I in common that you should visit my humble sanctuary, O worshipper of the Moon?'

'I'm looking for a white hare, fair votary – I believe it ran in here …?'

'This is a sanctuary, wizard, it protects *all* creatures from harm. The hare came and is safely gone.'

'Then please allow me to enter and be converted to your magic, dear Mildgyth, because *I* never saw it leave!'

'If there is any magic in it, it is of God's grace, not of me,' she said severely. 'But enter if you must, Merlyn's Heir, and may you find His peace within this place.'

She led the way, and he followed alert to discover anything that might be untoward or out of place. He had to admit to himself that it all appeared innocent enough. Perhaps Nemway had simply used the nun's name to lure the Mabyn King in this direction.

Tiny even by faerie measurements, the chapel contained no more than a small prayer stand and a crucifix on an alter, but the polished stone walls surrounding them shot up into a carved tracery of a dome so intricate it rivalled the delicate ruins of Fountains Abbey which he had once visited as a mortal in his travels through Yorkshire.

He bowed formally to the crucifix out of respect for Mildgyth's religious convictions; then looked again, his attention caught by an unexpected realism and unusual depiction of its occupant. The figure stood not nailed but with arms outstretched supporting the whole weight of the transverse beam across the palms of its upturned hands. The head held no wreath of thorns but bore a plain gold ring crown much like the one he had last seen on the head of the bogus 'Arthur' the previous night. He stared and blinked in bewilderment at the features themselves delineated below it. They teased him with a memory until he realised that they were also those of 'Arthur' whom he had left in the forest as Alder's successor. Myrddin had fashioned those features himself from a tiny piece of astral ectoplasm he had taken from a boy called 'Impy' – more properly named Jack Hundell – whose nickname had reflected his thin, lopsided features and long, almost pointed ears. Myrddin had found him a mentally retarded young man living alone with his grandmother. Not having expected to find his predecessor incarnated in such a form, he had left the boy until last when he had been looking for the-Wychy-that-had-been before him. Even then, when he couldn't find him, he had only visited the boy, feeling honour bound to leave no one out.

No one in the village had doubted that the youth had the gift of seeing the faerie, but mocked and taunted, Impy had long stopped saying anything about it except to those he trusted.

Myrddin had found him sitting on the grass in Wisher's Mead, his knees drawn up to his chin, staring straight ahead, and been startled to hear him say: 'I 'members thee, Mr Fairy.'

Myrddin remembered his astonished: 'What do you remember, Impy?'

'I 'members wearing black, like thee, and had a magic Wand, a' well.'

Myrddin remembered his shock at thus finding the greatest Wychy of all time; one who had somehow been able to turn the human Augustus Autrey into an elf and back again to mortal. A wise and kindly Wychy whose Wych as well had been at his side to rescue the rebellious half born August from the might of Dragga's wrath; a Wychy whose Weird Myrddin had then seen withered; his Wand casting him away – one who had then had to go and pay his debt to Dragga. Myrddin had wanted to take Impy back to the forest then and there, but Impy said his Nan had told him he wasn't fay no more but a baptised Christian, so he couldn't go back. How incensed Myrddin had felt. 'We'll see about that, Impy,' he had promised. 'I'll come and give you something tonight when you're asleep–'

Impy shook his head. 'T'won't work, Mr Fairy,' he said.

And nor did it, although Myrddin administered enough Wizards' Woe to have slain a horse. Impy simply woke the same as usual and none the worse. Myrddin had failed to remember the scripture that says: '… and when they will drink deadly poison, it will not hurt them at all …'[1]

So Myrddin instead had taken a little ectoplasm of the living boy when he had been sleeping, intent on fashioning a babe that had nothing of Impy's lopsidedness, but perfect in feature, because he was so determined that something of his predecessor should live on in the forest. He had also realised that, without his predecessor, his own successor, Redweird was now the last Wychy – for Myrddin could never take on that role again without having first paid his debt to Dragga. It was fortunate he had noted the fact in the shared book of wisdom lying in Black Wand's Retreat on The Wandle; a book that held a record of each successive Wychy's notes and experience to remind each of them as they resumed the Office of what had gone before, or still needed doing.

And here in the Chapel, Myrddin was being shown the Christ raised and come again bearing the cross of his ancient martyrdom signifying that through him, all ancient feuds would be resolved and the Faerie, however lowly in form, be re-united as one in all their former freedoms and perfections.

Forgetting Mildgyth's presence, he went slowly up to the altar and sank to his knees in humble amazement.

How is it possible? he wondered. *How can a scrap of astral ectoplasm that I fashioned with my own hands have become a symbol like this? No,* he assured himself. *It hadn't. It's pure coincidence.* It could only be that the same ideal that had

---

1   Mark 16:18

motivated his own ideal of 'Arthur' had also inspired the owner of the hands that had sculpted this likeness of the Christ. After all, he reasoned, hadn't the fake 'Arthur' he had made fooled everyone in the Forest into thinking it had been the true one? Even Nemway and her brother Amyas believed it.

As he stared and reflected, however, he became convinced that he need look no further for a retreat. This had to be the place where he would bring his treasured belongings to leave in Mildgyth's care. It seemed fitting that she should also have charge of the plain gold Wealspring Cup. When filled with water from either of the blue fountains outside the Chapel, it would transform the Mung back to their Mabyn origin and free them from their wretched existence. Also, the vicinity of the Chapel being sacred ground, where better to hide the Mabyn until he was able to contact Amyas who might know of a nearby Underway through which they could journey safely to the forest. At this point, he remembered Nemway's message to Amyas, so rose and went back to where Mildgyth stood watching him.

'How many before you have served in this holy place, most worthy of guardians?' he asked.

'Three,' she said. 'But not in continuity. There have been years between when none has entered – even to pray. The sanctuary is old and despite its legendary blessings, few – so few – ever come here now.'

'Do you know anything of any Underway near here?' he asked.

'Two,' she said. 'There's one in the Chapel garden here, and another nearby in the woods.'

'Are they used? Who comes and goes through them?'

'I have never known the one in the garden here to be used. I have no knowledge concerning the other. Come, wizard, I will show you ...'

She conducted him through her austerely furnished cell, into a walled garden blooming in a riot of tiny, exquisite and colourful, faerie flowers. He saw no opening to the mound she pointed to, but this didn't discount a magical doorway, and an obvious escape route for the hare.

In spite of Mildgyth's conventional attitude towards his being a wizard, they began to find understanding of a kind between them and so form a friendship. She questioned him curiously about the Weirdfolk. What their beliefs were and how they worshipped.

He told her that they believed in magic and worshipped the spirit of love.

He learned that she had a cousin in the nearby faerie Constable of Eden's Ford, and it became clear that her model of faith had applicability in Mortleroy's realm where the impulse of mortal living appeared to continue with all kinds of feasting, wars, gratuitous violence and cruelty – things unknown to the Weirdfolk hidden away in Weir Forest.

Because he felt time pressing, he made his excuses with regret and rose to take his leave.

'So soon?' she asked. She sounded disappointed and remained seated. 'I thought you had might have found a new peace in my ancient sanctuary, great Am-mar-el-lyn.'

He could be truthful. 'Yes, such peace as I have seldom known since leaving the forest. But I have work to do.'

'Not many come this way, Am-mar-el-lyn, and of them all, I find *you* the least easy to understand. You are kind and gentle, and courteous, nothing like a wizard at all. Tell me, can magic be equal to faith?'

Myrddin answered cautiously. 'Anything that appears to happen out of context and contrary to all experience, can appear to be magic' he replied. 'Sleight of hand tricks the eye and is called 'magic'. Access to powers unknown to physical science *look* like 'magic'. Even He that is imaged on your Cross performed miracles that *some* might call 'magic'. To raise people from the dead; change water into wine, provide food for thousands from a few mere loaves and fishes. Personally, I would say it is the work of faith to work miracles like that.'

She looked up at him, her eyes keen and askance. 'And what is the magic *you* do, Am-mar-el-lyn?'

'I believe that whatever I wish – or even command – to happen, happens by virtue of Merlyn's magic.'

'Then you are a true and perilous magician, Am-mar-el-lyn,' she said with a seriousness that belied the wistful smile that softened it. 'Such power would destroy a mortal–'

'And possibly immortal?' he asked with a wry smile, affected by her concern. 'Who knows? It could be like the sin of immortal Lucifer who believed he was equal to God.'

'Then I will pray for you, Am-mar-el-lyn,' she said with a deeply earnestness and seemed to think on his words even more than she had done earlier. She said then, as if debating with herself: 'It cannot be wrong to accept a service even from a pagan if it is for the comfort of one of God's creatures … And yet if that were so …' She paused, then asked with an abrupt frankness: 'Am-mar-el-lyn, why did you pursue the innocent hare that came to me for sanctuary?'

'Because it wasn't a normal hare, Mildgyth. It was an artifice made by a sorceress, a thing designed to delude and cause the death of a good and great King who is my friend. I had no wish to trouble you with such things because they are not of your world.'

It made her look thoughtful – and troubled. At last she got to her feet, saying: 'Lately, a bird, seemingly as you have just described, has come into the garden. It was not of a physical kind, as I now recognise, but so beautiful that, if it *is* fae, I would love to have near me. Could you, with your 'magic', command it so, Am-mar-el-lyn?'

'I could try,' he said at once, wondering what new decoy of Nemway's might be lurking in the trees.

Mildgyth went into the garden and made a soft cooing noise, and almost at once a tiny flash of white flew between two bushes.

Shades of Merlyn! he thought, recognising at once the mysterious White Dove of the Weirdfolk. No wonder he hadn't been able to overtake it when he'd flown after its presumed departure west. He raised his sceptre commandingly and whistled musically. The dove left its hiding place and came to settle at his feet while Mildgyth looked at him in awe.

Where before when it had appeared in the forest to deliver its message it had been of mortal size, here with Mildgyth it appeared to have reverted to its fae proportions. Myrddin held out his sceptre and the dove rose at once to perch on it. He passed it to Mildgyth and as she took it fluttering onto her fingers he explained:

'This is no artifice. This is the sacred White Dove of my own people which has been lost to us for a long, long time. It has no power to harm and I know of no better place for it to live than with your love and in this garden.'

She gave him a smile then that transformed her rather like a child receiving a much-desired gift from a thoughtful and loving elder. 'How like it is to the Dove which appeared from the heavens when our Lord was baptised by John,' she said happily.

Before he left, he also gave her the cup, saying gravely: 'Mildgyth, guard this well, it is a most holy treasure. And, I beg you, for the sake of Him whom you love and serve, to please give refuge to those whom I shall bring with me when I return. I promise you shall see a miracle.'

'This sanctuary is my Lord's,' she said softly. 'I shall expect you when I see you.'

When he took wing again, he did so well out of sight of the Chapel. He had no wish for the trusting and innocent Mildgyth to see him taking the form of a black falcon.

CHAPTER 5

JESSANT DE LYS

Myrddin would have flown straight back to the outhouse at Weir Court for his possessions if the sound of hooves hadn't sent him winging instead to a vantage point in a tree at the edge of a rough clearing in the woods.

To his delight, it was Amyas. Crowned, and wearing a richly decorated jerkin, hose and high boots, the nine-inch high Mabyn King came trotting into sight on his beloved and equally diminutive white unicorn, Icefire. From his left hand and in proportion to his size there hung a great spiked ball attached to a heavy looking chain which he swung gently to and fro and singing to it under his breath as if it were a living thing: *'Hey there, Moldwarp – hoe there, Moldwarp …'* while threading his way unhurriedly over the open ground littered with stones, some like boulders compared to his size.

Myrddin would have made himself known, but his friend appeared preoccupied and wary, glancing behind every now and then, clearly expecting someone or something to follow.

He had got halfway across the clearing when the undergrowth at his rear erupted with movement and shouts. A war party of knights no taller than himself, fae-at-arms and archers burst out of the bracken. His pursuers knew their job. The knights charged forward with lances levelled, their horses' caparisons streaming in the breeze followed by the fae-at-arms with swords drawn, while the mounted archers spread out in the rear ready for the kill if those in the fore-front failed.

It looked like the end for Amyas. The mabyn could not possibly reach any cover without falling to one or other sides of the rapidly forming pincer movement. To the magician's astonishment, however, the King stopped, turned his mount about and rushed recklessly back on his enemies whirling the flail round his head as if it were a toy. Only mortal feet from the nearest lances, he released it in an even wider orbit into the ground between them. Like a powerful battery of mortar shells exploding in a row, clods of earth and boulder-sized stones and pebbles rained down painfully on his attackers while a gouged out arc of earth yawned between him and them. Instead of staying on the safe side, however, Amyas and unicorn had leapt the trench and shot between the knights unharmed while they collapsed into the furrow, separating riders and horses, maiming and killing the former and scattering the latter head first to the ground.

The scene had taken only a second, leaving the unprepared archers still sitting with their mouths open. Before they could draw breath or bow, two more whirls from the warrior King's chained ball sent such a rain of earth and dust down on them, they were blinded, and most fell. A third swing horizontally into their midst then sent shattered archers and horses flying in all directions.

Leaving the bewildered riders and struggling retainers to sort their muddle, the King leaped back over the ditch and trotted on.

Myrddin flew ahead of him unseen until, well clear of the fracas behind them, changed his form and stepped out from behind the bracken beside the path as the rider drew level.

His sudden appearance caused Icefire to step sideways as Amyas brought her to a halt.

'Black One!' he exclaimed. 'Is it really you? Your White

One told me you were gone to pay your ancient debt to Dragga.'

'Ah, and that is the way a Wychy goes, noble Amyas, but I am Merlyn's Heir and have another destiny. Yet why are *you* here? Have you received a message purporting to come from Mildgyth?'

Amyas looked startled. 'What would you know of it, if I had?'

'I know it wasn't Mildgyth who sent it – it was Nemway.'

The Mabyn's expression relaxed, his eyes lighting in mild amusement that creased his rather grave face with a smile. 'Mildgyth's name is code between us for messages, and no, I haven't received it. What was it?'

Myrddin realised his need of quick apologies, which he made, and went on: ' … I turned the messenger back the way it had come in order to resolve the mystery – and it vanished in the Chapel of Blue Fountains. The message rather cryptically said "Mildgyth waits for you at the Chapel of Blue Fountains. Hear me and none other until I can send word again".'

The King smiled and nodded. 'Thank you, Merlyn's Heir. It tells me she is still alone. I am indebted to you in many ways,' he went on. 'This morning two mungs and a certain ex-Elder of the High Travellers were directed to me?'

'Gawain?'

'The same. He told me how you restored him to his ancient estate. So magician you truly are, for up until then, I have never been able to make contact with any of these, my own people.'

'I've told them to gather here in Cyngsfold Woods in order to get them to the Forest of Weir,' said Myrddin. 'However, it seems to me that the Chapel of Blue Fountains is far better placed for healing and hiding them, wouldn't you say?'

'Indeed, I have just taken Gawain there. To the People of the Ancient Mounds there are underground ways that are entirely safe, and an entrance to one lies in the garden there. Speed will be of the essence, though. Such a large gathering in the woods here *is* unusual and I am not the only one who has been told of it.'

Curiosity nagged Myrddin. 'How do you manage to keep so well informed?' he asked

'The Sage of all the Seers is my sister Nemway's son. He keeps me informed.'

'The ruler of the Denefolk,' said Myrddin ruefully, remembering a painful episode when the Sage had brought about his downfall as a golden eagle. 'Yes, you could say I have made his acquaintance. It was you rescued me and brought me back to the forest, remember?'

Amyas nodded, and went on: 'When Gawain told me what his people were doing, the Sage had me directed to where I could deal with one of the war-parties that are now on the look-out for them–'

'I watched you,' Myrddin said with a nod at *Moldwarp*. 'I have never seen such a weapon in action before. You are brave, Amyas.'

'I have *Moldwarp*,' the King said, shrugging the tribute aside. 'My people have nothing. If you will restore the rest of my enslaved kin, I swear King Arthur shall have a thousand warriors at his command to whom there are no equal.'

Myrddin inclined his head and returned no more than a brief: 'I will find them …'

*

He thought it just as well, even if dangerous, to have to take on the form of a golden eagle again when it came to looking for Mung. He doubted that the rest of them knew about the grey feather of the black falcon that he had shown the three elders. He therefore kept his eagle shape small, and had found them by mid-morning.

Pleased as they were to see him safe and in one piece, getting them to the Chapel proved another matter altogether.

'... It is one of the forbidden places, Lord Myrddin,' explained Koo, the chief elder, his gravelly voice trembling, his hairy face looking terrified. 'It is a holy place, like Avalon and every place where the enemy has a stronghold.'

'There are no enemies in the Chapel of Blue Fountains,' said Myrddin firmly, trying to be patient but having little time to waste. 'There is no one there but a holy woman who has the power of miracles at hand. So you either follow me, Koo, or remain the way you are forever.'

'Yet Lord, it is *forbidden* that our feet should ever touch the ground,' the mung wailed. 'Even if we're not killed, it is said that such a desecration will bring calamity ...' He tailed off at the approach of a female, her greying fur and flabby breasts showing her age as she edged forward to kneel before the wizard on the wide bough.

'Lord Myrddin ...?' she begged. 'Lord Myrddin, I am old and don't have long to live. I shall soon fail and fall to the forbidden earth. Please, let me dare the doom. If I survive and your magic supports me ...?' She reached out hesitantly to touch the symbols on his robe in longing appeal.

He held out his hand to raise her but Koo, shamed by her words, grasped it himself, begging to be first. Even then, when they arrived at the oak opposite the Chapel where Gawain, now clothed in jerkin and hose, and Mildgyth were waiting for them, Koo hung half paralysed for some moments to the lowest branchlet before obeying the magician's insistent command to let go.

With an eldritch groan that sent a shiver of fear through the crowd above, he at last obeyed.

Myrddin caught him as he fell almost senseless into his arms and Mildgyth, standing ready at the Chapel entrance, nearly dropped the Chalice in horror at the sight of such a crude and repugnant looking bundle of matted hair, crossing herself.

'Mildgyth, the Cup, please?' Myrddin prompted, as he knelt to nurse Koo into a sitting position. He could imagine she must have found it difficult to smother her feelings as she stooped to administer the Chalice. But when the hair faded and the form slimmed into the gnome-like proportions of a mabyn, emotion overcame her.

'O Lord God – praise be!' she whispered, clasping the cup to her breast.

Myrddin helped the amazed and delighted elder to his feet, except that he at once fell to his knees in tears, kissing the hem of the magician's robe and crying in a voice he had never been able to use before.

The lower branches of the adjacent oak were now crammed with eagerly appealing, outstretched arms, but Myrddin beckoned the unlovely female who had asked him first and was making no gesture for his attention. She fell into his supportive arms and lay contented, her arms around his neck, her head resting tiredly on his shoulder. What else could he do, but kiss her shrivelled lips before them all in thankfulness that she had been so willing to show them the way. Her subsequent transformation into a wiccy of the Weirdfolk just one of many other surprises in the task of catching and bearing each to the Chapel Porch. Most turned out to be Mabyn in origin, but here and there among the four to five hundred wraiths there were three who exhibited the proud, keen features of the Kin of Beauty – one of whom had been the Elder Nori. Just as Gawain had remembered his name on being changed, so Nori also cried out in awe: 'I am Jessant! Jessant de Lys!' Besides these, there were two others so curiously etherealised it witnessed that they had to be kin to the elusive Denefolk. Myrddin had never actually seen any before then, only sensing their presence. These, after a dignified expression of their gratitude and appreciation, begged to leave the company and go in search of their own kind. Another, regaining his form as a mabyn, looked around at them all, blinked, shook his head as if to clear it and went to Gawain.

'Gawain!' he said, with joyful simplicity embracing him. 'It's Percivale!'

When all had been restored, the wizard showed them how and where to gather astral material and, with Mildgyth's help, instructed them in making hose and jerkins for themselves. As soon as the first were clad, he set them to excavate a mound he had located just outside the chapel for the mabyns' protection and habitation. Mildgyth had assured him she had no reason to believe it held any entrance to an Underway.

During this, Jessant came to him: 'Lord Myrddin, when we were gathering, some of us heard news of the Evil One's forces coming together sooner than we thought. Not all parties are going to Weir Forest but ride from east to west. We have heard they are riding to another great war for the Kin of Beauty are coming from the Realms of Annwyn in large numbers.'

'The Kin of Beauty!' exclaimed Myrddin with some asperity. 'If that means King Gwyn has at last despatched an escort for the Weirdfolk, he's left it a bit late.' He spoke it more to himself than to the other but Jessant at once took him up on it:

'If we could learn how to arm and defend ourselves, Lord Myrddin …?' And left the question hanging, but watched the magician's face with eager and hopeful eyes.

It made sense to Myrddin. He had already helped the mabyns' close cousins, the gnomes in Weir Forest, with the making of high calibre arms and armour. If everyone here worked hard enough ...

CHAPTER 6

NEMWAY'S PLOT

Leaving the mabyns hard at work, Myrddin refashioned the eagle into a black falcon and flew off to reconnoitre beyond the confines of the wood and came across two elfin riders.

One, wrapped in the folds of a distinctive and voluminous blue cloak and wearing a white wimple, he recognised as Nemway on her all-white mare, Windfleet. The other, a knight, made Myrddin check his flight and circle round for another look. The shield across the rider's back bore the device of a bloodied sword.

Accolon! Nemway's misguided and misused dupe who had been tricked into fighting mortal Arthur with Excalibur, and here he was again, only now a fae and *still* in her company. Would he never learn? Wasn't it enough that his name was now infamous for treachery?

A fae-sized wolf leaped unexpectedly onto the path that the two were following bringing them to a halt. It yelped a brief message to the knight and bounded away again.

'A force approaches this way, noble Lady,' said Accolon. 'It would be better for us to detour than give them any reason to be mistrustful of where we're going.'

'Why are you suddenly so timid, Accolon? You said I had safe conduct, didn't you?'

'*Your* safety is not to be questioned my Lady. It's the granting of the boon that makes me doubtful. It is unthinkable that the King would have thought you might ask for the safety of the Weirdfolk wizard. He has issued orders that *none* shall leave the Forest of Weir and live.'

So, thought Myrddin. *The lady has not yet learned of my rescue by her brother and return to Weir Forest. Which means she doesn't know yet that I'm no longer Black Wand.* It did nothing to dispel the wizard's doubts, however. He knew that Nemway had reasons of her own to want him safe and none of them were friendly.

'But *I* have left the forest,' she said to Accolon.

'But Noble Lady, you have proved you are his ally by slaying the Weirdfolk Dragon,'

Nemway laughed, but gave no reason why other than to say: 'Accolon, I think you act wisely to avoid awkward questions. Even so, won't the wolf that brought the news of them to you, take news of us to them?'

'Of course it will,' he replied, and nodded ahead. 'But that field of corn will hide us better than a thicket.'

If a mortal can lie unseen in a cornfield, how much more so can two nine inch high riders vanish with their horses between the tall rows of golden stalks – although it had its drawbacks. While they might be safe from questing eyes at ground level, they couldn't see far enough themselves to evade others equally curious, nor hide from overhead observers. It seemed inevitable, therefore, that when they left their cover to carry on their journey south-westward Myrddin should see them run straight into the path of an armed party riding east.

The pair came to a halt, clearly aware that turning back would look not look good.

''Tis Sir Edric of Eden's Ford,' said Accolon recognising the leader's shield, and drawing his own down from across his shoulder to be seen. 'Peace or Death to you, Sir Edric?' he called belligerently

Myrddin remembered that Mildgyth had claimed kinship with the Constable of Eden's Ford, who appeared almost as wide as tall with a vast plume of red feathers towering from the crest of his helmet to reinforce the impression.

Electing 'Peace', he rode forward with one attendant knight. 'Greetings, Sir Accolon of the Bloodied Sword,' he said, but looking intently at Nemway as if anxious for introduction.

Nemway showed her dislike of him on sight and stared back, not at his face but, with withering contempt, at the fountain of feathers above it.

Accolon answered: 'Upon our Liege's head, Sir Edric, I demand safe conduct through your ranks for myself and the Lady Nemway whose person, by decree, is sacrosanct.'

'The Lady Nemway, eh?' repeated the other, looking surprised. 'Yes, the decree is known to me, Sir Accolon, but not the Lady. If she can prove her claim, the decree will be obeyed.'

'Claim!' cried Nemway arrogantly. 'One does not *claim* to be who one truly *is*. Thus …!' And her magic whip, Lightning streaking out scattered Sir Edric's mighty plume to the wind like wisps of flame.

Before the paralysed eyes of his followers, his charger bolted under the lash, nearly hurling its mortified rider from his seat. No one moved until he brought the horse back under control and returned looking more like a tinful of boiling brimstone.

'What brings you so far from your domain, Sir Constable?' Accolon asked, before the other could express his wrath.

'War!' The explosive reply appeared to relieve Sir Edric's emotional indigestion. 'The rebel Gwyn harries the garrisons of the west, and the forces of the Northern Wold have been ordered there, leaving the besieging of the Weirdfolk under my command – as well as hunting down a band of miscreant Mung reported to be gathering here. And where are *you* going, Sir Accolon?'

'The place and purpose are in accordance with the decree,' answered Accolon with suave diplomacy. 'And now, if you will be so courteous, Sir Edric, you will not delay us longer – or we may all incur the anger of our Liege.'

The Constable had no option but to let them pass whilst he himself continued into the woods.

Since Nemway and Accolon were headed in the direction of Three Weirs, and Myrddin wanted to collect the rest of his belongings from Weir Court, he hung back to find out what they were up to and saw a fae-sized hawk fly to Accolon's gauntlet.

The knight listened to its message. When it had flown off, he turned to his companion who appeared lost in thought: 'Lady, the Baron of the Northern Wold has had word of a terrible massacre nearby–'

'Then we must ride directly back to Sir Edric,' said Nemway urgently, appearing to come to an abrupt decision and, taking his bridle, tried to turn his horse. 'If we do not they will be annihilated by this Mabyn of Mabyn.'

'Sir Edric will have heard of it by now,' objected Accolon, pulling away. 'The Baron will have sent his scouts in search of the terrible Mabyn while Sir Edric was on his way from Three Weirs. He knows the Mabyn of Mabyn is in the Forest. The Baron's archers and bowmen will be occupying the highest points of vantage whilst his squadrons wait concealed ready to charge from cover as soon the quarry is sighted.'

'Those tactics are useless.' The scorn in her tone made Accolon's mouth tighten, and caused Myrddin a grim inward smile. 'I need to find Sir Edric and explain,' she went on. 'The King of the Mabyn seldom travels above ground.'

A shout from behind on the track they were following, brought them to a surprised halt.

'Accolon! Sir Accolon!'

They turned. A mounted fay-at-arms clad in a stout leather jerkin and wearing a cap of mail was riding towards them, a cross-bow and quiver of bolts slung across his back. Accolon made to lower his lance aggressively.

Nemway hissed a warning: 'He knows you, and calls as a friend. Speak to him!'

The fay pulled up level with them and raised a hand in salutation. 'Sir Accolon, please allow me ride in company with you and your lady. I have terrible news to take to Sir Edric, and it would be good to have your testimony to support my own. I don't think you will have seen the bolt I shot–'

'What bolt?' Accolon asked in astonishment.

'I aimed at the mighty Mabyn, noble knight, but then it seemed the whole earth opened beneath us and tore our whole company to pieces. It was awful,' he continued apologetically. 'I fell back and made off to give warning and to find help. I have seen no knight, hawk nor even wolf until I saw you and your lady. Have you heard anything?'

'A hawk has brought us news of this–'

Nemway interrupted with a tactful: 'Sir Accolon, please let this honest fae come with us to bear witness to what we were hurrying to tell. In view of our last encounter I have to confess that I doubt Sir Edric will give much credence to our unsupported news.'

And what greater proof of betrayal than that! thought the listening magician with amazement and followed the pair closely as they galloped back the way they had come.

*

Sir Edric scowled at their reappearance. It was reasonable however that they should have turned back to warn him and helpful to have an extra fae-at-arms he could add to his company.

Whatever plan it was that had sent Nemway back to the Constable, she began with an apology. '… Alas, I have a terrible temper,' she said. 'But if you will accept my amends, I promise I will replace the feathers with a sheaf so wonderful, that everyone who sees them will be green with envy.'

Sir Edric inclined his head politely. 'Lady Nemway, thank you. It would be appreciated.'

'Furthermore, I have a plan …'

Listening to what she had to say, Myrddin could hardly believe his ears to hear her promise the Constable that he could destroy the Mabyn of Mabyn and enslave the whole of the Weirdfolk at one stroke if he took her advice. It confirmed the wizard's worst suspicion that she was hand in glove with Mortleroy but he could only wonder what made the lady hate her brother so – unless she loved the usurper king the more.

'Please say on, lady, because up until now nothing has stopped the Mabyn King, and I am sure my King will reward you even more amply. With the Mabyn of Mabyn breaking loose, and destroying everything that stands in his path he draws my forces away from besieging the Forest of Weir.'

'Then listen to me …' and Nemway explained how the Mabyn used the ancient Underways, but she would send him a message asking for safe passage through his realm. This would draw him into the open from an Underway within the woods where she would be waiting. Amyas, believing that she only wanted safe passage, would not therefore have *Moldwarp* ready for action. The Constable's men, lying in ambush, could then kill or capture the Mabyn King as they liked, and lo and behold the Underway would be theirs for their invasion of the Forest.

Snatching at every detail, Myrddin hung in to listen.

*

Edric saw a snag. He did not want any word of it reaching the Baron until he had the whole glorious victory sealed and settled in blood, yet a hawk had just dropped to his wrist informing him that a Royal Falcon had been seen surveying his troop movements, and the Constable panicked.

`Lady, we are undone!' he cried. 'The bird will return to the King and report I am not stationed according to his orders to the Baron.'

'So what of it, Sir Edric?' Nemway asked sweetly. 'By the time your movements are reported, and the King sends back a bird asking your purpose, we shall be well on our way underground *into* the Forest. But,' and she shrugged, 'if not, then simply say that in accordance with his royal decree, you are assisting the Lady of the Lake to achieve the boon he has promised her – *any* boon,' the Constable found himself reminded significantly.

With that kind of reassurance, his enthusiasm returned in force, trusting Nemway's instruction with organising the ambush. When another hawk arrived soon after with the news that the Royal Falcon had disappeared without deigning to communicate the purpose of its visit, Edric was not surprised. As he said to the Lady Nemway: 'A Royal Falcon would never communicate with anything as lowly and inferior as a hawk, and I have sent a hawk of my own to the Baron that I have been only shortly delayed from the siege …'

*

Myrddin flew off to find Amyas. He went back to the Chapel of Blue Fountains, taking care to change out of his avian guise before reaching it.

When Mildgyth said she had seen nothing of the Mabyn, nor received any word from him, the magician was alarmed. How was he to find Amyas in time?

He flew back to where the ambush now laid waiting beside a mound just as Nemway, poised advantageously just outside it to raise the alarm the moment Amyas appeared, made him realise why there had been no chance of ever getting word to the Mabyn. Amyas must have received her second messenger and gone underground.

Even as Myrddin arrived, a gaping hole appeared in the side of the hillock and the warrior King mounted on the white unicorn stood framed in its blackness.

His reaction on seeing Nemway seemed a little odd to the wizard, for the Mabyn made no effort to greet her but at once swung his mount around to race back down the tunnel as she spurred Windfleet after him, shouting: 'Hurry. Sir Edric. He has seen us and turns …!'

The speed of it appeared to take Accolon and Edric a little by surprise. By the time they charged into the open tunnel with the remainder of the Constable's force in hot pursuit, Nemway was well away ahead of them.

All Myrddin could think of then was to fly hard for Weir Forest and warn the Master of Gnomes of the coming invasion. There was only one way he could do it, though. He knew there was no way he could avoid Redweird seeing him but, if he moved with enough speed, he could be down the shaft leading into the underground passage that the gnomes had excavated between their Mansion and Merlyn's Mount, before the Wychy had time to make sense of what was happening. It meant Myrddin having to fly in as a golden eagle, because Dreadful would attack a black falcon. It was something Myrddin had trained him to do and it took precious moments though to reform the falcon into an eagle. The wizard promised himself that it was going to be a number one priority to get hold of enough ectoplasm as soon as possible to make both kinds of bird.

Other forms, too, he thought. *It would be useful to have several different kinds – but they'll have to wait for now.*

*

He found the plump friendly form of the Master of Gnomes waiting for him in the passageway beneath the Mount.

'Hael and wyn, great Merlyn's Heir! Hael and wyn,' he said heartily, as Myrddin changed from eagle to himself.

'I fear you are mistaken; Master,' his shocked visitor urged at once in a low voice. 'I am Am-Mer-El-Lyn, a Prince of Damascus, and you must show me where the entrance to the Underway is. It has to be magically sealed – and quickly.'

Without further ado, Omric at once indicated the place on the wall where they were standing. It was where Amyas had, in fact, once burst in bearing Myrddin's unconscious form.

Previously, as a Wychy, Myrddin would have needed a Wand to draw the great seal of a flaming eye across the invisible entrance, now he used his sceptre.

Even as he was drawing the great sigil, it occurred to him that Amyas, realising he had been betrayed, might have opened up another route away from the Forest to divert the army that was chasing him. Nevertheless, Myrddin could not take the risk of leaving this entrance unsealed. For all he knew Amyas could be dead by now and Nemway might know the way in herself. At least his potent seal would keep *her* imprisoned.

Still in a hurry, only now to retrieve his stuff from the out-house at Weir Court, Myrddin saw no need to discuss the situation further with Omric, but bid him a swift farewell and took off under the Master's wondering gaze flying up the vertical shaft above them to the open sky.

*

Omric was left scratching his head. Am-mar-el-lyn had given him no chance to say that Amyas and Nemway had escaped the tunnel safely ahead of their pursuers, and closed it with *Moldwarp* before riding hard back to the woods near Cyngsfold to seal the other end in the same way.

CHAPTER 7

'SAVE THE WIZARD!'

It was a simple matter for Myrddin then to pick up his bag of belongings and fly everything back to the Chapel of Blue Fountains.

Thanks to Amyas' destruction of the war party that morning, and Sir Edric's force probably lost in an underground maze, all had remained quiet and it was gratifying to find how quickly the rehabilitated Mabyn had become familiar again with the work of re-discovering the ores and minerals they needed. The earth was their natural element after all and their renewed contact with it seemed to resuscitate skills long overlaid and forgotten; it also underlined the double cruelty of the bondage that had separated them from it.

With only an hour's interregnum that coming night, when neither sun or moon were above the horizon and the majority of Mabyn would be unconscious, they not only had time to excavate and build a large underground shelter, but also to copy the examples of arms and armour that Myrddin had left with them. The wizard now supervised the heating and quenching of their efforts, so that by moonset there were nearly two hundred suits completed and work begun on one entirely in black for himself.

Leaving over four hundred Mabyn safe for the short period of unconsciousness that followed, Myrddin refashioned his form to that of the black falcon and flew off once more on his delayed endeavour to find Caburn Hill.

*

It was still before moonrise when, after flying south, he saw a party of mailed riders when they appeared out of cover travelling slowly in a westerly direction. At first he took it that unlike the Weirdfolk and the transformed High Travellers, the rest of faedom was free of any restriction on their consciousness during the interregnum. However, when he flew nearer for closer inspection, he saw it was an escort in black riding at walking pace for a large number of knights all chained together and shuffling along like zombies, each with a hand on the shoulder of the one in front. And if that wasn't puzzling enough, he was astonished when the entire party disappeared the next moment as if the earth had opened up and swallowed it. He wondered if he had just come across a faerie path. Amaranthus had written of the track ways being fast and, theoretically, he supposed that could mean at the speed of thought depending on how much of the terrain one might wish to see between one place and another. But there was nothing around to indicate an end or the beginning of one, or any portal. As for an explanation of what he had just seen, it was beyond him at that moment, especially as, in that one brief glimpse, he could have sworn he had seen gaping black wounds, but no blood.

But he needed to fly on. He was on the lookout for the Kin of Beauty still not knowing whether or not they were subject to the same law of faerie blackout that affected the Weirdfolk and the Mung. It was not until after sun-rise, however, that he found them so the question remained unanswered.

A force of perhaps fifty knights with fae-at-arms – and of course archers – came into sight with a green banner bearing the device of White Owl crowned in silver. This he knew to be the emblem of Gwyn ap Gwyn, even if the party was approaching from the east when it should be coming from the west. Although, their archers would probably shoot a black falcon on sight, he felt it safer overall to trust to luck that he could morph into his guise as an eastern magician before they saw him. He was about to fly down, change and wait for their arrival, when he saw another, larger party coming directly from the west. Both were on course to meet head on and shortly.

Myrddin promptly flew ahead of the first party, changed into his eastern appearance to await them at the base of a tree; prepared to make a dramatic appearance and set them on the right road for the Forest.

The smaller party arrived ahead of the larger one but to his astonishment ignored his appearance and greeting.

He hurried after them, waving his arms and shouting and the cavalcade halted. The archers turned, fitted arrows to bows and covered him while a knight trotted back to investigate.

'Greetings, Sir Knight of the Kin of Beauty,' said Myrddin. 'I, Prince of Damascus and Heir of Merlyn, stand before you.'

'Of Merlin, all have heard,' said the other looking nonplussed. 'But of his heir nothing. Explain your business.'

'I am come to greet your lord, King Gwyn – if he is near – and direct you to the Forest of Weir – you are going in the wrong direction here.'

The look of frank astonishment on the knight's face puzzled Myrddin, so he asked: 'Are you not Commander of the Escort that your king promised to send to guard the Weirdfolk on their journey to his keep in Avalon?'

To his surprise, the other roared with laughter and beckoned to his followers. 'Indeed I am, O Heir of Merlyn.' he replied with another mirthless laugh and cried out: 'Seize him!' And, when his fae-at-arms hurried up, added: 'Don't harm him. His Majesty will be *very* happy to meet him.'

Myrddin backed hurriedly as mailed hands reached out for him. The arrival of the vanguard of the larger second party, however, saved him. It burst into view flying a green banner also bearing a white owl, and the effect was electric.

'My lance!' yelled the knight who had given the order and couching the quickly presented weapon under his arm, he pulled down his visor, turned his charger and spurred forward towards the newcomers with a roar of: 'Á Gars! Á Gars! Peace or Death traitors! Take down that accursed banner and follow me. Yield! Yield, I say, in the King's name …!'

No one paid Myrddin any further attention.

The second party promptly launched itself in a headlong gallop with lowered lances. Men and horses went down under the impact of their meeting. Swords flashed and fell, arrows flew and blasphemy filled the air.

The wind of an arrow skimming his ear brought Myrddin to his senses. Changing into the falcon, he flew for his life into the tree he had waited under and wondered what chances there were for the Weirdfolk when the Kin of Beauty was so divided that its factions fought each other like this all the time.

The ranks of knights, or what was left of them, passed through each other, turned, reformed and charged again. Of the smaller there now remained ten knights, four mounted and six on foot. These nevertheless turned to engage again but the sound of a clarion brought the majority of the reforming second party to a halt, leaving only the same number of knights to take on the remainder of the first. This did not apply to the fae-at-arms or archers on either side who continued in murderous combat irrespective of their unequal numbers.

After a long and heroic fight had laid most of their opponents in the dust, there remained just five left standing of the first party.

The trumpet sounded again, and everyone stood or sat as they were, as if allowed breathing space.

'All honour to you, Sir Gars!' cried the leader of the larger party, addressing the only knight still mounted of the five

'To you also, Sir Avellane!' the other replied, with some difficulty. 'Of your courtesy, noble enemy, refreshment for my companions …?'

'Wine! Wine!' shouted Sir Avellane, turning in his seat and beckoning to his rear. 'A stoup of wine for every knight still standing.'

A packhorse, laden with wine-jack and provisions came up and large goblets of wine were distributed to the condemned first and then to Sir Avellane and his own knights.

Sir Avellane raised his flagon towards his opposite number. 'To your prowess, Sir Gars,' he called. 'If I kill you in the next encounter, I promise your name shall be inscribed on the walls of the halls of Annwyn forever.'

Myrddin was impressed. *What a way to fight a war*! He had seen nothing like it in his life before. It was a point he later realised had made him blind to the fact that although a number of knights lay slain, it had been an entirely bloodless encounter.

'All honour to you … Sir Avellane,' gasped his adversary. 'If I survive I swear … I will drink to your memory in the holiest of cups … in blood, from the Sacred Skull that …that …' and he reeled, dropping the goblet before pulling himself together. Grasping his lance with failing arm, he settled unsteadily into his saddle crying out: 'To the last encounter, Sir Avellane …!'

He fell from his horse before it had even broken into its charge and Sir Avellane lanced him through where he lay.

The reference to a skull meant nothing to Myrddin, but that of Sir Avellane to the halls of Annwyn showed his party to be of the true Kin of Beauty and Sir Gars', therefore, a deception of Mortleroy's.

Reverting to himself, Myrddin bounded with elfin lightness down through the branches and walked sedately towards Sir Avellane, holding up his open right hand in peaceful greeting:

'Hael and wyn, Sir Avellane!' he cried, and stopped at the sudden array of weapons he found turned on him. He chided himself inwardly. He really should have realised that the People of Beauty, being in the middle of a battle in a foreign land, would regard him as a potential enemy. 'I come in peace,' he said firmly. 'I am Merlyn's Heir, lately Black Wand of the Weirdfolk. My name is Am-mar-el-lyn.'

Sir Avellane, who had just finished off another of the knights, motioned his fellows to put up their weapons, raised his visor and waited until the acclamations on the death of the last but two had died down, before answering: 'These are noble claims, wizard. But how shall I know that you are not also an enemy disguised? The Weirdfolk, as we all know, are peaceful spirits who abhor the arts of war.'

'This is true, Sir Avellane, which is why your noble King promised to send us an escort in defence against the dangers of this outer world, and so I find it strange that you should be travelling in the wrong direction for our Forest–'

'Not as strange as finding *you* so far from your People.' returned the knight with undisguised suspicion. 'If you are truly–' He broke off to look round at more shouts of joy. Another of Gar's knights was dying in single combat unable to rise further than his knees. His sword was broken, his shield gone, but he still drew his dagger rather than submit.

To Myrddin's surprise, his opponent at once dropped his own sword and drew his dagger rather than wield an unfair advantage. He even put out his free mailed fist to help his enemy to his feet to further cheers from his own party. When the wounded fay, balancing on one leg then went down within seconds, accurately stabbed through the neck, his death met a respectful silence. No one was cheering what amounted to a military execution. The last two contestants moved towards each other, and Myrddin looked back at Sir Avellane to find the latter observing him. The Commander had a slender, beautiful face, yet sharp with keen features not seen among the Weirdfolk. He seemed about to continue their conversation when a knight came to his side.

'Sir Avellane, there is one here – an archer – who says he has news of this strange magician.'

Sir Avellane nodded the archer's approach who stared hard at Myrddin as he spoke: 'My lord Avellane, I saw this same magician talking with Sir Gars when we rode into battle. I loosed an arrow at him but he changed himself into the likeness of one of enemy's Royal Falcons and flew up into the tree – there,' he said, pointing.

And how was he to answer a charge like that? Myrddin wondered.

Sir Avellane looked back at him with an expression of mocking askance.

'Sir Avellane, it is not as it looks,' Myrddin hurried to say. 'Yes, I did choose the form of a black falcon but only in order to distinguish friend from foe more easily. I am no friend of Mortleroy's – I am his fatal enemy. I have already slain two of his falcons, and nearly succeeded in bringing the traitorous Lady Nemway to her doom–'

For the second time that day, the order came: 'Seize him!'

He stepped back, just as he had before, but this time no distraction came to the rescue. Swords were out and bows drawn in case he turned back into the hated black falcon. As hands reached out to secure him, he pleaded desperately: 'You will take me to your King, Sir Avellane?'

'*That* I promise you.' the knight assured him with grim determination. 'Gwyn ap Gwyn ap Nudd is the greatest of *all* magicians *and* kin to the Lady Nemway! He will surely avenge her upon you for such a betrayal.' His voice became brisk: 'Seat the wizard on a horse, tie his ankles securely beneath its belly, and someone guard him well.' And with that, Sir Avellane showed no further interest in the matter.

It had been late morning when Avellane turned to the knightly disposal of the last of his enemies before reassembling his force and continuing north-east under the banner of the Owl towards a hill. The dead were left scattered behind him where they had fallen, causing an idle thought to cross Myrddin's mind:

I wonder who clears the remains of battles? He was riding in the rear with his horse's bridle looped over the mailed arm of knight whose shield bore the device of two mailed arms bent and linked together. The wizard tried a conversational opening by asking the other his name.

'Bras-de-Fer,' the knight answered in lofty disdain. 'It means–'

'That your arm has the strength of iron,' Myrddin guessed in an attempt to show no ill-feeling. 'And from what I witnessed in the field back there, very aptly so. But tell me, Sir Bras-de-Fer, why did Sir Gars' party and yours both bear the same banner? I thought the White Owl was the emblem only of the Kin of Beauty?'

'One can but guess,' replied the other with a shrug. 'A ruse to trap us? I understand the Evil One has employed the device before. Fortunately, our noble commander, Sir Avellane knew that we had outstripped all other parties recalled from Glastonbury for the siege of Reading's Citadel, and so recognised them for the enemy they were – may Shaitan take their souls for their iniquity.'

'But if you come from Glastonbury, why are you riding so far to the east? Aren't you the Escort promised by your King to guide the Weirdfolk to the sanctuary of his stronghold in Annwyn?'

'I know nothing about any such mission, wizard. We ride ahead of others to bring reinforcements to the siege of the Citadel of Reading.'

'Reading is over sixty mortal miles away to the northwest as the crow flies from Lewes,' Myrddin said, trying not to sound contentious. 'That's a long way for a mortal – big as they are! How much more to us who are tiny by comparison?'

Bras-de-Fer was contemptuous. 'For a wizard you are not very intelligent,' he said, awarding Myrddin a sideways glance. 'Mortals – are – slow – wizard,' he enunciated the words slowly as if speaking to an awkward child. 'That – is – why.'

Myrddin gave him the point in silence. It wasn't the one he had been trying to make – which was to ascertain why they were so far out of their way. After all, the reason could be as simple as Avellane having taken the wrong turning somewhere along the line – literally so, for they seemed to be travelling in a straight path that always appeared to be there. It went along roads, through hedges, over ditches and bridged water. Occasionally it got bisected by another such path which Avellane either took or ignored. However, Myrddin knew it would be useless to point this out to Bras-de-Fer. The knight's Commander was his hero.

Apart from their slight misunderstanding, Bras-de-Fer proved a willing, if not a very intelligent talker. His main interest was in pride of arms, as Myrddin had already admitted he had seen demonstrated. Warlike accomplishments were the be-all and end-all of his existence, and he looked forward to meeting an opponent who could be his equal. '… Such is my prowess,' he went on, without a hint of modesty, 'I have entered the lists with no less than five of my ladies' favours on my arm – yes, and afterwards proved myself as worthy in the lists of love with each of them.'

Myrddin was not in the mood to enquire after any ensuing details. He asked instead: 'And does King Gwyn intend to be present at this besiegement, Sir Knight?'

'So we understand – and regarding him, have no delusions, wizard. Our King is the greatest of magicians since Merlin – whose name you take in vain. He flies freely where he will in the guise of a White Owl unharmed by the Evil One's black falcons.'

'Yet, Sir Knight, I saw such an owl devoured by seven black falcons not even as many days ago,' Myrddin said in a mild voice.

Sir Bras-de-Fer favoured him with a superior smile. 'You would need a thousand eyes to see the true Bird of Gwyn, wizard. His messengers are many, but few know him, himself. Prophecy says that none shall slay the King except in battle …'

After some time in profitless conversation, it became obvious there was no change to be got out of Bras-de-Fer, so Myrddin gave up the fruitless interrogation. After all, he reasoned, once he'd had a tete-a-tete with Gwyn, he'd learn a lot more in five minutes than he could glean in a lifetime from the bloodthirsty moron at his side.

It was at this point that their progress came to an abrupt halt and an order arrived from Avellane. 'Bring up the wizard!'

On Myrddin's arrival at the head of the column, Avellane pointed to a newly built supermarket looming over the way ahead. 'Remove it!' he said imperiously.

Myrddin nearly laughed out loud. *But give the fellow his due*, he thought. *What was the point of having a wizard with you if you couldn't use him to do something as simple as eradicating a supermarket?* Aloud, he was blunt. 'There's nothing I can do. The mortals who built the thing have to remove it themselves. And how do you tell that to *them*?'

Avellane raised a mailed fist, shaking it. 'A curse on them!' he cried.

Myrddin lifted an open hand in restraint. 'Sir Avellane, have mercy,' he said. 'They don't know what they have done. Your curse can only bring misfortune and misery to the innocent–'

'Mercy!' exclaimed the outraged knight. 'I have a war to fight – I can't afford mercy!'

'Yet you showed fairness even to an enemy knight only this morning,' Myrddin found himself reminding him. 'These mortals are ignorant. They have long forgotten us–'

'Then more the reason to remind them!' roared the knight drawing his sword and pointing it at the obstruction. 'I say a curse on these infidels!'

It was performed with such conviction, that Myrddin could only wonder why he didn't see actual bolts fly from the weapon. 'It will return on you,' he warned the Commander in a low voice.

'A pox on you, also!' returned the knight with equal assurance, and gestured Bras-de-Fer. 'Take him away – the useless impostor!'

*

It took time, but the track was eventually found again by late afternoon issuing from one of the other sides of the building and they were able to continue on at a good pace.

With Bras-de-Fer now silent, Myrddin paid more attention to the passing surrounds and their speed which he found difficult to estimate. The ever changing scenery viewed from very nearly ground level was apparently flying by as if their column had the express rate of a train. However, as dusk fell, they were brought to another unexpected halt and word sent back to Bras-de-Fer to bring the captive wizard again to the front.

In the deepening twilight, Myrddin arrived to see a ghostly White Owl gripping Sir Avellane's mailed fist and the Commander looking radiant.

'Know, O Wizard-of-Much-Pretence that my King, being busy elsewhere, no longer intends to lead his Host in person and has honoured me with the supreme command of the assault on the Citadel of Reading.'

'And I'm expected to offer my congratulations?' Myrddin asked. 'The only reason I agreed to come with you was because you promised I should speak to your King. As that is no longer possible, set me free and let me return to my People.'

Avellane surprised him with a thin smile: 'Willingly, if that is your wish. However, I'm afraid you will find your going somewhat hampered. I cannot spare a horse and the way is long if you are to walk – unless, of course, you would prefer to fly …?'

Myrddin was trapped. If he even had time to draw his sceptre which, despite his being man-handled, was still up his sleeve, the very sight of it could invite could invite instant attack. Mounted archers with broad grins on their faces were already spreading out from the party each drawing an arrow from his quiver.

'Loose him,' ordered Avellane, signalling the archers that they would be free to fire at will. With the rasp of a sword leaving its scabbard coming from beside him, Bras-de-Fer sounded only too willing to beat them to it if it would please his Commander.

In the half-light, with everyone's eyes on the doomed magician, there came a great cry from behind them: 'Save the wizard!'

CHAPTER 8

PEREDUR

Much later, Myrddin was to learn that if anyone deserved the 'Mortleroy Medal for Conspicuous Initiative' that night, it had to be Ranulph, erstwhile Baron of the Northern Wold, and now Earl of the Southern Marches. During the thirty years following the previous Earl's departure, he had held both Offices anyway from the ancient and pleasant Citadel of Reading, which was the Earldom's focal point. His acting unpaid appointment had at last become substantive and, in Ranulph's view, not before time. He believed he deserved it. Twice during the previous year, the People of Beauty had sacked the strongholds of Warwick and many others, but had never gained a footing in Reading. More than that, he had kept the threat of an increasing number of mortals at bay. The thickly wooded Dome Hill with its strange bare crown had become legendary in the neighbourhood for bad luck. So many eerie things, even fatalities, were said to happen to tramps, campers, hikers and motorists alike who spent more than an hour or so there, that it was known among the locals as Doom Hill and therefore avoided like the plague.

It was the never-ending campaign against mortals which kept Ranulph's garrison on its toes and he knew his reports tickled Mortleroy.

Instinct told Ranulph that Gwyn's next onslaught was bound to come in an all-out effort to cancel past defeats. The Earl had therefore made every preparation he could to meet the threat and when he saw a rather smaller force than anything previously gathered around his perimeter at dawn, Ranulph smelt the rat he had long anticipated.

In spite of advice from Mortleroy that the sacred stronghold of Glastonbury was under heavy attack as well as Warwick, which was the key to the Western Marches, Ranulph persisted that both were a feint. He was sure that Reading was the ultimate objective. He became even more convinced of it while he suffered the day-long ritual of sending out small parties of his more expendable knights for skirmishing and even individual combats – conducted with meticulous chivalry on both sides – because his hawks had brought him news of secretly hidden weapons not previously used against a beleaguered fort. Any kind of projectile other than arrows and quarrels – even the latter now frowned on – was outlawed. But this time it seemed the Knights of Beauty had brought rock-throwing implements and *fireballs* with them. The latter implied that King Gwyn was resorting to magic, in which he was an expert.

Ordinarily, fire had no power over the faerie, but astral fire could burn and kill and only a magician knew the secret of controlling it.

Ranulph knew that Mortleroy had no magician equal to the task. Algaric, the only one the King ever had, was rumoured to have met with a fatal accident in the more recent past. It was Algaric, at the beginning of Mortleroy's reign, who had turned resistant Mabyn into Mung, and other Kins into Wellsprite and Cave-wight. He had also given Mortleroy the wolves and falcons to harry them, as well as the Royal Falcons to be the King's own ears and eyes everywhere, plus a host of Troll to slave and toil as a workforce without rest.

Late that afternoon when his steward arrived to tell Ranulph that a hawk from Sir Gars had arrived, the Earl was surprised.

'Sir Gars?' he repeated askance. The knight was close to the King, and Ranulph wondered uneasily what he could possibly want with him.

'Without doubt, my lord Earl, and dispatched most urgently for it still bears jesses – and the golden bell has Sir Gars' own signet.'

The bird stayed long enough to deliver bad news. There had been an unforeseen meeting between his party travelling southeast, and a larger party from the northwest flying the true banner of the Owl. Neither Sir Gars nor any of his knights had survived the disastrous clash that followed.

The intelligence came as a terrible blow and, when his scouts further learnt that Sir Avellane was continuing southeast in the direction of Ranulph's Citadel, it confirmed Ranulph's premonition that Dome Hill was the main target. However, another of his hawks returned with a stranger but more promising report. Gwyn's second-in-command had apparently captured a magician whose mantle bore magical symbols and designs. News that the wizard was reported to be tied to his mount, made Ranulph drum his fingers for a while. Although it showed the wizard to be an unwilling party, it could also mean the fellow hadn't even magic enough to free himself. But the Earl's need was desperate and he had to take the chance of rescue that it presented. He therefore rejoined his knights and shattered them with the demand that he wanted a sortie made within the hour.

'But, my lord!' objected shocked voices. 'Such conduct would be dishonourable. The hours between sunset and sunrise have always been sacred. There can be no legitimate combat until dawn.'

Ranulph then told them the full story; the new threat menacing the King's arms in the person of the Mabyn of Mabyn, who had brought shameful defeat on their compeers that morning, and capped it with his knowledge of the new and illicit weapons that Gwyn would use against them in the coming dawn.

Even with that information, they took a lot of convincing that their ancient enemy could descend to such dishonourable tactics. Their triumphs that very day had proved the rebel forces were still inspired with the very soul of chivalry and honour.

'Then must I go to my death alone?' Ranulph fumed with a passion they had never seen before. 'I swear by the Skull I would rather die than surrender this ancient Citadel without a blow! You ride with me along a secret route I have prepared, or stay and die by rock and fire – I don't care which. Steward!' he yelled. 'Call servants! My arms! My horse! And get me mailed! You will also despatch a hawk to my Liege with these my dying words: that Reading fell because my knights–'

The instant uproar of voices clamouring for arms drowned the rest of his sentence.

*

In the event, Ranulph chose the hour well. He led his astonished followers out of the bowels of the Citadel through a lengthy descending passageway which none of them even knew existed. Sapping and tunnelling were another of the arts of war 'not done' by knights. They knew and accepted that Gwyn used them in order to move his forces secretly by underground ways from distant Annwyn but he had never used such artefacts against the strongholds he attacked.

Naturally, they asked how this marvel had come about, and Ranulph gave the brief answer that he had used an army of trolls on the project. All knew the creatures worked without stopping at any task they were set to do; they asked no questions and, without tongues, betrayed no secrets.

On arriving at the massive gate just before the well-hidden entrance at the foot of the hill, the Earl halted for a last minute conference with his second-in-command, Peredur, to assure himself that the knight understood his instructions to the letter. They then waited until two hawks arrived separately with their news. From each, it was good. The coast was clear and the enemy unsuspecting.

*

Peredur went first, leading the smaller of the two parties to the northeast, loosing yet another hawk to scout ahead and keep track of his target's movements.

With their cry of: 'Save the wizard!' they fell on The Knights of Beauty before Myrddin could be freed from his horse or Avellane's task force prepare themselves to meet the unexpected attack, arrows went home and, after them, the thunderous sound of clashing mail and arms.

*

The onslaught swept through Avellane's ranks and Myrddin found himself taken with it. A strange knight, seizing his horse's bridle, thumped the animal's rump with the flat of his sword setting his mount into a startled gallop. Myrddin almost fell, but the stranger held on to him, and swept him away into the closing night.

To Myrddin it seemed no more than a delayed death sentence. If his new captors were enemies of Gwyn; then their interest could hardly be friendly. He therefore concluded that Mortleroy must have learned of his capture by enemy forces, and was taking no chance of losing his vengeance on the magician of the Weirdfolk who had caused him so much trouble.

No one said anything as, pursued by Avellane's outraged knights; his new escort took him in a mad gallop towards what looked like a bonfire on the side of a large hill. Skirting its foot, however, they conducted him through a well-hidden hefty looking portcullis entrance that rose at their approach and fell behind them with the silence of a well-oiled piece of machinery well ahead of their pursuers of whom there was no further sign. All relaxed to a walking pace up a large sloping tunnel through a series of imposing gates before reaching a brightly lit and roomy vault.

Here, the leader of the party halted, motioned a couple of fae-at-arms that they should release the prisoner, and threw up his visor to say: 'Welcome to the Citadel of Reading, Lord Enchanter. Lord Ranulph, Earl of the Southern Marches will receive you shortly and add his apologies to mine for your rude attachment, but his orders were specific. No dalliance for chivalrous contests, but to secure you at all costs and bring you here immediately.'

Myrddin later learned that the Earl had just as explicitly warned his second-in-command, *not* to release their captive before they were back – a tied wizard being better than a loose one who could defend himself.

Peredur was continuing: 'I promise no harm was or is meant towards you. When the Earl learnt of your capture by the rebels from the Underworld, he thought it dishonourable not to attempt a rescue.'

Myrddin took the cue with relief that no one seemed to know his real identity, and while his wrists and ankles began to be untied, replied with ponderous dignity: 'Sir Knight, your explanation is welcome. I confess that in my journey so far through this ancient land of Brython, I was beginning to think it was your barbarous custom to maltreat all visitors to your native land.'

'Then you are a stranger, wizard?'

'Forgive me, Sir Knight, but does my attire *look* as if I am a native of this country?' Myrddin spoke with gentle irony. 'Yet know that you have before you Am-mar-el-lyn, a Prince of Damascus and inheritor of all the lore of the East.' He gave it all the gravitas he could and Peredur nearly fell from his horse he was in such a rush to dismount.

'Am-mar-el-lyn?' he stammered and, with an dazed expression of shock and unbelief, thrust aside the fae-at-arms, and hurried to complete Myrddin's unfastening himself, saying 'Most revered of Princes, had I known who you were, I would have saved you this indignity a long way back.'

Assisting Myrddin from off his charger, Peredur addressed his companions: 'Brothers-in-arms, I order you to treat this noble Prince with royal honour and respect for he is, to my knowledge, the mightiest magician among mortals and immortals both.'

It was Myrddin's turn to blink in astonishment. A case of mistaken identity and a great deal to live up to. There was no alternative, however, but to play to it to the best of his ability.

He inclined his head gravely to the awed acclaim, but demurred modestly: 'You are kind, Sir Knight, but an exaggeration, surely? I have heard that the Overlord of this land is no mean magician himself, which is indeed why I have journeyed so far to meet him.'

That appeared to go down well, for his rescuer responded: 'O Prince of Undying Fame, know that I, Peredur came to your land in days long gone in company with Sirs Percivale and Gareth seeking the Holy Grail. We would have given much to have met with you then.'

'I have heard of you and your companions, brave Peredur,' Myrddin could say with truth. 'But I learned too late of your heroic end in Hindustan.' In fact, he had only just heard the long tale of the Quest from Gareth himself when he had related it to the Weirdfolk in the forest the previous week.

Peredur was nodding. 'Yet it was a kind fate, noble Prince, for since being reborn in this realm, I have learned the quest was vain. Although I have not seen it, I now know the Holy Grail yet remains within these shores.'

Myrddin could not ask how he knew, so he awarded him a benign smile and assured him, again with truthful words: 'The sacred vision shall indeed be yours, Sir Peredur, this I promise. But what of your companions, Sirs Percivale and Gareth? Have you re-met them in this realm?'

'I have not, noble Prince. Sir Gareth was mabyn in wraith, and the Mabyn, being spirits of the earth, I believe him lost in the darkness of some terrifying underworld.' Peredur sighed unhappily, before adding: 'Sir Percivale came of even stranger race. Once, when he was in a dangerous fever from his wounds, he raved of hills, hollows, and places where water ran and music played by the wind in the trees. I therefore think he was of the Denefolk. But it is known that all lies originate with them, and all manner of mischievousness; that they poison the water with their contrary magic and therefore we slay them when we can – which is difficult as they are often invisible.' And Peredur sighed again. 'Yet Perceval seemed so true a knight ...'

Myrddin clenched his hands. Mortleroy had to be a spirit without a conscience. This systematic brainwashing appeared to have vilified the characteristics of every Faerie Kin except those that served him, and the sheer enormity of the situation came home to him when he remembered there were only four great divisions of the Faerie in Britain: The Weirdfolk, the Denefolk, the Kin of Beauty and the Mabyn – and asked himself to what other Kin could these adherents of Mortleroy belong?

The answer was staring him in the face and shook him to the roots. Not only Mortleroy himself, but everyone of his underlings must have originated from one or other of these four great Kins over whom he ruled.

He looked around at the listening group of fae-at-arms and knights and believed he could have identified the true origin of each one of them. Mortleroy had not only enslaved the fae in the form of Mung, Wellsprite, Cave-wight and Troll, but these around him also in their apparently free and loyal support. In which case, it could be said that the Overlord of Britain had the whole Faerie Realm of Brython in the hollow of his hand – even the Weirdfolk of Weir Forest who had had to be hidden, and the People of Beauty who were forced to fight.

This new understanding had a profound effect on Myrddin. He no longer looked on these spirits as innately hostile. They were no more than innocent, misguided fae.

Peredur conducted him up many flights of stairs to a richly furnished chamber to wait for the Earl, whom Peredur went off to find, and Myrddin composed himself to think.

He was well aware that he had not been rescued by whim but for his magical ability and remembered Mildgyth's question: 'And what is the magic *you* do, Am-mar-el-lyn?' His reply that he believed that whatever he wished – or even commanded – to happen, did so by virtue of Merlyn's magic, still remained to be proven in its entirety. In his Office of Black Wand in the forest he had learnt that magic wasn't something that could be read and then said to be mastered. There had been principles to learn; means and methods to memorise, but success, like a musical composition, would always remain the result of spontaneity, genius and what Mildgyth would have called faith but which he interpreted as self-belief. And something was telling him that such a moment had arrived. Here was his chance to put on such a performance that Ranulph would be in no doubt as to what kind of magician they had rescued and needed to respect.

CHAPTER 9

RANULPH

With the kind of luck Ranulph had had that night, Peredur's news that he had rescued the wizard safely, and could speak for him as the genuine article, was a welcome relief. His own foray had been a disaster. Although his party had taken the besiegers by surprise – they were carousing in anticipation of the firestorm they intended to unleash – the removal of the first few fireballs had brought an end to the exercise before it had really begun. Ranulph's orders had been precise; each set of missiles found were to be attached to the finders' saddlebows before riding off to find the next cache. His spies had reported the things to be the size of gooseberries with their openings plugged, suspended from low growing bushes, His guess at what had happened surmised that when the van of the raiding party found the first, some overzealous knight had stabbed at it with his lance or, more likely, a ham-fisted archer had failed to secure one properly to his saddle. If one of the culprits had survived to tell the story of what had happened, he might have been a wiser Earl. But none did. As it was, the instant blaze that lit the sky was impressive and roused the revellers like a swarm of angry bees. Ranulph's small force had had to retire in a hurry, with the vengeful camp commander, Gaheris, and his knights in hot pursuit. Gaheris almost shattered his lance against the imposing portcullis which was down almost before the last of Ranulph's party were inside.

Gaheris shook his fist in righteous anger at the forbidding stronghold, crying: 'Beware the dawn, Ranulph, you cornered rat! A hundred fireballs still wait for you, craven Earl!'

Ranulph hurried to the battlements and hurled back an imperious challenge to personal combat on his persecutor. It was put in such uncompromising terms of rudeness and vilification that Gaheris could not wait to accept and rode away, regardless of the shower of arrows that flew after him. Such a meeting would at least decide something between them.

*

One benefit from the accident, however, was that it had taken the heat off Peredur when Avellane diverted his pursuit on seeing the fire which then took the combined efforts of both commanders to bring under control.

Ranulph had returned to his stronghold with the worrying fear that there were still unnumbered fireballs left to fling at him in the morning. And when Peredur came to advise him with the identity of their captive, the Earl hurried to make his guest welcome and to apologise profusely for the manner of his abduction.

When his excuses were waived aside, Ranulph regretted sounding so fulsome but his experience of Algaric had made him nervous of wizards and, under the cool, appraising eye of this one, doubly so. He was being weighed up and looked to be found wanting. He wished he had been more his usual self, to show his implacable loyalty to duty and – with an impressive assortment of practical skills – to open ways of thinking. It was the kind of scrutiny, however, that made him realise that Peredur had done a good job in calming the magician down. If his second-in-command hadn't managed to assure their guest that he was needed as an expert and capable wizard, Ranulph did not like to think what might have happened.

He was by no means out of the woods, however. When Am-mar-el-lyn began to speak, saying how, many moons ago in his own country, he had read strange signs and omens in the stars which could only be found in this far off northern land, Ranulph tried to express polite interest despite his impatience to get down to his own troubles.

He interrupted with a respectful cough: 'If you would care to tell me what form these signs and omens took, perhaps my modest understanding of events here might be of help, noble Prince?'

The Prince of Damascus gazed into the far distance with an air of mystery and spoke with deep gravity: 'Firstly, it would seem best to tell you of a great roc that fell from heaven to the earth–'

'A great rock!' repeated the Earl, thinking his guest might have had a vision of Gwyn using an even larger ballistic missile against him even than those the Earl had seen. 'I assure you no such bolt has fallen on us – yet.'

His guest looked disdainful. 'I speak of a bird, mighty Earl – not a thunderbolt,' he was corrected. 'A roc is a fabulous bird of golden plumage with talons as keen as swords, and beak sharper than a ploughman's harrow. A sacred bird that appears out of nowhere with portents and messages from the gates of Heaven itself.'

'Ah!' enlightenment dawned on the relieved Ranulph, and he went on to volunteer: '*We* call such a bird a Golden Eagle. And one actually *was* seen only a day or so ago. It looked so monstrous; the King's own Royal Falcons and our bowmen's arrows slew it …' he trailed off, his heart sinking at seeing his guest's expression had abruptly darkened: 'Please, don't tell me what we did was wrong?'

The Prince, looking outraged, had sprung to his feet

with a cry: 'What kind of barbarians are you, you people of Brython?'

When he then began pacing the room with long, angry strides, Ranulph tried again, 'But great Prince, we believed it to be a hostile image sent by some enemy magician to bring about our destruction–'

'Magician?' The interruption was uttered with withering contempt. 'What *magician* has been known in these islands since Merlyn?'

And how am I to answer that? thought Ranulph, remembering that even Algaric hadn't quite measured up to this legendary Enchanter.

When the enraged Prince then raised his hands to heaven and cried passionately: 'O Great Merlyn, master from of old, whose lore I sucked with my mother's milk, how is your name crumbled into dust in this doom-racked land of rogues and lechers! What vengeance do you command I wreak upon such villainy–?'

The Earl interrupted with alarm: 'But mighty one, we don't defile the name of Merlyn. We *revere* his memory.'

'Silence!' the wizard thundered, flinging out his sceptre to evoke a gush of flame between them. Ranulph had no way of knowing if it was a hallucination or not. It looked real enough to him, and the fact that it set nothing else alight only made it the more terrifying while the wizard continued: 'You stinking offspring of a camel's putrefying dung! Who were they but your own ancestors who slew the Great Master of the Heavens?'

It wasn't the injustice of the accusation that worried the Earl; his petrified gaze was fixed on that column of fire. It proved that this mercurial prince was a master of his craft and left Ranulph wondering how he was ever going to placate such a heaven-sent visitor.

After a few more uncomplimentary words were expressed about the state of the country, the wizard again demanded heaven to tell him know what kind of punishment he was to inflict on the Great Enchanter's erstwhile murderers.

In the silence that followed, Ranulph waited in a state of profound dejection, thinking of all his deep-laid schemes and the entire existence of his beloved Citadel that lay in the balance.

When nothing happened and no blast came to hurl him into oblivion, Ranulph allowed himself to relax a little and lifted his head.

The apparently all-powerful magician turned slowly and announced solemnly: 'Be thankful, vile infidel. My spirit tells me that heaven's wrath is not yet to be … I know not why …' He dismissed the column of flame with a flick of his fingers, '… I merely obey.' He then sat himself with much dignity on the nearest couch and voiced an invitation that sounded more like a command: 'Come, misguided servant of a wayward monarch, sit here beside me, and I will tell you more of my visions, and you shall answer me *truthfully* what you may know of them.'

But the Earl would only perch on the edge of the couch. He needed to be ready to be up and out of harm's way before the next outburst.

'In the heavens,' he was informed in ponderous sentences, 'I saw also the likeness of a monster so huge and terrible that its green immensity seared my mind. It seemed the shape of a dragon yet not invincible for the noble beast was writhing and shrivelling beneath a blast of lightning like a whip–'

'Not guilty!' cried Ranulph starting to his feet at once, holding up his hands. 'Neither the King nor I, nor any of our people destroyed that noble beast, O mighty One. It was the Lady Nemway. The Lady of the Lake that long ago lured Great Merlyn to his doom. I will swear it, mighty Prince; on whatever holy relic you might care to choose.'

The Prince nodded sagely. 'Be at peace, Ranulph,' he said, his tone quiet. 'My spirit tells me that you are speaking the truth and that it is indeed that vile witch who is the guilty one.'

Ranulph resumed his seat, although still wary, and explained: 'We knew it as one of the four ancient Protectors of this Realm – and the most dreaded. Great Merlyn placed the Great Green Dragon of the South as guardian over the forest of the Weirdfolk himself. Do you think that that could be why the witch Nemway slew it?' It was a devious invention off the top of Ranulph's head. He couldn't forget the other three of the great dragons had been imprisoned by Algaric.

'Possibly,' he found his words sagely accepted. 'But you spoke of four such "Protectors" of this Realm. What of the other three – where are they?'

Ranulph swallowed hard before answering: 'At the very beginning of our King's reign, a certain magician, Algaric, implored them to do homage to their rightful sovereign. This they did, and have lived obediently ever since under his mighty patronage.'

'So why?' he was asked. 'Why doesn't the King use these powerful protectors against these rebels that you fight?'

'We don't think it's chivalrous to employ such magical forces against our enemies,' Ranulph said, his tone virtuous. 'Up 'til *now*, they have never used such unfair methods against us.'

'Until now, you say? So what unfair methods are these, then? And what magicians do they have who can accomplish it?'

'Their King, Gwyn Son of Gwyn Son of Nudd, has the reputation of being a most capable warlock, O Prince – and that I can believe. I had news today that his forces have brought unlawful weapons with them, weapons that hurl rocks and stones – but, most dreaded of all – balls of fire against which we have no defence.' And Ranulph left it there, hoping the challenge would stay in the foreign magician's mind.

The wizard nodded, pursing his lips in thought.

Ranulph held his breath, hoping against hope that his guest would understand that only someone of equal or greater knowledge could now save Reading from annihilation.

When the wizard asked for further details, Ranulph recounted his disastrous attempt to capture the incendiaries that evening and found his listener sympathetic. It seemed he could appreciate that a dozen valuable fighters destroyed in such a foray was no joke. The fact that a great many more fireballs remained, Ranulph knew, gave his guest the ace of trumps that he could play as he wished. But the Earl found himself kept on tenterhooks just a little longer.

'There is one other omen, noble Earl – the third of my celestial visions that needs interpreting,' he was told. 'I had vision of a male child; a royal babe crowned in glory and descending from the clouds with all the insignia of kingship – and my spirit made known to me that his name was *Yathra*.'

For a moment, Ranulph was dumbstruck. The name was an understandable mispronunciation of Arthur by a foreigner, but there was no doubt regarding its meaning. *Truly*, he thought, *this Prince of Damascus was a Seer of all Seers. How else could he know of the one advent that Mortleroy demanded above all things that his loyal adherents should quickly send news of when it happened?* Again he swallowed, and found his voice almost a whisper. 'Yes,' he said, 'we know of this also. Then, with a burst of inspiration, added 'Which is the very reason why the rebels of the Underworld have invaded our territory, isn't it? Don't the forces of Evil always array themselves against the forces of Good? Weren't they about to kill *you*, noble Prince, when, by the grace of heaven, we rescued you?' He added it as a daring, but artful point with the intentional irony that the wizard might now acknowledge that he owed his life to Ranulph, which meant he *really* was under a certain amount of obligation …?

'So you believe that these People of the Underworld have surfaced to fight against the coming of the Celestial King?'

The Earl nodded at once, reminding the enchanter how the illegal weapons, which could destroy every stronghold on the face of Britain, could also destroy the Child of Heaven.

His guest looked thoughtful. 'And you have no defence?' he asked.

Again the Earl nodded. 'All that remains of Algaric's magic is this: that our wolves, our falcons, our weapons, our servants – were all designed and made by him, and when these have been slain, broken or finally destroyed, the noble realm we have ruled so long must end. And worse, it is now apparent that Algaric for all his gifts was never a Lord of Fire – as you have already proved yourself to be.'

He waited, hanging on his guest's next words. Either he had said too much, or too little, but he was prepared to say and to give a great deal more if it would persuade this great Prince of Damascus to intercede on their behalf.

CHAPTER 10

FIRE OVER READING

Myrddin couldn't help admiring Ranulph. The Earl had courage and integrity. He should have been in command of the forces arraigned against him on the outside – not Avellane.

The wizard frowned. 'Your plight affects me deeply, noble Ranulph. Tell me, if these toys of fire were quenched, and the rock-hurling inventions of your enemies reduced, could you then hold your Citadel?'

Hope lit Ranulph's eyes. 'Most noblest of Princes, nothing would be more certain.'

'Then I must know more,' said Myrddin. 'And, I need a promise.'

Ranulph hunched his shoulders and spread his hands. 'Noble Prince, whatever – anything.'

'I need you to swear that whatever I decide – or do – that you shall not question the wisdom of my acts, my needs, my comings or my goings. Do you so swear?'

'By the Holy Skull, I swear it!' Ranulph exclaimed, crossing himself.

Startled, Myrddin said curiously: 'Your oath is strange one, noble Earl. Whose skull is this, and why is it sacred enough for your oath?'

''Tis a most ancient and holy relic guarded in the King's stronghold at Glastonbury, great Prince. Every year the highest in the land gather to honour the memory of the once and future king – he who is to come even as your vision showed – by virtue of his shrunken astral skull.'

Myrddin frowned. 'I don't understand,' he said. 'How? When?'

'On a certain day – we never know until it is announced – the skull fills itself with the mystic essence of his blood which mysteriously fortifies all who drink of it.' He shrugged and again spread his hands, this time disclaiming: 'There is a rumour even now that Arthur is already born to the Queen of the Weirdfolk – only that is impossible for they are a barren people and far too spiritless anyway to be chosen for such a hero. But our King has issued an edict that all new births among our kind must be reported, and the stars studied, so that the royal babe can be taken to him, and fostered in his own stronghold.'

This was as potentially hopeful, as well as being the most worrying, piece of news that Myrddin had heard until then. Believing he had foisted a changeling on the barren Queen of the Weirdfolk, it troubled him deeply that the spirit of Arthur would be born again among these misguided people. Hopefully, however, he was now in the right position with Ranulph to learn of the event when it happened, to arrive on the scene first and to declare the babe was indeed Yathra. The name had been no mispronunciation, but a deliberate choice on his part in the hopes of getting it adopted to distinguish the fake Arthur of the forest from the true one still to be born. It was more than worrying to think that Mortleroy could still get there first. It seemed plain to Myrddin that the King believed in the time-honoured tactics of Herod. He had only to welcome Yathra as the one to whom he would humbly kneel and submit his crown, for its proud mother to hand the infant over. Then, in the course of time – a very short course no doubt – there would be the inevitable unfortunate and lamentable 'accident'. It meant that he, Myrddin must do everything he could to be the first on hand to rescue the babe and see him spirited away and nurtured secretly; in much the same manner as Merlin had wiled away the mortal Arthur.

Satisfied the Earl believed he could swear no greater oath; Myrddin rose and asked to be shown around his garrison and fortifications.

Ranulph expressed his delight and summoned Peredur to accompany them.

When they emerged onto the moonlit ramparts, a pall of smoke drifting up from the besieging campsite indicated where a small but still burning fire remained, and the distant shouts floating up to them were eloquent of the difficulty Avellane and Gaheris were having to organise its complete extinction.

'You certainly gave them something to think about,' Peredur said with a grin at Ranulph.

'Aye, but have set them on the alert!' the Earl said. Then gestured their guest's attention to what they had to show him.

Myrddin had never seen the outside of a citadel before, let alone been shown around the inside, he was therefore impressed and astonished. Between twelve towers ranging along twelve faces of the star-shaped curtaining walls, ran a buttressed gallery, battlemented and plentifully loop-holed to allow a quick operating of the compactly modelled city's high defences. Within the walls the faerie town laid set with buildings and streets; small parks and here and there small lakes all invisible, he knew, to the mortal world. Even a moat surrounded the walls outside fed from a spring only a few feet from its northernmost point. Overlooked from the many strong points, there was no way of damming or diverting it.

Peredur was proud of its defence. 'Only once has any attempted crossing been successful.'

Ranulph indicated embrasures along the gallery each with neat heaps of rocks and stones piled ready. 'But we are well prepared to repel them. Beyond each heap there is a loosely bricked hole which will give way the moment the first rock is pushed through it. No enemy has ever survived who got that far. And, as I promised, with the fireballs destroyed, our proud impregnability will remain has it always has.'

'It would appear so,' said Myrddin, who had been assessing the strength of what he had seen. 'But I doubt these walls could withstand an assault from *every* enemy.'

'How do you mean, great prince?' Ranulph asked his voice sharp with anxiety.

In demonstration, Myrddin delivered a quick blow with the edge of his sceptre on the battlemented wall over which they were leaning – and pulled the Earl back just in time as it crumbled into a irregular breach.

'A poor magician, who raised such walls,' he said. 'One blow from the Mabyn's *Moldwarp* would shatter them to their foundations.'

Ranulph's look of shocked surprise told him he had dropped an outsize in bricks *extra* to those that had toppled into the moat below.

He covered it with a bewildered frown, saying, 'Noble Ranulph, tell me – what means *Mabyn* and *Moldwarp*? Such arcane sayings come to me often.'

*

By the time Ranulph had finished explaining; he was ready to serve Myrddin on bended knee and congratulated himself on having already sent news to the King of the rescue of such a wonderful ally. It would surely bring Mortleroy hotfoot to the Citadel to reward their new wizard suitably – if he definitely agreed to help. With this in mind, Ranulph held nothing back. Having shown the Prince of Damascus his heights, the Earl and his second-in-command then gave him a conducted tour of the Citadel's secret depths; dungeons that held the repellent examples of faerie distortion that he kept imprisoned there under their guard of trolls.

*

Myrddin stared horrified at what he saw. The trolls themselves were unspeakably misshapen, some had but one eye, others no ears, while all were maimed and hideously distorted.

His eyes went from them to a couple of Mung cowering in a cage. 'These are no witless images,' he exploded indignantly.

'Great Prince, they are all as they are,' said Peredur defensively. 'When and how, I don't know, but this is the way they have always been–'

'And those?' Myrddin interrupted, pointing at another cage in which three attenuated forms hardly more than skeletons had shrunk into a corner hiding their eyes from the light with claw-like hands.

'Wellsprite,' said Ranulph dismissing them with contempt. 'Another rebellious kind that needs keeping in subjection. We keep them caged like this so that our wolves, hawks and falcons learn to recognise them whenever they meet them.'

'The things plague our highways, infect our wells or sneak from caves to kill the King's deer which is unlawful,' said Peredur, 'For the King's comfort, therefore, we destroy them when we can ...'

Myrddin wasn't listening as he tried to smother his feelings. In justice, the two were only airing their indoctrination. They were not to blame for the travesties themselves, or their brain-washed attitude towards them.

What a diabolical set-up this King Death of theirs has contrived, he thought with a shiver. It was evident now that Mortleroy wasn't even the magician that Myrddin had believed him to be, but had all the instincts of Satan to manipulate his rule.

Ranulph wanted to show him their newest captive, caught that same day, but Myrddin turned away with distaste, making it obvious that he had seen enough. It seemed Ranulph got the message, for he hastened to invite him to the evening's festivities.

The mysterious wizard's appearance in the banqueting hall brought a sudden hush. Every knight and lady rose to greet him, because Ranulph had made it known that the visitor was an honoured guest.

He was introduced to the wives of Ranulph and Peredur, and met Peredur's son, Osric – a serious faced youth who took him aback by asking:

'Please, sir, what is it like to be a magician?'

Non-plussed, Myrddin said: 'Why? Do you want to be one?'

Osric looked at his father, shook his head almost violently and shuddered. 'Oh no, sir! Never.'

'Then why do you ask?' Myrddin asked made curious by such an answer.

Before the boy could answer, his father said: 'Probably just nosy and wants to know what he's missing.' And to Osric: 'Go and sit down with your mother, boy, and another time, don't be so impertinent.' He turned to Myrddin. 'Please …?'he said, with a gesture that ushered Myrddin to a seat on Ranulph's right between the Earl's daughter, the Lady Ustane, and Peredur's sister, the Lady Alys.

Acknowledging them and taking his seat, Myrddin's mind stayed a moment longer on Osric as he shook his head and reflected: *Were I a Lord of Earth, Air, Fire* and *Water, I would still never have the power to know the inside mind of another person!*

He then soon forgot the oddness of the conversation in the novel experience of the meal. Servants came and went bearing viands of all descriptions: boar's head, venison, swan, capon, goose. Like everything else, none of it physical.

'Tis a royal meat, dear prince,' said Lady Ustane, catching his look of astonishment at the haunch of venison that had appeared before him. 'Is this noble beast unknown in your own country?'

'Not at all,' Peredur intervened, answering for him: 'Rather, I think our guest is without a dagger.' And proffered his own.

Myrddin accepted it with murmured thanks and cut himself a cautious chunk. He had another surprise when he bit into it, it was perfectly cooked; tender and as delicious as anything he remembered in mortality but reminding him how ill he had felt when he had once sipped mortal gin when he had first met the maladjusted fae trying to live like men and women in Weir Forest. He marvelled now as he tore another mouthful from the piece at the end of the knife. Surely the ancient magician Algaric, who appeared to have provided all things needful, couldn't have made the amount of images, even of one kind, to supply centuries of consumers. Perhaps it was magically renewed …?

Ranulph beamed at his guest's delighted expression and assured him with pride: 'The hunting in these parts excels that of any forest in Britain. In Reading we breed only the best.'

Myrddin nearly choked on the meat. '*Breed*, my lord Earl …?'

'Indeed. The deer mate and bear young the same way as we do. Isn't it the same with you?'

'I had no idea such magic was known to you?' Myrddin said, his voice faint to cover his astonishment.

'Not known to us!' the Lady Alys exclaimed, looking daggers at her rival, the Lady Ustane's unnecessary support of the hand Myrddin was using to hold the knife. 'The great Algaric made a gift of its secret to us a long time long ago.'

And how had the magician done that? Myrddin asked himself. The fellow couldn't even reinforce a solid piece of astral masonry and had no knowledge of fire.

'A secret he had from Merlyn, so 'tis said,' Ranulph said, seeing his guest's frown. He seemed anxious to avoid the disturbance of any professional feelings.

'The wretched hordes from the Underworld also have it, so they're very nearly as good at hunting as we are,' Peredur added.

'But as soon as we have slain the rabble at our gates, I promise I can show you some good sport, great prince,' Ranulph hastened to contribute.

This struck Myrddin as a rather pointed reminder of time and the job still waiting to be done. But he needed time to think. There was something here that was nagging away in a corner of his mind.

'Allow me,' he said with a smile at each of his female admirers. He carved a morsel for each which they took daintily – and in that moment he realised the enormity of what he and they were doing. They were *eating meat – dead* animal meat, and revulsion engulfed him. A vivid picture of his first ever meeting with White Wand filled his mind. It was when he had sat, nervous and trembling, hugging his knees and tugging idly at a blade of grass, that her silver slippered foot had moved, making his hand tingle and causing him to cry out in protest at the shock: 'Destroy no life, August,' she had said. 'Only mortals do that ...'

And here he was now in Mortleroy's Kingdom; where King Death saw to it that his subjects were fed with death; and ruled that their whole way of life should reflect mortality to the extent that they even *appeared* to die like ordinary mortals.

So what really happens to them? he wondered. They had no tradition of returning to mortality like the Weirdfolk, only of being re-born as fae – or something worse, apparently. What *kind* of magician had Algaric really been who could have worked such a powerful subjugation?

He wanted to jump up, to cry out – anything to wake them up to what was going on – but wisdom and prudence held him fast and dictated: *You are not the one to free them. Only the true Arthur can do that. What you have to do is find him.* It was true, and brought him back to his next step. There was no denying that King Gwyn had let him down atrociously in the matter of sending an armed escort for the Weirdfolk. More than that, his commander-in-chief, Avellane would have had Myrddin slain without a second thought but for the timely intervention of Ranulph's party. But now, with one blow, Myrddin could repay the Earl and teach Gwyn a lesson he might never forget. It was highly treasonable, of course, to give aid and comfort to the true Arthur's enemies, but that was of secondary importance just then. With the knowledge he had gained of the Citadel's defences, he felt confident that, under his directions, Amyas would be able to break it wide open again, and thus redeem Myrddin's apparent betrayal.

As he returned the knife to Peredur with his thanks, something in his expression, distaste perhaps, must have betrayed the shock he was still feeling, because Ranulph looked startled.

'You are offended?' he asked anxiously. 'Something we've said …?'

'On the contrary, dear Earl, I am sorely tempted to sample more it is so delicious –' *Which was true enough,* he thought, although it was testing his powers of diplomacy to say so, '– but it will soon be dawn and such indulgence would be detrimental. I need to be away while it is still dark enough if I am to deal with the threat that hangs over you.'

Ranulph's look of relief told him that the Earl must have been waiting in extremes of patience to discover whether the Prince of Damascus really *was* going to deliver what he had already as good as promised, and might well have been on the point of wondering what other kind of veiled reminder would draw the wizard's attention to how late it was getting.

'How will you go, noble prince?' he asked 'The surest and safest route I can offer is the tunnel through which you were brought in. The exit is well away from the enemy's surveillance–'

Myrddin cut him short with a laugh. 'I shall fly from your battlements in a guise that I believe will astonish you,' he promised.

*

Standing with them once more on the great walls surrounding the city, they saw him step back and a moment later, when a Royal Falcon leapt into the air to soar away high above Dome Hill, an electrified Peredur and Ranulph stood petrified until Ranulph fell to his knees and whispered: 'Peredur, woe is me. I told him we had no magic against Gwyn's fireballs – yet *who* but our Liege himself would dare change into one of his own beloved Falcons …?'

*

Dealing with the fireballs took Myrddin far longer than he anticipated. They were scattered all round the perimeter of the besieger's encircling camp and each group was now under a strong guard against further attack.

Avellane, miraculously surviving Peredur's onslaught in the rescue of Myrddin, had established overall command in the absence of Gwyn. The fire had been extinguished at last, and the remaining fireballs secured. Then all relaxation was cancelled. Avellane wanted a council of war.

Myrddin was in time to eavesdrop a moment for a flavour of what was being said by hiding his fae-sized bird shape under the flap of Avellane's pavilion. It soon became clear to him that no one wanted Avellane's plan for an all-out attack at dawn to stand as it was – apart from a personal encounter between Ranulph and himself which had to be meticulously fair. Should Avellane fall in combat then Gaheris would assume command and after him, Bras-de-fer. Then the order was: first the rocks to make breaches in the walls to distract the defenders and then fireballs to rain death and destruction upon all within.

A number of voices were speaking out loudly against it. They had come to fight honourably as became the People of Beauty, not to break in and burn like common robbers and assassins. Such a holocaust would leave no one in the Citadel alive to fight. They hadn't liked the idea from the beginning and had readily agreed among themselves that they would have the strongest of words with Gwyn ap Gwyn when he arrived. Now that they had heard he wasn't coming, they were prepared to have even stronger words with his Commander in Chief.

The protests grew increasingly loud and came to a head when Bras-de-Fer swore roundly that unless he was allowed at least a dozen personally conducted single combats he would pack it in and make tracks for home. The announcement received a roar of applause that nearly brought the tent down.

Leaving them at it, Myrddin started work, still able to hear them arguing. In the end, Avellane reached a compromise: he would permit combats á l'outrance – which Myrddin now understood to mean 'to the death' – until midday but, after that, the fiery cannonade must begin.

They had just reached this agreement when the first of the fireballs, sneaked away by a mortal-sized black falcon, whistled down like bombs on two nearby catapults.

Everyone poured out of the tent like a disturbed wasp nest; Avellane issuing orders to catch and slay the raiders at all costs, and Gaheris and Bras-de-Fer, with malicious intent, giving contrary instructions to douse the fires first and let the raiders do their worst. The more fireballs destroyed, the longer everyone could spend in honourable combat. They had to change their minds, though, when messengers reported that the fireballs were somehow targeting the catapults. No one minded the fireballs' destruction, but they couldn't make the necessary breaches in the walls without the catapults. Then news came that the cause of the havoc was one of the enemy's Royal Falcons …!

Pandemonium reigned. In the midst of the encircling inferno, which none of their efforts could quench, grassland, shrubs and trees had caught alight. Soon burning branches were falling and trees bursting with the heat, hampering not only the Knights of Beauty, but Myrddin also. Not wishing to injure any of them, he had to resort to all kinds of wiles to lure the guards away from the simmering fruit on the branches above them while their arrows drove him off more than once.

*

Watchers on the ramparts of Reading's faerie Citadel stood transfixed in wonder at the extent of the conflagration.

'Truly, our Liege is a Lord of Fire,' whispered Ranulph, wishing he could have cried it to the heavens, but knowing he had to keep it between himself and Peredur. It was a sobering thought that, but for the intervention of their noble King, all this might have been taking place within his walls instead of outside them. It left him feeling awed – even if a little puzzled.

CHAPTER 11

THE EYE OF THE HORSE

By the time mortal fire-engines were rumbling slowly to the scene, Myrddin had incinerated every catapult and, with only one or two exceptions, the fireballs as well. By then the false dawn was in the east, and he needed to be gone if he was to check on Weir Forest before returning to the Chapel of Blue Fountains. But how was he to get there? He had been abducted near Lewes and again from the fast track that Avellane had been following before reaching Dome Hill. It could be anywhere. But simply travelling southeast in a straight line was not the answer to his problem, he knew. There had to be a better way. From where he was above Dome Hill, the hills a few miles away to the south reminded him of his intention to visit Mount Caburn even further south. These nearer hills lay in the general direction of where he wanted to go, so it was worth a quick survey to see if there was an Iron Age Hill Fort among them as well.

He shouldn't have been surprised – although it was a pleasant one. It was more that he hadn't remembered how close Reading lay to the White Horse at Uffington. Now it spread beneath him in all its white splendour – Myrddin could have sworn that its eye winked!

Intrigued, he flew low over the eye itself and saw it pulse again with another shaft of light, only this time in a different direction. Hovering above it, he saw the pulses increase with the sun's growing appearance, until the eye was blazing out in all directions: *Rayed for all the world like a trig point!* he thought in amazement. And it was. Dropping down for an even closer look, he found the illuminating beams running in every direction of the compass path to every place on the map and beyond – and there was Mount Caburn! He leaned forward towards it – and a bolt of energy hit him.

Like someone thrown down into deep water, he threshed about in a wild, uncoordinated struggle for stability and when he regained it a moment later, still flapping his wings, he was there above the bare grassy slopes of the 480ft isolated peak of Mount Caburn with a single stone below him.

It was impossible for him to be out of breath, but it felt like it.

'Talk about the speed of light!' he muttered, morphing out of the falcon into himself. He leant against the stone – and as quickly jerked away. It was alive! Energy, like a slow heartbeat pulsing in spiralling waves up from the earth to flow up and away down again like a stream of living water.

It was a lot to think about. Amaranthus had written: *It is also recognised among these races of the faerie kin that they may also be known to each other through the eye of the horse. ...* He remembered with a jolt how his partner, Ann, had described the vision of a Unicorn she had seen in the Eye of Mona: '*... It turns now and is galloping towards a hill. But it is changing – melting – turning itself into one of those chalk effigies ...*'

But first things first, though. He had sought and found a direct route over sixty miles in quite literally the blink of an eye. He still had twenty to go, so back to his falcon form for an overview.

A clear straight track ran northwest. He followed it, his flight fast, smooth and gentle. He knew exactly where the path was going and where he needed to turn off onto another.

Obstructions were no problem, they slowed him down, but he could fly over or around them and pick up on the path he was following easily enough. *It's odd I've never noticed these lines before*, he thought. But then he hadn't done a lot of flying before leaving the forest, nor had he known anything of what he should have been looking for.

*

When he reached the vicinity of Three Weirs village, he was surprised to see the Constable of Eden's Ford, his followers, knights, fae-at-arms, and bowmen, wolves and hawks arriving in a field on its outskirts from the direction of Cyngsfold, all in one piece and apparently unharmed. The sight at least assured him that he had been in time to stop them invading the forest via the tunnel. Or had he?

Wondering just what he was going to find in the forest, he plunged through the Veil of Invisibility and became aware that the two Wychies were doing their best to contain a crisis. He hovered a few moments above the Mead.

If Dreadful was still intact and on guard, the creature should come at once.

It did, the forty-foot virulent green immensity of form that Myrddin had made for it scintillating in the sun as it hurtled towards him out of the trees with a gust of fire.

In his anxiety, Myrddin had forgotten he was still in the shape of a black falcon. He dropped like a stone to the ground, reverted to his eastern appearance as Am-mar-el-lyn, and had hastily re-applied a beard by the time Dreadful had turned, landed and skidded to a surprised halt before him. Commanding the beast back to his normal one metre of golden size, Myrddin ordered the dragon to take his compliments to Black Wand, and ask if Am-mar-el-lyn was welcome.

But the glittering black appearance of Redweird was already on hand.

'Hael and wyn, Am-mar-el-lyn.' he greeted him, his tone grave. 'You come at a sorry time but most opportune. If anyone can help us, it must surely be you. Arthur appears to have left the Forest, alone and unarmed, and we are still trying to establish what happened.'

Myrddin hurried with him to Queen's Glade where Arthur's black charger, Windflame was standing quietly with four strange and terrified riders clinging to his mane and to each other. After all that the wizard had seen in Ranulph's dungeons, he had no difficulty identifying an attenuated and skeletal wellsprite, wearing Arthur's gold and purple cloak, clutching at an awkward and ungainly cave-wight wearing the youth's tunic, while clinging to a misshapen troll and a hairy mung; the last two sporting the royal hose, shoes and cap between them. It was an extraordinary sight, and Myrddin couldn't begin to imagine what had happened to account for it.

White Wand had her back towards him while endeavouring to get the occupants off the horse, and both Wychies were keeping the fae from seeing the strange and terrible looking arrival – as well as prevent them from realising that Arthur had gone.

They had been unable to protect Queen Gwen, however. She had retired to the privacy of her bower where she was weeping in silence. The Seneschal and Chamberlain were coming hot-foot at Black Wand's summons, while the Master of Gnomes, and Arthur's knight, Gareth had just arrived from the Wynn.

On Redweird's arrival White Wand turned to speak to him, and Myrddin, who had taken it for granted that she would be his previous partner, Ann, was stunned to see it was her understudy, Stella. It could only mean that Ann had taken the bane and gone the Way of Unbecoming back into mortality.

It was a shock he had to put to the back of his mind as Stella first greeted her partner before she turned to Myrddin. There was no sign of recognition in her eyes only visible relief at his being there. 'Great Am-mar-el-lyn,' she said, appealing to him: '*you* know the ways of the world beyond the Veil of Invisibility, please, tell us what we should do?'

Myrddin went straight to the frightened mung. Stroking the creature's tangled and matted fur, he managed to calm and reassure it; his love and understanding reaching past its fear and, to the amazement of those around him, he soon translated the barely audible and uncouth sounds that came in answer to his quiet questioning.

It appeared that Arthur had rescued them from some hunters, who were always on the lookout to take them captive with wolves, hawks or falcons. Their oppressors had been confronted by Arthur and ordered to hand over each of the maltreated creatures as he had come across them one by one. He had given each of the strange beings a piece of his clothing in exchange for their rags before ordering Windflame to take them to the Forest of Weir at full speed.

The terrified riders, who had never before been on any kind of horse, had simply clung to each other and to Windflame's mane in abject terror until they arrived trembling and still unable to understand where they were or what was going to happen to them.

After Myrddin had explained all this, Gareth, whom he now knew to have been the erstwhile companion of Peredur when they had been together in mortality, at once made sense of it.

'It's all my fault,' he said, coming forward almost in tears. 'When Arthur came with us to the Mansion of Gnomes after refusing to draw the sword, the noble Amyas spoke of the weapons of the outside world and tested my shield with *Moldwarp*. It never even dented it. The great Mabyn marvelled at it and said that it must be of Wayland's make because no child of Wayland could ever hurt each other. Then Arthur took me aside and asked me how people went about when they didn't want to be recognised. Well, you know how curious he is about *everything*, so I thought nothing of it. I said that they simply disguised themselves. And Arthur says: "I realise that, Gareth – but how? How can anyone make themselves *look* different from the person that they are?" So I said that if I were a king for example, I might disguise myself as a beggar – because nobody expects a king to be a beggar. "And how do people *look* like beggars, Gareth?" he asks, and I said "Well, Sire, they wear rags and they beg for money to buy bread." "Well, thank you, Gareth." he says. "Please, don't let me keep you longer from joining the Master and our guest", – that was Amyas–'

'That must be when Arthur then came to me for rags,' the closely listening Seneschal interrupted. 'I was very surprised but told our young Liege that the Weirdfolk had no rags. "That's all right," says Arthur, thanking me. "I'll see where I can find some." I thought then that he returned to his mother the Queen here in the Glade here, but it must have been *then* that he took his horse Windflame from the Royal Stables …' he tailed off, spreading his hands helplessly.

Myrddin turned to Black Wand. 'Great Wychy, if I might make a suggestion …?'

'Please!'

'Let Nyzor provide a suitable potion for calming and restoring the spirits of these – your new arrivals. I would then suggest that these two …' and he indicated the cave-wight and wellsprite '… will be happiest in the Wealspring grotto for the moment …' He turned to Omric. '… And you, Master, if you could have pity on our brother the troll and let him shelter with you and the gnomes in your Mansion?'

'He will be made most welcome, great Am-mar-el-lyn,' Omric's deep voice assured him.

'As for our brother, the high-traveller,' said Myrddin, looking back at the Wychies. 'I beg he may be allowed the freedom of the trees. There he will feel most at home and be happiest. Please then excuse me. I will go immediately in search of Arthur–'

He was interrupted by Gareth running forward and falling on his knee before him. 'Please, oh please, great Am-mar-el-lyn, take me with you!'

Myrddin looked at him non-plussed. 'But I have no horse for you, Gareth–'

'There's Dreadful …?' he said eagerly.

'Who is needed here in the Forest,' Redweird cut in at once, but in a gentle manner.

'Then mayn't I take Windflame for my Liege – for when we find him?'

Myrddin looked at Omric. 'Master, Gareth is part of your company – it must be your decision?'

'If you will have him, great Am-mar-el-lyn, then I say he should go with you.'

While Gareth hurried off to suit up in his armour, Nyzor appeared with his dray of barrels to administer suitable potions all round, and Myrddin had time to regret he had not brought the cup with him which would have turned their four guests back to their true shapes. He consoled himself however that Nyzor's potions would at least soothe them, and so helped the Wands and the Royal Vintner with their ministrations.

As soon as he could, he took Stella to one side and asked what had happened to the Wych-that-was. Something in his voice must have betrayed his emotion for he found Stella looking at him with wide and startled eyes. He immediately veiled his own but knew it had only confirmed her recognition. The Wychy-that-had-been had so often veiled his gaze the same way in the past with her.

'Black Wand!' she said softly in astonishment, the old habit of his title dying hard.

'Am-mar-el-lyn,' he corrected in as low a tone. 'Please, tell me, when did it happen?'

'Your Wych so pined for you, Am-Mar-El-Lin, she took the Mortal Sickness. It was some time ago now, as we sat together in her Retreat on the Wandle, her Wand simply passed from her hand to mine. She begged me for the Bane, which I had to give her, as you know–' She broke off as Gareth came clanking back into view, and drew away from the wizard, saying clearly: 'So you see how it is with us, great Am-mar-el-lyn?'

Of course he did and his mind raced with the implications. Ann had gone back to mortality, and it was his fault. It was ironic that he had unthinkingly infected her with the mortalness of Merlyn's human form at a time when they were trying to rescue every incarnate wraith in the village that they could find before the forest disappeared and left them without a home to come back to. He shuddered to think of her dying as a mortal and finding herself at the mercy of the larger Faerie Realm under Mortleroy. He couldn't help wondering at the providence that had saved himself from Dragga which now made it possible for him to go in search of her and bring her wraith back to the Weirdfolk.

Gareth's need for attention broke in on his thoughts. Stella had gone to the Queen to tell her what was happening, and Gwen came at once to thank them both and to give Gareth her grateful blessing. The two then said their farewells to the Wychies and, with the fae now allowed to crowd around in excited admiration, the Master of Gnomes helped Gareth to mount the vacant black charger.

'What an adventure for him!' they sighed blissfully to each other. 'What tales he will have to tell us when he returns!'

Myrddin saw the look of relief that passed between Redweird and Stella. They knew they had done well. Their charges had no idea of what had happened, or that Arthur was missing – which was just as it should be.

*

As soon as they were by themselves in Wychies' Lane, Gareth remarked how uncomfortable it felt to have the great Am-Mar-El-Lin walking on foot beside him.

Knowing how difficult and pernickety the knight could be on all points of etiquette and procedure Myrddin felt obliged to remind him that they were on a rescue mission.

'Don't worry, I shall provide myself with a horse as and when necessary. What you need to do is to remember that you are with me as my personal Knight-at-Arms. Your loyalty is to me alone – however contradictory things may appear. You will obey *my* orders, and you will keep *your* mouth shut no matter what you might want to say. Our lives will depend on it – is that understood?'

Gareth nodded.

'Good. Now the 'enemy' is in a field near Three Weirs village, and I will do the talking. Firstly though, I must scout ahead, and will do so as a black falcon. You will wait just here inside the Veil until I return. Is that understood?'

Gareth assured him it was.

CHAPTER 12

KINDRED OF THE GRAIL

Flying over the village, Myrddin noted the Constable still deploying his force on the outskirts.

For Myrddin the slow moving, loud and heavy rumble of the mountainous mortal world had become a backdrop; a part of the landscape which he hardly noticed anymore. Back with Gareth, though, he realised it how new it all was to the knight – and not a little unnerving – as indeed was his own company. The wizard had been aware of the knight's awe and wonder when he had changed back to his eastern persona and fashioned a horse for himself from plant plasma.

'Gareth, you'll get used to it,' he said, as they weaved their way ahead at lightning speed around cars, lorries and cyclists and pedestrians. 'Wizards are wizards. And it isn't the mortal world that you need to be afraid of,' he went on, dodging the sudden lunge of a dog and waving it aside with his sceptre. 'I spoke of the 'enemy', didn't I? But it's a figurative term. In the main, they are simply misguided fae. You remember Peredur?'

Gareth nodded. 'A good knight, and my best friend,' he answered, his expression surprised and eager. 'You have seen him?'

'You'll meet him as one of the figurative 'enemy'. He remembers you–' he broke off. They had reached a quiet outskirt and one of Edric's knights followed by a wolf, had cantered into view to challenge him. 'Say nothing,' Myrddin reminded Gareth in a low voice before declaring himself with a haughty: 'I am Am-mar-el-lyn, Prince and Magician of Damascus. Now let whoever is in command of you advance and give account of himself, and say why he dare so discourteously obstruct the Saviour of Reading and friend of the Earl of the Southern Marches.'

*

Edric, still wearing his plume-less helm and still trying to find out what had been going on while he had been lost in the underground maze, received the message with some astonishment and rode his horse in a hurried response. Introducing himself as Sir Ranulph's Constable of Eden's Ford, he asked for an explanation of the Prince's words.

It was given to him along with a factual description of the Citadel's personalities, its defences and the kind of surprising armaments that the People of Gwyn had levelled against it. The Constable then found himself heckled about his own activities. What had he been doing the previous day in the company of the Lady of the Lake and Sir Accolon of the Bloodied Sword? And where were the two of them now?

Blinking in guilty amazement, Edric wondered how the foreign Prince could possibly know so much; quite apart from why it should even interest him. *So what might have been reported to the Earl?* He bluffed it out; saying he had laid an ambush for the King of the Mabyns '…We were within that much …' he demonstrated graphically with finger and thumb '… of catching him, but when we followed him into an Underway, he escaped us by fetching down a load of rock to block our way. We returned along the same route only to find the passage blocked there also! We eventually found our way out by following a wave of fresh air coming in via another entrance early this morning in the grounds of a Chapel.' He didn't add that their arrival had surprised a great number of armed Mabyn, and that he had been roundly told off by his cousin Mildgyth for breaking the peace of her Holy Place, and had wasted no time in getting away from it. He did say, however, that he had sent word by hawk to Sir Ranulph. '… I am therefore most anxious and worried, Great Prince,' he went on. 'I am afraid of what must have happened to the Lady Nemway, to whom my Liege has given the greatest of privileges because of her brave annihilation of the Green Dragon of the South. I fear she and Accolon may have been crushed by the rock-fall.'

'Believe me, Constable,' he found himself informed dryly: 'the Lady is in less danger from the King of the Mabyn than you will be if you ever try to enter the Forest of Weir again. He is none other than her brother. They both lord it there and have gnomes mailed and armed far, far outnumbering your force – even without the mighty weapon of the Mabyn of Mabyn. As for the Green Dragon supposedly slain by the witch, it was a simulation. The real thing is still alive there, and only *I* can control it.'

Edric promptly slid off his horse and fell at the magician's feet. 'O mighty Prince, Saviour of our Citadel of Reading, I implore you save me! I went against the Earl's orders; seeking glory for myself by thinking I could seize the Forest of Weir. What shall I do? How shall I account for my long absence?'

'Not easily,' he was told, and had the impression of the matter being given profound consideration before the wizard continued thoughtfully: 'Personally speaking, I couldn't hold it against you. What hope has any honest warrior who pits his wits against a woman's wiles – especially a vile witch like Nemway? I can only promise to argue your case with the noble Earl as soon, and as strongly, as possible …'

But Edric remained terror stricken. *What if the efforts of the Prince of Damascus were not enough?* Mortleroy was notoriously short-tempered with bunglers: he usually had them stripped of their apparel and ignominiously thrown to the wolves before the eyes of his approving knights and ladies. He then held a select banquet at which the victim's head – or rather its contents – were consumed by a favoured few as an extra-special delicacy. And that wasn't all. It was believed and held as a tenet, that the spirit of the departed would be re-born a bestial mung, *if* he was lucky. If he wasn't, then a spidery wellsprite or – if you can get even lower than that – a mindless troll …

The voice above him was continuing: '… In return, however, I want a promise from you?'

Edric could only respond with an emotional: '*Anything*, O mighty Prince.'

'Then swear to me that you will never again go within one mortal mile of the Chapel of Blue Fountains whence you emerged, unless you wish to incur the full weight of *my* wrath and displeasure.'

'But I have already sent word to Sir Ranulph that the place is besieged–'

'Then you had better send another – and quickly – that you have been deceived …!'

*

Myrddin's alarm at what might be happening in the Chapel of Blue Fountains made him in a hurry to leave the Constable and the village. He was thankful for Gareth's obedience to keep silent, but suspected it was more in fright at his, Myrddin's behaviour with Edric that the knight was hardly daring to speak to him at all, although Myrddin knew there had to be many questions the fay was dying to ask. But the wizard had one for him.

'Gareth, in the Forest before we left, you said that Arthur had refused to draw the sword – what did you mean?'

'W-why, that was when Arthur was presented with Excalibur at High Moon, after Black Wand-who-had-been had left us. Arthur declared it was not Excalibur and gave it to the Master of Gnomes to identify. And truly, Am-mar-el-lyn, Omric confessed that the sword was the one that *he* had made, at the behest of the Black-One-that-had-been, to replace the sword that the Lady Nemway had brought. Then Arthur asked how the Master had forged it, and Omric said: "I did as the Black One directed me, Sire. But after it was done, and knowing it was not Excalibur, I took it secretly to the Wealspring, with Dreadful. Three times I bid Dreadful to breathe fire upon it, and three times I quenched the sword with water from the Wealspring, making a wish each time. One that it should reveal Arthur; two, that it should bring him victory and three that it should have healing powers." Then Arthur thanked the Master and said it was most perfectly fashioned. He smiled when he said this – and you could see how proud it made Omric. Then Arthur said a strange thing. "But," he said, "I shall not draw this sword until the hand that holds Excalibur has slain me. Then I shall draw this." When the Lady Nemway returned yesterday morning, and heard what had happened, and saw Omric's sword, she was extremely grieved and angry. She said she would go at once in search of the true Excalibur.'

Myrddin doubted it was Arthur's own perception that had told him the sword wasn't Excalibur. More like Nemway would have warned the young Pretender before she left the Forest that he should have nothing to do with it. So of course, she would go off again in pretence of finding the real thing, and return with another just as impossible to unsheathe as the first had been. All part of her dastardly plan to reveal Arthur as an impostor – which he was – but Nemway didn't know that. She really believed he was the genuine article but, as Mortleroy's agent, she wanted to destroy him. As for being 'slain by Excalibur'. Well, yes, he supposed that when the true Arthur held the true Excalibur then the false Arthur would be literally 'slain'. Smiling thinly at the irony of it all, he gave his attention to getting back to the Chapel of Blue Fountains. He had never meant to be away for as long as he had, but then he could not have foreseen his adventures with Sirs Gars, Avellane and Peredur.

'I shall fly ahead of you as a black falcon,' he told Gareth. 'We're making for the same woods where Nemway took you last time you were out here. I need to get there quickly so lead my horse and please keep up with me as nearly as you can.'

*

They arrived at the Chapel without incident and, just as he had expected, it still hummed like a disturbed wasps' nest, with Mildgyth especially and unaccustomedly agitated. Every mabyn who had arms or armour was fully clad and scouting parties were in permanent circulation.

Koo and Nori, now Tors and Gawain respectively, came in high excitement to explain what had happened. It appeared that they had left their wiccies to carry on making clothes and armour while, in the interests of everyone's greater safety and unknown to Mildgyth, they had started excavating another underground home, this time into a promising looking hillock within the Chapel garden itself. Hampered by their new arms and armour, the work was done in the all-together. They had commenced cheerfully with their bare hands, or with splinters of wood for leverage; having all agreed that to use their swords and shields as picks and shovels would be a sacrilege. The long latent genius for working in earth had strengthened, so that the excavation, which was well organised, had become consistent and rapid and, to their astonishment, opened up an ready-made refuge which they explored and found to be an Underway.

Tors had immediately gone to report it to Mildgyth. The next moment a sudden hubbub of warlike shouts and yells of anger and dismay brought the pair of them out to see the whole workforce running towards them, with warning cries: 'To the trees, brothers! To arms! The trees! To arms!'

And while everyone disappeared in quest of their arms and armour, mailed and mounted figures had come charging out of the Underway in pursuit accompanied by a flight of hawks and a number of red-eyed slavering wolves.

It was with admiration that Tors told Myrddin how Mildgyth had taken one look at their leader, and walked swiftly into his path. Raising a commanding hand, she had spoken with dignity: 'It is the law that there shall be no war upon this sacred ground. Neither God, nor King will condone such a violation of this Chapel.'

That had made them pull-up immediately and in obvious consternation. They called back the racing wolves, while their leader, whipping up his visor, exclaimed: 'Most reverend Mildgyth, no sacrilege is intended. We did not know the Mabyn's Underway would lead us here. Of your charity, dear cousin, forgive us. We will leave at once.'

'With that and your apology, I shall be content, Cousin Edric,' she said quietly. 'But how is it that you are here at all? This is an Underway of the Mabyn, which they never use, anyway.'

Ordering his force to retire, Edric dismounted heavily out of respect for his sainted kinslady whilst, seeing the truce, the hastily arming Mabyn stopped mailing and Mildgyth's companions lowered their bows.

'It's a long story, cousin,' said Edric, and explained the plot that had gone so wrong, and how the King of the Mabyn was to have been beguiled into coming into the open at the other exit.

'But why? To what purpose?'

Tors said her cousin had looked surprised that she should need to ask and, apparently without thinking, he blurted out: 'That we might slay him–' realised his mistake at her look of horror and corrected himself '–that is to say, to speak with him on certain matters vital to us both because–'

'Edric, you said "slay",' she had reminded him severely. 'And it seems you designed a wicked and dishonourable plan to trap a single mabyn with so many.'

'He is an enemy of our King! In one hand he also carries the means of despatching fae one hundred at a time! Unless he's removed–' He stopped short again, aware that the reason why the Mabyn of Mabyn needed to be removed would sound even more unpleasant to Mildgyth's ears. He therefore turned it to a virtuous account of how he had been hoodwinked by the treacherous King of the Mabyn.

Mildgyth made it clear, however, that she was not on his side, and in no mood to argue the pros and cons. '… I have no concern with these worldly matters, cousin. Now go, please, and leave the solitude of my ancient sanctuary in peace.'

Solitude! The look of amazement on her cousin's face as he stared around at four hundred armed mabyns betrayed his thoughts to everyone: *The whole place is crawling with an army of Mabyn! They have her prisoner here. This has to be reported …*

*

Myrddin was able to reassure the nun that her cousin had cancelled his news to the Earl, and set about calming everyone down; telling them it was a one-off incident but quite right that they should be prepared. He then introduced Gareth as his second-in-command who was going to train them in the arts of war.

'… And you, my people,' he said. 'You who are no longer the High Travellers, have a new name. You shall be known as The Kindred of the Grail.'

It was perfect. He knew it, and they knew it.

So it was that as he supervised the work, he kept up a sequence of instructions and commands. Every wicca, as soon as he was fully armed, would spend a set amount of time in vigil and then be dubbed Knight with his own sword – unless they remembered any title they had had in mortal form, as had Sirs Tors and Gawain, Hector, Jessant and Geraint. The rest were pleased to be invested with such romantic titles as Sirs Maliot; Allardyne; Unwaine and Gryflet that Myrddin bestowed on them. The wiccies adopted new names, more often based on their own choice of a softer, wiser rendering of their grotesque originals.

Myrddin had a special name for the wiccy who had once been the old mung begging to be first. She had turned out to be one of the Weirdfolk and therefore most beautiful of them all.

'I name you Faith,' he told her, 'for you believed in me and were brave enough to want to show the others the way. Will you –? Shall you be my squire?'

'That I will!' she said happily and from that moment hardly left his side.

'And how will you call yourself, Lord of the Grail?' asked the watching nun, fascinated by the civilising effect of all these moves on their charges.

'What else but Lord of the Grail?' he said with a shrug, already thinking ahead to his next task – which was to forge a missile more than equal to *Moldwarp*. He wanted something which would cleave through anything that his enemies might possess.

What emerged was a three-in-one piece of weaponry. At his instant thought it would transform itself into a lance, a sword or a mace. He named it *Earthshaker*. No one, but no one, he swore to himself, was ever again going to have the Lord of the Grail at a disadvantage. And the first thing he did with it was to undo all the hard work that had been put into opening the Underway in the Chapel garden. Three times he hurled his new missile at the yawning hole and, as a result, sealed an entrance that only *Earthshaker* would ever be able to open again.

CHAPTER 13

BIRTH OF YATHRA

Myrddin left Gareth in charge of training the new Kindred, and flew back to the Citadel as a Royal Falcon. It was quicker than making the journey by horse and he wanted an overall view of what was happening on the way. When he spotted a number of companies streaming west that were flying the Banner of the Owl, he was not surprised. Nothing remained of the besieging force on the blackened summit of Dome Hill. With fireballs and catapults gone, there was little point in staying, and Myrddin rejoiced in the satisfaction of a hard won but well achieved victory that he could look on as all his own work.

As soon as everyone learned that the mighty Prince Ammar-el-lyn had returned, the entire Citadel rocked in a fever of excitement. The Earl had to lead the magician forth on his balcony to meet a roar of applause. Shouted acclamations came from every quarter, scarves and banners waved, and heralds blew themselves out with fanfares.

When Myrddin at last had the Earl on his own and asked for the latest news of the war, Ranulph enthused: 'The cowards melted away, most noble Prince. The three hours after sun-up were devoted to single combats, for which it seemed they had no great heart. We laid them on the grass three to our one and then, when it was agreed to retire to meet their onslaught; they fell by dozens knowing their cause already lost.'

'Sirs Avellane, Gaheris and Bras-de-Fer?' asked Myrddin, grieved to have had such a part in their defeat.

'Sir Avellane was spared – I know. For the rest ...' Ranulph shrugged, 'we vanquished them by the score! They fell like corn before the scythe. And everywhere the tide of victory has swung in our favour. Never has there been such a short and glorious war. The sieges of Warwick and Glastonbury have been raised and everywhere the enemy is in full retreat.'

This was not good news for his hearer. Myrddin had been relying on the war's continuance as a bargaining counter with Mortleroy but with Gwyn going back underground, the Weirdfolk would find few friends above it when it came to leaving the Forest. He was therefore doubly thankful for the new Kindred whom he had already earmarked for the special duty of guarding the awaited infant when it appeared. Which reminded him to ask if there been any news concerning the heavenly babe he had seen in his vision?

With a face radiating joy, the Earl told him that indeed, a hawk had arrived even that very morning from the Constable of Eden's Ford with a message informing the Earl that an angel had appeared to his wife the previous day. '... apparently he announced heaven's blessing upon her, saying that that very evening the child she was expecting would be born, and should be named Yathra ...'

That made Myrddin blink. *How on earth ...?* he wondered as Ranulph went on to say how the babe had duly arrived, '... now Edric's sent an appeal for a special escort to bring his wife and child into the security of Reading, being engaged as he is on the blockade of Weir Forest. I have therefore despatched a company under Peredur, and am waiting to hear when he will be back,' Ranulph finished.

Myrddin's astonishment was complete. Not only had the heavenly visitor named the child correctly, but it seemed that fate was going to deliver the said Yathra straight into his hands without his having to do a thing about it: *And if I can't contrive to get possession of the child on arrival and spirit it away to deliver into Mildgyth's charge, then my name isn't Myrddin and I'm not Merlyn's Heir!* he reflected with satisfaction.

*

Ranulph himself, keyed up and energised, also reflected with satisfaction that with this news, and if the Prince of Damascus and the King really were one and the same, his own good fortune was assured and would outshine all others in glory. Who knew– a Dukedom, perhaps even an unprecedented Princedom!

He *really* had to mark the occasion with an extraordinary week of festivity and entertainment. He would impress all the mummers, jugglers and acrobats he could find; despatch invitations to a huge jousting spree – open to all comers – and crown the whole thing with a Roman holiday. He had enough trolls he could use for a distraction, and would send a search party to round up some more mungs, wellsprites and cave-wights. He would have them armed with clubs and stones and set a hundred wolves on them. He was sure the Prince of Damascus would be delighted with the novel entertainment and might even produce a magic lion or two, himself, to add to the glorious confusion. Of course, the trolls would run for their lives and get in everyone's way but that would only make the scene the more hilarious.

With these pleasantries in mind, he hurried away to the bird loft and had an enjoyable time impressing hawk after hawk with messages, along with some ravens and crows, before hefting the lot out of the high opening. He then came across on a hawk he had forgotten he was expecting. It was the one that had been despatched with Peredur to send news back as soon as possible of the success of his mission and when the Escort was to be expected to return to Reading with mother and baby.

The bird was fast asleep, which often happened when left unquestioned on arrival. He wondered what the Head Falconer had been doing to be so dilatory, then shrugged when he remembered the carte blanche he had given everyone to make the most of the celebrations. When he shook it into wakefulness he received a message that Peredur had arrived at the Keep of Eden's Ford only to find Dame Margaret and child already on their way to the King under the aegis of the Lady of the Lake. And, please, where did his bewildered second-in-command go from there …?

It did the Earl no good when he hastened to explain to the Prince of Damascus that the Lady of the Lake was an honoured and privileged protégée of the King. The Prince appeared to believe otherwise.

He fumed that the Lady of the Lake was a devilish witch who had sworn undying fealty to the spurious King Arthur living in the Forest of Weir. She had engineered the kidnapping of Dame Margaret's child to embarrass the King of Brython. They must find the evil witch immediately, rescue the Babe and its mother and bring them into the safety of the Citadel just as the Earl in his wisdom had originally intended. Ranulph must therefore dispatch every available messenger he had, and bring all obtainable force to bear on the matter.

Ranulph, not only confused but in a dilemma, realised that everything that had any right to call itself a messenger had been dispatched. Even the one from Peredur had been sent out again. All were impossible to recall and much valuable time would pass before the first returned. After explaining this to the already frustrated and angry Prince, Ranulph tensed for an explosive reaction, hardly knowing what to believe. It had already dawned on him with a mixture of disappointment, some relief and a growing wariness, that the magician couldn't possibly be Mortleroy in disguise after all. So far as he knew, the King's safe conduct for the Lady Nemway hadn't been rescinded. He had, therefore, reluctantly to conclude that his awesome guest's anger pointed to some private war. And while Ranulph was eternally grateful for Reading's deliverance, he had no wish to play at being 'piggy-in-the-middle' between Mortleroy and this unknown but mighty magician.

*

With the Earl's expression becoming guarded, Myrddin realised he had come close to overplaying his hand. He had to recognise he was becoming more and more paranoid where Nemway was concerned and that, besides confusing himself when it came to convincing anyone else of her wickedness, it was alienating Ranulph. He calmed himself at once; he assured the Earl that he wouldn't dream of holding him responsible for a turn of events that he simply could not have foreseen and that he had already thought of a way in which he could avert the threatened evil, anyway. He would leave at once and, with wit and with magic, bring the Child and its mother safe to Reading himself.

It was a relief to see Ranulph's caution giving place to delight at the restored prospect of custody and its reward from Mortleroy. Myrddin smiled at the thought that if it hadn't been necessary to keep some dignity in front of the servants, the Earl would probably have been on his knees in thankfulness before him.

*

As for Peredur, while he waited for the return of the hawk for further instructions, he had spent the time in a careful interrogation the servants and the handful of fae-at-arms at Eden's Ford Keep. The Earl would require a full account of what had happened, apart from which his Second-in-Command was curious himself – and it was an odd tale that he gathered.

It began with Dame Margaret's agitation when there had been no word from her husband for the whole of the previous day. Not only was her pregnancy a rare enough event in itself, it also promised their first child and Edric had been sending a hawk several times a day for news of any change in her condition. When she at last sent her servants to the top of a vantage point in the late afternoon for any sight of his return along the road, there had been no one seen but a solitary rider on a black charger. The Dame therefore had them bring whoever it was into the Keep for news of any possible sighting they might have had of her husband.

Everyone agreed that the strange youth with whom they had returned, had made a deep impression on them. He had the manner and bearing of a king; was richly clothed and rode a magnificent charger, yet in his gentle behaviour and courtesy with everyone, servants, fae-at-arms and Chatelaine alike, was quite *unlike* any Lord they had ever known.

In other words, Peredur thought, with some irritation, *a fair description of some rich young fool with more possessions than good sense. Who else but such a fool would travel alone and unarmed through a country up in arms and treat commoners as equals?* There was a still, small voice within him that nonetheless did whisper how much he wished he could believe it true.

He was told that the Dame had questioned the youth, who said he hadn't seen the Constable or his party, and was concerned for her when she began weep, saying she was frightened that something terrible had happened to him.

The young stranger had then placed his hand on her head and said in a quiet voice – although all heard him clearly: 'Be at peace, Mother, and heaven bless your child. He shall be named Yathra and will be born this night.'

Everyone agreed the action, and that those were the exact words used. Then the strange youth was gone, and Dame Margaret confided in her maid that she felt she had been visited by an angel.

By evening, her baby had arrived and, by early morning, not only was there was a hawk from her husband, apologising for his silence and asking after her but also news they had received of Reading's deliverance. She had sent a hawk back with the joyful news of the birth and the 'angelic' announcement.

In the light of what had been said to have happened next, Peredur deduced that the Constable, unable to leave his post, had sent his request to the Earl for a strong escort to take his wife and their wondrous child into the safety of Reading. However, before Edric could, in turn, send news to his wife that Ranulph had despatched Peredur as escort for her and his new born heir, the Constable had found himself under attack from one of Gwyn's returning cohorts.

News of Sir Edric's death had arrived with the Lady Nemway. Without an escort, and bearing his helmet, she rode up to the Keep with great boldness, declaring her name and showing her famous whip Lightning.

Everyone received her with respect knowing that the King had promised preferment to anyone who could bring the Slayer of the Green Dragon over to his side and, in the Constable's absence; this honour would now fall to Dame Margaret.

Nemway told the Chatelaine how she had come across a battlefield where she had found a whole company of knights and their retainers done to death by an unknown foe and, at their centre, a warrior brought down by a hundred wounds. Since the device on his shield revealed him to be the Constable of Eden's Ford, she had tenderly relieved his body of its shattered helmet which, miraculously, had renewed itself and most astonishing of all, had changed its previous tower of red plumes into a cascade that now looked like one of living fire.

Dame Margaret, seeing the wonder as another sign of heavenly blessing, received the news of her husband's demise with stoicism. Since the present Overlord of all Britain had promised to abdicate in favour of his long-awaited successor, her only regret was that her husband had not lived long enough to bask in the glory of his new fatherhood. She could not now wait to bear both child and helm to her sovereign lord according to his decree. But, alas, as she explained to Nemway, her husband had taken every available knight with him.

Nemway then offered herself as escort. Who else could be more heaven-sent than she, the Slayer of the Great Green Dragon? Her Whip, which had slain such a mighty creature, would be more than a match for any mere force of the Underworld. Let Dame Margaret prepare herself and the Babe quickly for the journey and the problem was as good as solved. She even went with the overjoyed Chatelaine to oversee the preparations and the servants had seen, watched and heard her crow in delight with Dame Margaret over the infant, commenting with wonder on the child's generous proportions and unmistakeable royal appearance.

By mid-morning and still no message from the Earl, Peredur decided he had better head west for Glastonbury, the most likely direction the Lady Nemway would have taken and try and catch up with her before Mortleroy could blame the Earl for not sending sufficient escort.

*

Myrddin's prompt flight back to the Chapel of Blue Fountains from Reading was swift. An anxious Gareth met him, eager to know if he had had any news of Arthur. What with the news and worry over Yathra, Myrddin had all but forgotten the youth *was* missing. He could not tell the Knight about the birth of Yathra, however, since it was Gareth who had recognised the Holy Grail, and at once presented it to 'Arthur' and sworn him fealty.

'No – no news, Gareth, I'm afraid,' he said, 'but much work to be done. If we are to find him, I must make hawks and train one of the Kindred to care for them as their Falconer, then we can send the birds out in search of Arthur. How goes the training of the Kindred for war?'

It appeared that Gareth had pursued the Kindred's instruction in the martial arts with zeal and vigour, and was proud to give Myrddin a list of their growing accomplishments. '… And did you know …?' he asked in earnest excitement 'Gawain is here! Gawain was with Peredur, Percivale and myself when we set off for Hindustan …'

But Myrddin wasn't listening.

*

Telling him to keep hard at it, the magician went to look for Faith. She was not in the chapel, but something else was. At the foot of the Cross, carefully laid out, was every piece of his new black armour, emblazoned with a golden cup, and all the accoutrements that he had asked for. It was evident that Faith had placed them there for safekeeping as his especial property. He found her in the garden busily engaged with a number of others on making suits for the archers, and banners and long slender pennants.

He thanked her for the armour, and asked if she minded him using some of the material she had collected for his hawks.

'You may use this,' she pointed to a heap, 'but that …' pointing to another, '… is reserved for your standard. It shall be black with the device of a Golden Eagle bearing the cup in its talons as befitting the Lord of the Grail.'

Faith was proving herself a capable squire, well in command of what she was doing, and with all that was going on. Myrddin smiled at his new title.

He made the first two hawks, attaching seals inscribed with the symbol of the Grail and the Knight's name it was intended for, and then chose one of the Kindred who appeared suitable for the office of Chief Falconer. Teaching him how to get the birds to obey his instructions and the way in which the gathered information had to be extracted on their return, Myrddin left him to pass on the skills to four others while he rapidly made six more hawks. The recruits practiced their new craft so well that it was not long before each of the four companies into which he was dividing his force, had two hawks apiece. It took until sunset and, in the near one and a half hours of interregnum before moonrise while the Kindred were unconscious, Myrddin made a lot more horses with the help of the Elders Gawain, Tors and Geraint who were not subject to oblivion like the others of their kind.

When the rest of the Kindred returned to consciousness, they were able to ride off in four companies, east, west, north and south, letting loose their hawks before them. Nor did they need any instruction on finding and using faerie pathways, he realised. They had always known and travelled them. Only the Weirdfolk who had never ventured out of their forest home had remained in ignorance.

Myrddin, clad now from head to foot in black armour as befitted the Lord of the Grail, glowed with satisfaction. *His Companies!* They rode out fast, two and two, their lances streaming with the long narrow black flags bearing the golden emblem of the Grail, which was also emblazoned on their breastplates. He had warned them that unless they were attacked, they must not attack any force bearing the banner of the Owl. Time and circumstances permitting, the Kindred were to make it plain that they were equally the enemies of Mortleroy.

*

The hawk of the company under the newly knighted Sir Jessant de Lys going west, returned to the Chief Falconer with news of having sighted the witch Nemway riding hard ahead of him with Dame Margaret and the babe.

The hawk, which Nemway had apparently recognised as a spy, had had a narrow escape from her whip. At the time of the encounter, she had been many miles away and by then could be twice as many again.

Myrddin sent out three of the remaining four hawks to divert the other companies to turn and join the chase and returned Jessant's hawk to him with instructions to keep pressing on as hard and fast as he could.

CHAPTER 14

NEMWAY VANISHES

While Nemway was racing to take Yathra and his mother to Mortleroy and Myrddin was occupied with the Kindred, Earl Ranulph had begun receiving his messengers back. Hurrying to catch up on interrupted intelligence reports, he at once sent them out again east, west, north and south requiring every piece of news they could glean.

The one to Eden's Ford returned with the information that Peredur, after fretful consideration, had gone west – concluding it was the most likely direction the Lady Nemway would have taken. A returnee from the southwest confirmed the sighting.

Surprised and relieved that, contrary to what the Prince of Damascus believed, it appeared the witch *was* on her way to present Dame Margaret and her babe to the King, Ranulph despatched the news to Mortleroy, and relaxed. With the situation now safe enough to disown all further responsibility, he had recalled Peredur to Reading.

*

A hawk hovering above Avellane made him give a nearby archer an almost imperceptible nod that beckoned him to his side.

Avellane mouthed at him a silent instruction: 'I want that bird brought down. But don't kill it.'

The archer obliged, and the damaged hawk was brought to him. The column had stopped and Gaheris rode up to see what was happening.

'It's unusual behaviour made me suspicious,' Avellane told him. 'Fortunately so, as it happens. It's newly made and inexperienced. It bears instructions from someone entitled The Lord of the Grail to a certain Gawain of the Kindred of the Grail. He is to turn west, and find and report the position of our Lady Nemway and her companion, Dame Margaret, whilst staying out of range of her whip.'

'Never heard of the Lord of the Grail,' Gaheris said. 'Who do you suppose he is?'

Avellane's handsome features looked grim. 'Since it appears he is no friend of our Lady Nemway, then he is no friend of ours ...' And turned his company around to head back east at once, scenting fresh adventure and a chance to redeem the misfortunes of the day.

And so it was that when his scouts reported a strange company under the banner of a golden cup, it was enough. Avellane charged full tilt into Gawain of the Kindred of the Grail who received his onslaught with enthusiasm.

It was unlike any encounter Avellane had ever met before. *Anyone would think they were on some kind of jaunt,* thought the astonished knight.

The 'Holy Grailers', as he called them, were even exclaiming excitedly to each other: 'See that!' or 'Look at this!' and 'Whee-ee!' as they charged through his ranks. And it was Avellane's knights who were going down like ninepins without leaving even a scratch on their adversaries' armour.

Seeing the massacre, the Commander at last held up his open hand for a truce and retired with Gaheris and the few remaining knights of his company still standing. Not prepared to wait for the formal negotiation of sending anyone else with a white flag, Avellane nodded to Gaheris and they rode out together with it.

They found themselves paid the compliment of being met by their opposite number who, to their amazement, was full of apology.

'... I did not see your banner in time. The Lord of the Grail has no warlike intention against the Kin of Beauty,' Gawain ended.

'It seems a little strange you should take the trouble to mention it so belatedly,' Gaheris said, looking pointedly at his littered companions.

'And just who is this so well intentioned Lord of the Holy Grail?' Avellane asked.

Their late adversary opened his mouth to reply and shut it again without explanation. When he tried again to explain, all he could manage was: 'The Lord of the Grail *is* who he is – the Lord of the Grail–'

He broke off under the impact of Peredur's returning company that came at them out of the blue like a thunderclap. When it was seen that these knights wore the embattled Tower of Glastonbury on their breastplates, as did all the armies of Mortleroy, the fight was on.

However, taken completely by surprise as they were, the onslaught rolled the Grail Knights to the ground leaving their archers to avert disaster. They poured their arrows into Peredur's smaller force and then unsheathed their swords. This gave the Kindred's knights time to rise and fight beside Avellane and Gaheris, whose greater expertise against their traditional enemy was proving deadly although it was the invincible armour of the Kindred that eventually won the day.

Peredur, also aware of increasing losses, at last retired a distance to wait for reinforcements after sending hurried messengers reporting the advent of these strange new warriors who, though overthrown, had yet risen to fight again.

By this time, Avellane and Gaheris looked a mess in their broken and disordered armour which stood out in stark contrast to the Kindred's almost unmarked mail. The two looked, marvelled, and demanded wearily to know what artisan had made it.

'The Lord of the Grail,' was Gawain's simple reply and, apparently anxious to be on his way, added: 'Now, how say you noble knights, we have fought a common enemy shoulder to shoulder, will you stay in our company? As I have said, my Lord has no quarrel with the People of Beauty, and we would not have fought you if you hadn't come upon us in such a warlike manner.'

Avellane, remembering his reason for turning back and falling into such a disastrous battle, challenged him: 'If the Lord of the Grail is so well disposed towards the Kin of Beauty, why does he spy on the Lady of the Lake who is kinslady to our King, Gwyn ap Gwyn ap Nudd?'

'I didn't know she was,' Gawain said, showing his surprise. 'What I do know, because my Lord told me himself, is that she has abducted the heavenly babe that is Arthur-to-be, and his mother, to deliver them into the murderous charge of Mortleroy.'

'By the Wonderful Head, *that* I will never believe!' cried Avellane angrily and he and Gaheris fell back a little in order to re-present their lances. 'I would rather fight to the death than hear our Lady's name used in such a way. Advance, false knight, and engage us singly in combat á l'outrance.'

*

Loath as he was to disobey his Lord, Gawain had no choice but to fall back in the same manner to allow suitable distance for the charge but couched his lance unhappily. Both his opponents bore wounds and had had their armour shattered. His own armour being flawless, and himself still in one piece, he raised his visor leaving his face unprotected.

He was remembering a code of chivalry long ago instilled by the Knights of Beauty to whom he really belonged. To his surprise and respect, Avellane abruptly checked his charger and, throwing down his battered spear and buckler, stood motionless.

Gawain at once dropped his own lance and shield and rode to halt at his side. He stared hard at his adversary saying: 'Very well, brother-in-arms, let us dismount and proceed on foot.'

It became apparent however that they were still unmatched.

Avellane had only half a sword.

Gawain at once threw his own aside and drew his dagger.

'By the sacred Owl, you unman me!' Avellane swore, hurling the broken sword away. 'You see I have no dagger! Do you really want us to fight with our bare fists?'

'What kind of argument is that?' asked Gawain. 'If I had disarmed you fairly until now, would you then have cried that you were unmanned? Wasn't it you, yourself, at the Battle of the Fords soon after Lyonesse, sent the very enemy, Mordred your own horse because you saw him without one?'

Avellane's eyes widened in amazement. 'Only one other mortal knew of that incident,' he said slowly staring at Gawain in disbelief. 'Because we were the last to die that terrible day – and that person was my mortal brother ...'

'I know!' cried Gawain. 'We could have run Mordred down, but you would not. He had been unhorsed, I offered you mine. But he slew you in the first charge, as you knew he would with Weyland's lance. I took your horse then, and went the same way. Algaric seized my family when I was born into this immortal realm and turned us into Mung. And now the Lord of the Grail has come and given us to drink from this Holy Vessel I wear emblazoned here – and we were delivered.'

A mixture of shock, pity, and incredulity had swept across Avellane's lean features. 'A mung,' he whispered. 'By the Venerable Head, *that* is an even greater wonder that you tell!' Then, raising his hand in a gesture of acknowledgement and peace, he added quietly 'I cannot argue with your new loyalty, Timeless Brother, and your rebuke is accepted without rancour, yet neither can I desert *my* liege.'

Without further word, he remounted his horse and rode away, beckoning Gaheris to follow.

Filled with new unhappiness, Gawain watched them go.

*

To Myrddin, it seemed obvious that Nemway was bound for Glastonbury, which would appear to indicate that she had had news of Mortleroy being there.

The Knights of The Grail, now thundering over a wide area of the Sussex countryside, had been riding an hour or so, before Gawain's hawk came back to Myrddin with the news of his encounter with the Knights of Beauty and Jessant's hawk returned with news that their quarry had vanished off the face of the earth.

CHAPTER 15

KIDNAPPED

Nemway reined to a halt, her way barred by a knight armoured head to foot in green. He had ridden out of the bracken shadows into a patch of sunlight that lit his breastplate emblazoned with the Red Dragon of the West and a shield showing the emblem of a White Owl crowned in silver. His face, alight with hearty good humour, beamed at Nemway through an open visor. Gwyn son of Gwyn was the most bluff and generous hearted of souls but, as all knew, his fiery temper and erratic sense of humour made him unpredictable.

Nemway was inclined to be cautious. 'Hail and Wyn, glorious cousin.' she greeted him. 'What brings you here – your latest war against kingly sovereignty?'

She was no match for her kinsman, though. She knew it was deliberate on his part to misunderstand her but was surprised when he answered:

'War? I have no war with Royal Arthur? Did I not promise him the sanctuary of Annwyn before he was born, along with his mother and all the People of the Weirdfolk?'

'Annwyn?' she repeated. 'The White Dove's message spoke of an escort to Glastonbury.'

Gwyn frowned. 'One,' he said, 'Mortleroy holds Glastonbury. And, two: am *I* likely to have sent a dove? You know full well, my messengers are white owls – *not* white doves.'

'Then this is very mysterious, cousin. I rather think it would pay to share what we know together.'

Out of earshot of the Lady Margaret, she told him everything as far as she knew that had happened in Weir Forest: Arthur had come of age and someone had stolen Excalibur. She said nothing of her suspicions that the thief had been the Weirdfolk's recently resident magician. From what she had learned from Stella, Merlyn's Heir had long gone to Dragga and was likely to have already started incarnation as another mortal, so there was little point in stirring things. She said no more than that she was in search of the Sword.

'And your companion?' he asked.

His question answered her silent speculation as to his waylaying her. *What and how much has he learned?* she wondered. Aloud, she answered: 'I'm escorting the widow of the late Constable of Eden's Ford. I discovered her spouse's corpse this morning savagely slain in combat with one of your triumphant cohorts, cousin. She was in much distress – her babe new born. I took pity on them, and am escorting them to safety. You wouldn't deny her the comfort and protection of her own kind, even if you are at war with them, would you, cousin?' It was a dig she had been unable to resist but at once regretted when his reaction spurred his horse to the Dame's side.

Lowering the point of his lance to the dust in courteous deference, he greeted her: 'Your servant, fair Chatelaine of Eden's Ford. Gwyn ap Gwyn ap Nudd am I, by whose forces I understand your husband has lately died in battle. I am grieved to meet the widow of such a famous and courageous warrior. But I do not make war on the hapless and helpless. Of your charity, lady, command me that I may conduct you and your babe in safety to your own kind.'

But Dame Margaret, clutching her infant to her, stared at him in terror.

Nemway, knowing why, hurried after him. The wickedness of the King of the Underworld Rebels was legendary as far as the Dame was concerned. Every loyal subject of the King of Brython knew him and his people to be capable of infamous crimes – even sacrificing living children and babies to the Awful Head that everyone knew they worshipped.

Nemway spoke quickly: 'We thank you for your chivalrous offer, noble King, but the magic of my Whip is already pledged in Dame Margaret's defence.'

'And no better weapon could there be,' the Dame said gamely, although her voice quavered. 'I thank you for your courtesy, sworn enemy of my King, but with your leave, I would rather ride under the protection of the Lady of the Lake. Her Whip has slain the Great Green Dragon of the South–'

Gwyn turned on Nemway, his expression outraged. 'You have slain a Sacred Dragon!' he exclaimed. 'How could *you* of the Kin of Beauty so abuse your power–?'

With Dame Margaret listening, Nemway could hardly tell him the whole thing had been a hoax. 'The circumstances were accidental–' she began.

'*Accidental!*' He spat the words with a withering sarcasm, cutting her to the quick. Seeing his knuckles whitening under his grip of the lance he began to raise as if he were about to slay her on the spot, made Nemway loosen her whip, Lightning. Wayland had made both their weapons and neither could prevail against the other though they fought from dawn to dusk.

Slowly he let the butt of his lance down to rest beside his foot, bitterness souring his voice as he said: 'So be it, trait'ress. But I hereby pronounce you outlawed from our Kin. The evil you have done shall be known throughout the land and be certain your doom will come. What the children of Wayland may not do, the justice of heaven will surely accomplish.' And riding to one side, turned his back on her.

Nemway's lips straightened to a thin line. Never mind that broadcasting the deed afresh would enhance her standing with Mortleroy, her banishment from the Kin of Beauty now made them her implacable enemies. She wanted to weep knowing that even the removal of Mortleroy, if she could do it, could never outweigh the killing of a Sacred Dragon. The fact that it was also the one dragon that Mortleroy had never been able to capture made it all the worse.

*

Sometime later, galloping along the verge of a lonely lane fringed on one side by a dark line of woodland, Nemway and the Dame came across a figure seated below a towering milestone.

The unkempt looking male, clad in a half-robe of fae doeskin, rose on his staff at their approach, lifting a hand in benediction. Now that they were closer and Nemway saw his face, its severe beauty surprised her.

'Hugh, Hermit of the Bone, offers greeting and peace to you both, daughters of distress,' he said. 'The Oracle I serve commanded my presence here to meet you.'

Nemway had always been aware that hereabouts lay an ancient and secret hermitage, not unlike the Chapel of Blue Fountains, except older and always occupied by a male recluse. It was said to house not a bone but a tooth – a mortal one. The legend ran that it came from the head of a remote King of Britain, and therefore called the Bone of Bran.

She returned his greeting with gratitude; sure that such a wise and unworldly incumbent would listen compassionately to her dilemma, and perhaps help her in her spiritual anguish. She therefore begged hospitality for them both.

He responded with an inviting gesture and set off for the woods, leading them along a an almost invisible path through the high grass.

A triathlon, well hidden beneath a boulder of ironstone, fronted the entrance to his cave, a large rough hewn chamber containing no more than a couch of twigs and an altar on which rested the famous Tooth. The brazier lights revealed it deep yellow in colour, darkened on one side with decay.

She beckoned Margaret in with her. But the Dame stepped back in dismay from her glimpse of the interior. 'I'm not going in there,' she said. 'It looks a heathen place.'

Nemway managed to keep her temper with difficulty. After the long ride, her arm ached more than ever from the mauling it had received from her betrayal to the wolves. 'We need to rest, fair Dame, we have been riding hours and more. So if not for yourself, at least for your unfed baby's sake.'

The Dame peeked in again at the huge and unattractive tooth and shuddered. 'Such an ungodly place would sour us both. I'll rest and feed my babe outside in the fresh air, thank you. And I don't like that vagabond's face,' she added as she backed out. 'It looks more like some savage rebel from the underground than any saint's.'

Nemway turned to apologise to the hermit, but he was already kneeling before the altar with his back to her.

She followed the Dame outside to find a more suitable nook in keeping with her pride – now inflated to glory by her elevation to Mother-of-the-King-To-Be. Nemway dreaded what the inevitable fall from grace would mean for the Chatelaine of Eden's Ford, when the truth became known that the puling scrap she nursed was as ordinary a wraith as was ever born outside Weir Forest. Nemway had known from the outset that it was not, nor ever could be, the innately royal personage that she had recently left in the forest but, now that she no longer had Accolon as escort –

and she had to assume he had elected to stay with Sir Edric – the infant was her only direct passport to Mortleroy.

She got the finicky mother settled at last, leaving Windfleet ready to alert her owner the instant there was any danger, and returned to the hermitage.

Hugh waved her apologies for Dame Margaret aside, and gestured she should take a seat on the couch of twigs. Believing him free of all worldly partisanship, and seeing him as an unbiased father confessor, she told him everything that had happened since the first news of Arthur's coming and, in particular, the truth about her supposed slaying of the Green Dragon, the cause of her hurt. She said nothing however about the pseudo divinity of the Dame's infant. Nor did she say where she proposed leading its mother in search of security.

The hermit listened with an expression of aloof compassion and was silent for some time before he said: 'Your worldly policies have no hold on me, sworn as I am to this solitary living, yet it maybe that the Spirit of Bran is aware of your troubles? Come, let us drink together the cup of unity that our spirits may be at one and pray for guidance.'

He brought a bowl filled with a rich red liquid, and presented it devoutly to the Tooth before holding it out to Nemway, inviting her to drink first.

*

He caught her, bowl and all, as she passed out and laid her gently on the couch. Dame Margaret had been correct when she had observed that he looked more like an underground rebel than a saint. Hugh was the youngest and least esteemed of the sons of Gwyn – at least by his jovial, energetic and warlike sire. But Hugh was no weakling, although he had no spirit for warfare he was content to serve as a guardian of this particular secret exit from the halls of Annwyn by which the Knights of Beauty could emerge at will and take

Mortleroy's forces by surprise. A messenger owl from his father had informed him of Nemway and her companion, and advised him that the long revered and respected Lady of the Lake had turned traitor. Both females were to be given a sleeping draught and carried as soon as possible into the depths of Annwyn.

Glad to find that Nemway was not the traitor his father believed her to be, he hid her whip behind the altar – judging it safer there than in the hands of his sire – before carrying out the rest of his orders. By the time he had dealt a similar potion to Dame Margaret and the infant and carried them into his den, help had arrived and the Lady Nemway was gone.

Hugh made it clear to those who came back for the Dame and babe that Nemway stood innocent of the charge, and they must inform his father of the fact as soon as possible. He then decided to make himself scarce before Gwyn discovered the weapon was missing and came looking for it.

*

When Nemway recovered to find herself in a sumptuous apartment, she shot upright to see the sleeping Dame on another couch nearby.

'That cursed wine of Bran!' she cried furiously, her hand flying to her side for the Whip – only to find it gone. She sprang off the couch and made for the door, and met Gwyn on his way in.

'Where is Lightning, my whip?' she challenged him. 'And why have I been brought here?'

No longer jovial, Gwyn looked stern. 'I want the truth, cousin–'

'I want my whip, scurrilous dog! Remember? Weyland curses the one who has it, that he will die within the day if it isn't returned to me immediately …'

*

Full of curses on Hugh for not remembering the whip had to stay with Nemway, Gwyn set off for the Hermitage ....

He returned sometime later looking slightly the worse for wear, but bearing the weapon which he returned to her. 'And now, I want the truth,' he said. 'If you did not kill the Green Dragon of the South, what dragon did you kill?'

'None,' she owned cheerfully. 'It was a blown up pet of an ex-Wychy of the Weirdfolk. I wounded it by accident when the warlock betrayed me to a pack of murdering wolves.'

'Then I shall avenge you, cousin!'

'Too late,' she said sweetly. 'He is already meat himself to the very *much* alive Green Dragon of the South.'

'You managed that?' he said in astonishment.

'No. The wizard had to go of his own accord when his time came with the full moon just passed. It is the way of all the Wychies of the Weirdfolk. Now I have said my piece, it's your turn. Why have you kidnapped the Dame Margaret and me?'

'I understand the Dame believes her child to be Arthur-come-again as Yathra. It is interesting that the Queen of the Weirdfolk also believes that Arthur has been born to her.'

'Royal Arthur has been so born and, via a *Dove*, she and her royal child – and her People – were promised an escort to Glastonbury, which I now know to be a lie, since you say Glastonbury is in the hands of Mortleroy.'

Gwyn expressed exasperation: 'And where *have* you been all this time that you didn't know that? Anyway, as I have also already told you, my messenger was an Owl and it spoke of the Halls of Annwyn. I sent greetings to the Queen of the Weirdfolk. I thanked her for *her* dove that had brought us news of Arthur's imminent birth, and offered them and their people refuge here in Annwyn.'

'So nothing of any escort for them?'

'I said I had no fear for their journeying since they would have the protection of the most powerful of all our guardian dragons. But if, as you say, Royal Arthur *has* been born of the Weirdfolk Queen, what were you doing with the one I brought here?'

'Mortleroy believes Yathra's the genuine article – so, like a good citizen, I'm simply escorting Mother and Child to their destiny.'

A slow smile lit Gwyn's features. He turned and filled two goblets from a pitcher of wine he had brought in with him. Offering her one, he said: 'Then let us drink to that, fairest of cousins.'

And for the second time that day, Nemway slid into unconsciousness.

This time, Gwyn took her via underground to the Chapel of Blue Fountains. He did not want her in the Halls of Annwyn, and he certainly did not want the Sage of all the Seers to see her unconscious form in his charge and suffer the indignity of another drubbing from the Denefolk. He was still smarting from the first ...

CHAPTER 16

THE SCOURGING OF GWYN

Nemway's white mare had quite literally gone with the wind for help. She took off before her abductors could catch her, and when the Sage of all the Seers learnt of his mother's kidnap, he was out for Gwyn's blood.

It was known to Gwyn that Nemway had a powerful ally among the People of the Hills and Hollows. What he did not know was that ever since the ex-Wychy of the Weirdfolk had betrayed her so badly, the Sage of all the Seers had set a special watch on Nemway's safety. Through the far-flung eyes and ears of his nearly invisible People who moved with wind and water and disguised their voices in the rustle of leaves and murmur of brooks, he was aware of all events and spoken words on the surface of the land. He was equally acquainted with the meeting between Nemway and Gwyn and had heard Gwyn's furious words outlawing her from her kin. However, although the Sage was all-seeing and all-hearing above ground, he was not all-knowing. The Denefolk had no ability to read minds, or to know what was happening underground, in caves or any other kind of deep interior.

A Watcher had alerted the Sage when Nemway's mare was seen to shy away from a Knight of Beauty who came out of the Hermitage to take her. It was then an educated guess that Gwyn's people had abducted his mother and were holding her somewhere against her will beneath ground.

The Sage sent a huge gust of wind to help Windfleet's escape back to the Chapel of Blue Fountains. He then floated off himself on another breeze to watch the Hermitage. He knew the Hermit was Gwyn's son and, seeing Hugh leave the place with a set expression of mutiny on his face, it seemed reasonable to expect his father to come looking for him.

When a ghostly white Owl eventually flew out of the place far sooner than he expected, the Sage hit it with the fury of a hurricane.

*

Gwyn had indeed made an underground trip to the Hermitage. He had to question Hugh on the whereabouts of Nemway's whip. Finding the place empty meant he had to locate him quickly or lose himself to Weyland's curse.

The unexpected blast of wind that sent him spinning towards the trunk of a large oak should have damaged him severely but he managed to avoid the impact at the last moment. Another blast, however, threw him back like a shuttlecock towards an even larger one.

Gwyn evaded that collision by executing a neat twist, with an indignant squawk down his beak. He was too old a bird not to realise now the source of the attack, but could not account for it. So far as he could remember, there had always been a tacit truce between the Denefolk and the Kin of Beauty – in the main because he had never worked out a practical method of fighting them. Now he felt that if they didn't lay off this unwarranted attack, he'd call off his plans and go for them bald-headed even if it meant sacrificing himself and every one of his warriors in the attempt. When he was bounced off a third tree it occurred to him that perhaps they just weren't aware whose august person they were throwing around like a foot-ball.

'It's me, O People of the Hollows and the Hills,' he screeched into the tornado, 'the Lord of Annwyn, the Lord of Doom.' Then wondered why the heavens themselves appeared to open their wrath on him.

Watchers, Readers, and Seers weighed in on the side of their outraged Sage. They tossed him up, they threw him down; they flattened him into the earth, uprooted him again and scored him with icy streams of wind that pierced like knives; whipped him naked feather by feather with invisible fingers; then held him in a downdraught as securely and as rigid as a iron straightjacket to suffer the worst humiliation of his long existence.

Faintly, as if from a great distance, a thin voice demanded: *'What have you done with the Lady Nemway, the fairest of all your Kin, O spawn of the Underworld?'*

It needed an effort of will to reply, but Gwyn contrived it: 'What concern is that of yours, you hollow-bellied ghoul. Let me up and fight you face to face, skulker of the skies. Don't you know that none can slay me in this guise? Make your choice, you witless ghost: fight me fairly or live bedamned on the lips of all.'

He might have addressed a stone. The voice merely repeated the question with the piercing effect of a winter's blast.

Gwyn gave in: 'I haven't done anything to her,' he said irritably. 'I need her and she needs me.'

'Yet this very morning you swore she was your immortal enemy.'

'It was a misunderstanding,' he growled.

'You swear this on the Venerable Head?' asked the voice.

'Yes – and on the Harp of Lyr, my forefather, also. Now loose me.'

The voice obliged: *'Free him …!'*

Gwyn scrambled onto his talons and swayed dizzily. He was too frozen and battered to recover without help but warm winds blew on him, restoring his wellbeing and soothing his lacerations. However, as soon as he could he performed a lightning change and sat mounted, mailed and armed, in every respect himself.

'Now I am invulnerable!' he cried in ungrateful response at his unseen foes, considering the amends they had made. 'Show yourselves, and face the lance that Weyland made – and while we're on the subject,' he added quickly, 'if you're so concerned for the Lady Nemway's welfare, say what you know of the miscreant Hermit who has made off with her Whip? I came here to find it and take it back to her – *and* she'll need her horse returned.'

'*Your son went down a rabbit warren,*' replied the Sage evasively. '*Nor was he carrying the Whip when he went. But if you say the Lady Nemway lives and is unharmed, why was her Whip taken from her?*'

Gwyn made no answer because he now had all he needed to know. If Hugh had not taken the Whip with him then it had to be still in the Hermitage. He was no more than a mortal foot or so from its entrance at that moment, so took his questioner by surprise and had sped into its safety before the Denefolk could stop him. In his passion, he wrecked the couch and did not find the Whip. He overturned the altar – and did.

*

Nemway opened her eyes to find Mildgyth's arm around her shoulder and water from the Wealspring cup trickling into her mouth and down her chin. The constant agony that had possessed her shoulder ever since the wolf attack was gone and the bliss that enveloped her was heaven – but short lived. For when she exclaimed in wonder and relief that she was healed, she wanted to know how the cup had come to be there. Mildgyth answered:

'Merlyn's Heir gave it into my charge, beloved Lady.'

The nun's reply threw her into despair 'What!' she exclaimed, sitting up, her tone sharp: 'When?'

'Why, just after the last full moon was past,' Mildgyth said and stared in surprise when Nemway groaned:

'And here was I thinking we were done with him and his mischief making at last. So where is he now, do you know?'

'Looking for *you*, beloved Lady. Everyone is looking for you – except Sir Gareth. He's looking for Arthur–'

'Looking for Arthur?' Nemway exclaimed in astonishment and alarm. 'Why, where did he go? What has happened to him?'

Mildgyth mourned: 'If only we knew, beloved lady. Sir Gareth says he went missing not long after the full moon just passed–'

'How did I get here?' Nemway interrupted, feeling for her Whip to find it safe beside her.

'Beloved lady, you brought here unconscious by your cousin, Gwyn ap Gwyn.'

'And why is Merlyn's heir looking for *me*?'

'He says you have kidnapped the true Arthur and his mother, and are taking them to the King.'

Nemway gave a short mirthless laugh. 'Then Mona help us,' she said. 'For surely no one else can if he believes that!'

'My lady!' Mildgyth looked shocked.

'Don't you think that *I* of all people would know my own foster son?' Adding in frustration, 'And you, Mildgyth, you should know him. You worship the true King's living likeness every day.' She sprang to her feet in quick resolve, and then paused in her stride for the door to return and place a warm kiss on the nun's cheek. 'Blessed Mildgyth, thank you for your ministration' she said. 'And have no fear for me, I will return with the true Arthur I promise – not some puking infant I intended foisting on Mortleroy to gain my dearest foster-son some precious time …'

There was only one person who might know where Arthur was, and that was her son, the Sage. She rode into the heart of the wood where a Reader, Seer or Watcher might be and called softly:

'O People of the Hills and Hollows take my grateful thanks to the Sage of all the Seers for bringing Windfleet to the Chapel of the Blue Fountains, and tell him that Nemway was there in the forest when the Otter of the Denefolk came and promised Arthur the help of your Oracle.'

Like the indistinct reflection of a tree on the surface of a fast flowing river, a long willowy figure in tenuous garments appeared, rippling and swaying against its darker background.

The figure spoke, its whisper words sighing on the wind: *'The People rejoice to see you safe and well and again in possession of your Whip, Mother. The sacred Otter of the People of the Hills and Hollows spoke truly. What is it that Royal Arthur needs to know?*

'My son, it's what *I* need to know for his sake,' she said urgently, 'Arthur is missing from the Forest. His mother will be grieving for him, and I am afraid for him. Can you tell me where he is?'

'He went into a rabbit warren two miles distant to the north. There we led Gwyn's son Hugh, repenting his betrayal of you and in rebellion against his father ….' the wind-voice soughed away as the wraith-form faded.

Knowing her son was not one to waste words, neither did Nemway waste time. Spurring Windfleet to the north, she raced away allowing her mount full rein, wondering how, when and why Arthur had managed to get himself lost down a rabbit-hole.

CHAPTER 17

ARTHUR RETURNS

Arthur had not hesitated to use his horse to send his rescued subjects quickly into safe-keeping, but it left him looking for something else to ride.

He needed to know more about his kingdom before he returned home, so when he came across a wild rabbit he decided it was enough to serve his purpose.

It proved an inspired choice. Spooked by the sudden and invisible presence on its shoulders, the rabbit panicked and raced for its warren, scuttling down the first hole it came to. Quick as it was in mortal terms, Arthur still had plenty of time to flatten out between its ears to save his head, but the overhanging projection tore away the thin dilapidated tunic that he had swapped from the wellsprite.

The rabbit shook him off in the roomy centre of its warren where a crowd of troglodytes crept out to surround him with an air of stupefied awe.

For one thing, he was as near naked as themselves, for another he had arrived on an animal to whom they owed their shelter and therefore their lives, and for a third, he had come exactly as foretold in the universal legend of the Great King's second coming. The legend had been somewhat bowdlerised into terms they could understand but in essence it had sustained them in the belief that one day the Mighty King who had dominion over all things above as well as underground, would come exactly as Arthur had now arrived, naked on the back of Big Brother.

So they stared and marvelled at the white-gold hair and the perfectly proportioned, beautiful youth whom legend said would save them from their precarious existence in which hunting parties of knights chased them with wolves, while others sent dreaded ferrets down the burrows to kill them.

Arthur rubbed the parts of him that had taken the tumble, remarking with a wide grin that he had a lot to learn about rabbits.

They found he also wanted to know all about them; their names, and how and where they lived. No one had ever shown such an interest in them before or been willing to sit, listen and learn that, besides a precarious existence in rabbit warrens, how they also managed to survive in various rocky nooks or fox-earths. Two of their Elders, Ogmar and Lugshorn told him how they were hunted by fae-wolves and ferrets or captured to provide sport for those who lived in the Over-world.

Arthur in turn told them of a kingdom where none hunted or killed, but sang and danced, and were happy; looked after and cared for by magical guardians. The cave-wights began gathering from other places to listen, and with them came the skin clad Hugh the Hermit, son of Gwyn ap Nudd, curious to see what they were doing and where they were all going.

One look at Arthur's clear grey gaze of askance and Hugh fell on his knees in wonder. 'My lord, my King.' he said simply. 'How I have longed for this day.'

Relief shone in Arthur's eyes at seeing him: 'Hugh, how glad I am that you have come,' he said with feeling. 'I am concerned for my People here. They gather in such numbers I'm afraid they will begin to attract unwelcome attention. Please help me. Please help them to disperse carefully, and to take the news of my coming among all their Kin, and to prepare for the time when they will be summoned into my Kingdom.'

*

Nemway found the gathering of Cave-wight so focussed on Arthur and Hugh that they missed her arrival, which she guessed would have scattered them at once.

Her shocked eyes met Arthur's in time for him to reassure them all that all was well and that she came as his friend and therefore theirs.

They could be forgiven if they found this difficult to believe, because Nemway's immediate relief at finding him alive made her give way to anger. Seeing him clothed in nothing but a filthy rag that was barely decent – as well as sitting on the floor in the company of the hermit who had betrayed her, she scolded Arthur for his appearance and for the heartache and worry he was causing his mother.

'Oh dear,' said Arthur looking around at his new friends with a rueful smile, 'The Lady Nemway is quite right. It seems I'm not very good at looking after myself, am I? It was wrong of me to leave without saying where I was going. I shall need to go back with the Lady – but I shall not forget you,' he added quickly. 'I give my word that you shall come and live in my Kingdom. In the meantime ...' and he reached out his hands to the hermit and to Ogmar and Lugshorn who were nearest him, '... I'm leaving every one of you in Hugh's good care, and I want each of you to remember to prepare everyone you can reach, to be ready to leave with him. He will bring you to my forest ...' His eyes appealed to the hermit, '... won't you Hugh?'

Hugh looked taken aback. 'Sire, but where is your forest? And how shall I know when to come?'

'It's the Forest of the Weirdfolk, Hugh, and when you hear the sound of Excalibur unsheathed, you will know it is time to go there – quickly!'

Nemway watched and listened in silent amazement, unable to say a word, as the troglodytes crept up to and shifted close about Arthur, their heavy and misshapen faces alight with adoration, promising eagerly they would do everything exactly as he said.

Hugh helped him to his feet and all went with him to the entrance where they waited and watched sorrowfully as Arthur climbed up behind Nemway on her mare and vanished from their sight among the tall bracken.

*

No word passed between the two riders until they reached the Chapel of the Blue Fountains; there Nemway told him that Gareth was out searching for him, and she must go and find him with the good news.

Hearing voices, Mildgyth came to meet them and at the sight of Arthur's face, fell on her knees before him. 'My lord and my King!' she whispered in shock at seeing the object of her long worship standing alive before her.

Drawing her to her feet, he bowed his head, saying warmly: 'Mildgyth, I know you also, most good and loving lady. Has Sir Gareth returned yet?'

'Sire, I will send word to him at once that you are found safe and well,' she assured him earnestly, her eyes unable to leave his face.

'Good,' he answered with a grave nod. 'Then we will return to the forest, ' he said before adding quietly, and to Nemway's further astonishment: 'And do you come with me, Mildgyth, and be my Queen?'

'Oh my Lord, I am unworthy.' she whispered in confusion, dropping her eyes, unable to look at him.

Raising her face to his and smiling, Arthur asked her tenderly: 'Mildgyth, am *I* not to be the best judge of that?'

As he enfolded her, she looked up at him with undisguised love then down again in simple acquiescence, saying: 'My Lord, wherever and whatever your will, it is mine also.'

'My Lady Nemway,' said Arthur, turning to her. 'I thank you for coming for me. I would not keep you should you wish to leave–'

Nemway promptly slid off Windfleet and knelt at his feet: 'Sire, forgive me,' she begged. 'I should never have spoken to you as I did.'

'Nemway,' he chided gently, lifting her to her feet and shaking his head. 'You spoke in love and concern for me and all whom I love. What is there to forgive?'

Mildgyth hurried away to have the Falconer send a hawk to Gareth, and returned with some of her own handiwork to clothe Arthur, before taking him and Nemway to meet the Kindred who were at work in their underground stronghold.

The Kin responded enthusiastically to Arthur's questions; telling him of the wonderful wizard who had found them and the Holy Cup from which they had drunk and been transformed back to their proper shapes.

Mildgyth noticed Nemway raise an eyebrow on hearing how much love and respect they held for Myrddin, then saw her dear Arthur's grey eyes seeking those of the witch in smiling askance, as he assured her: 'Dear Lady Nemway, Myrddin always acts with my best interests at heart, just as you did with the infant Yathra. I know you acted to protect me, but Myrddin truly believes the infant to be the true Arthur – just as I meant him to.'

'So you were the 'angel' that Dame Margaret insisted had blessed her,' exclaimed Nemway in shocked surprise. 'But why, my Liege? Why?'

He drew them both aside before answering in a low voice: 'It is necessary you should know that Myrddin will betray me in order to disprove me …' He held up his hand to silence Nemway's indignant contradiction. 'It is the only way he will ever realise his mistake and in the end that is the only way to save him and every one of *you*, my people …'

*

When Gareth arrived back with Arthur's black charger, he took it upon himself in Am-mar-el-lyn's absence to recall the other three companies of the Knights of the Grail to escort Arthur back to the Forest. It was beyond the devoted knight's imagination to think it might not have been quite what Am-mar-el-lyn would have wanted.

Gareth also pointed out that the quickest and safest route for their return lay through the Mabyn's Underway that had been accidentally opened in up the Chapel garden by the Kindred and sealed again by the Lord of the Grail.

This was news to Nemway, who immediately sent for her brother. They not only needed him to break their way out of the Underway he had sealed with *Moldwarp* into Weir Forest but now to break their way open into the Underway in the garden.

When Amyas came and learnt of the Kindred's excavation of the mound in the Chapel's garden, of Edric's escape and the Lord of the Grail's resealing of the entrance, he shook his head despairingly. 'This is not the way to treat these Portals between Over-and Under-Worlds,' he said, his grave face even more severe. 'What I did in Weir Forest was an emergency – now completely wasted – and yes, you will need *Moldwarp* to re-open it. But I shall not use the weapon here to re-open this one. We must use the other portal nearby.'

Gareth objected: 'But Sire, surely that will be dangerous?'

The listening Arthur nodded. 'There must be no loss of life,' he said quietly. 'But Amyas is right; it is the way we go.

However,' he added looking around at all of them crowding to hear the discussion, 'I have seen the work you have done in your other excavation outside the Chapel grounds. I think it possible that if our good Amyas were allowed to explore the place; he might find another entrance into the Underways …?'

It was difficult to tell whether the Mabyn King was disappointed or delighted by the idea. It seemed he brightened a little at the prospect of another encounter with the enemy. But he agreed and in a short space did find and open a new entrance inside their stronghold.

With everyone assembled, Arthur addressed them, saying: 'Good and faithful servants and knights to Amyas, to the Lord of the Grail and myself, I see how hard you have worked on this underground fastness that you have made your home, and would wish you to keep it that way. With your permission, I will ask my good Amyas to close the entrance so that it shall not be discovered after you have left.' His listeners' approval was unanimous. He raised his hand: 'One thing more,' he said. 'Who among you would wish to stay and Ward our Chapel of Blue Fountains?'

Faith made her way forward to kneel at Arthur's feet: 'Please, Sire, I am The Lord of The Grail's squire. Let me stay for his return?'

'None better!' Arthur said, lifting her to her feet with a smile. 'Bless you, and may God be with you …'

Before she left, Mildgyth placed the chest containing all Myrddin's undisclosed contents into Faith's care but carried the Wealspring Cup with her as Arthur told her its proper place was with the Weirdfolk in the little kingdom.

The young King then took Mildgyth up to ride with him on Windflame, and the large party set off.

As they drew near to the forest end of the tunnel, Amyas became puzzled: 'I don't remember it being as wet as this,' he said.

Nemway made no comment. The previous time, she had been riding too hard to care or to notice anything, but their steeds were now splashing through great puddles of water.

A faint sound ahead of them, made Amyas hold up a warning hand for everyone to stop and listen. Someone had heard their approach and a distant voice was calling for help.

CHAPTER 18

ACCOLON

Nemway hadn't explained her intention to Accolon when he heard her persuading the Constable of Eden's Ford to set an ambush for the King of the Mabyn and invade the Forest of Weir via its Underway. It was the knight's misfortune that Nemway, with her usual single-mindedness, had expected him to act on her lead when she spurred Windfleet into the mound's opening the moment Amyas appeared. It was only as the distance increased between the pair in front and their pursuers behind that it dawned on Accolon what the two had had in mind. His race ahead to catch them up arrived only in time to be caught, and half buried, under the fall of rock that sealed the Underway behind the two still well ahead of him.

At first he had tried to free himself and then given up when his efforts brought even more rock down on top of him. He lay still and thought resignedly about the time he had died as a mortal, being quite sure he was now in for a second death. It wasn't something he particularly wanted to think about but Nemway had told him the incredible news that Arthur had come again, born to the Queen of the Weirdfolk in the Forest of Weir.

Lying there, lost and alone in the dark it now appeared Accolon would never be re-united with his true Liege after all but left with the bitter, unhappy recollection of having almost killed this dearest friend the last time they had met. Neither had known who the other was, both of them tricked as they were and lured into the fracas by Morgan le Fay. She had called on each of them separately to be her champion to kill the other, who she said was a traitor and had murdered her husband, King Urience of Gorre.

She had arranged it so that neither man had had his own armour with him. They had met each other mailed in plain unmarked suits, closed visors and with nothing on their shields to identify them. He remembered the growing respect he had reluctantly began to feel for his unknown adversary's strength, endurance and knightly forbearance.

How I couldn't work out that it was Arthur I was fighting, I just don't know? I knew him well enough. The times we went hunting together, Arthur, Urience and me. It must have been that Excalibur blinded me. What an experience wielding that sword had been! It had bitten into his opponent's armour like a knife through butter. He should have bled to death from a dozen wounds. But no, he stayed on his feet, parrying Accolon's blows with consummate skill – and that had been infuriating; the unknown's ability to stay on his feet, and keep up his attack.

Even when they had fought themselves to standstill, with Arthur dripping blood everywhere and Accolon himself with hardly a scratch … *It was my exasperation that gave me the energy to rush at him then, shouting: 'Rest? I'll give you rest!'* And to aim a blow that should have slain him on the spot. But no. The nigh on useless sword that Arthur was wielding with such practised know-how, deflected the attack back on Accolon's own head so that it was he who fell with a crash to the ground. The sheer force of it, however, had broken Arthur's weapon leaving only the hilt and crossbar in his hand. Accolon remembered how, when he had clambered to his feet and slashed at his adversary again, Arthur took the blow on his shield and struck Accolon so hard across his visor with the broken sword that the knight staggered back – *which was when I saw Nemway,* he remembered.

He hadn't seen her before but now, a hooded figure looking straight at him, her fingers were weaving some design at her waist and Excalibur's scabbard, which had kept him from being wounded, loosened from his side and fell in front of Arthur. The king caught it up, and was fastening it on his belt when, half-crazed, Accolon came at him again to strike him with force enough to have sliced him crown to chin – and again Nemway intervened. Her sudden gesture that twisted Excalibur from Accolon's grasp made it land point down in front of Arthur.

Then it was Arthur's turn to strike at Accolon; the force of it causing blood to burst from his nose, mouth and ears. *Which was me done for!* His opponent, standing over him with blood pulsating in rivulets down his armour, had Excalibur at Accolon's throat.

'Now I will slay you unless you yield!' he said quietly.

Accolon remembered managing to return a defiant glare while trying to speak through the bubbles of blood in his mouth. 'Then do it … for I will never yield … I will not live ashamed.' And to his surprise, the sword was lowered.

'Then tell me who you are, and whom you serve, for I find you a brave and honourable knight.'

Trying to speak without gurgling, the words had come thickly: 'I am of the royal court of King Arthur, and Accolon of Gaul is my name.'

'And how came this sword to be in your hands?'

'Queen Morgan le Fay … sent it me … reminding me I had promised to be her champion … against whoever she needed avenging … that the man I had to fight … had killed her husband, King Urience … But who are you?' he asked, because the other had abruptly dropped to his knee beside him.

'Oh, Accolon, Accolon, don't you recognise my voice?' he asked. 'I am your King.'

The horror that Accolon had felt; his tears, his pleas returned in full, so that he whispered again into the dimness about him the words he had said then: 'Fairest lord ... King Arthur, save me ... for I did not know you ...!'

And Arthur had replied: 'Mercy you shall have, for this battle was not your doing, but my sister's. She has deceived me also by her beauty and her magic wiles for she told me the same story. Now I will send her from my court.'

Their squires had had to hurry them both to a nearby abbey, and Nemway had come herself and nursed them both. But Accolon had not survived the night. As he lay dying, however, Nemway told them how she had come to be there at all. '... I knew it was a betrayal when word reached me of a combat á l'outrance between two unknown and nameless knights – one of them armed with Excalibur! I came at once – and only just in time ...'

In the faint earth-lit gloom of the Underway, with the bitter experience sharpened even more by the agony of regret that the joyful anticipation of seeing Arthur again would never happen to him now, Accolon gave in to despair. He had no idea how long it was going to take him to die but he only wished there was some way he could commit suicide. And then, it seemed an eternity later, came the sound of horses, the clinking of armour and chatter of voices ...

He was conscious of everyone striving with might and main to shift the rocks but the further they laboured into the fallen debris the harder it became, until Nemway recognised the problem.

'This exit has been *magically* sealed!' she exclaimed in disbelief. 'We're none of us going to get out this way.'

Apparently it was true. When they at last succeeded in dragging the injured knight clear, and Amyas was able to wield *Moldwarp*, the mace jumped back to his hand as if bouncing off rubber.

'So we find another way,' he said with dour practicality, stomping off to look for it, whilst Nemway knelt at Accolon's side, her tone full of remorse at her oversight. 'I thought you had returned to Mortleroy,' she said. 'I never thought to look back.'

'You couldn't have waited for me,' he said. 'I was too far behind. You said Arthur had come again in the Forest of Weir. He is my Liege. How could I go back to Mortleroy?'

It sounded unbelievable to Accolon when she exclaimed: 'Arthur's here now – he's with us!' And turned, calling the king's attention: 'Arthur! Arthur, it's Accolon!'

Arthur came at once and knelt by the side of the injured fay, taking Accolon's head in his arms. 'My friend!' he said warmly, before calling over his shoulder: 'Mildgyth, my dearest love, please the Cup. '

But Mildgyth was already on her way, the Cup filled from one of the many puddles. Taking it from her, Arthur held it to Accolon's lips for him to drink.

In wonder, the knight sat up, marvelling at his healing. When Arthur helped him to his feet, Accolon promptly sank on his knee before him, bowing his head. 'My Liege,' he said. My King–'

'And my good friend and companion,' Arthur interrupted warmly, drawing him to his feet again and embracing him. 'Remember the times we spent together–

'Sire!' It was Gareth hurrying over. 'Sire, this is Accolon of the Bloodied Sword – he nearly killed you!'

Accolon began to explain quickly: 'It was in penance, Sire, when I became a knight here. I chose that device so all would know–'

'Neither of us knew *who* the other was that day we fought,' Arthur interrupted his voice firm. 'I lost you, Accolon, also a great deal of blood without the scabbard that would have saved me.' He looked around at them all. 'That battle was none of this good knight's doing. In the event, he died that very night in mortality from his wounds – while I lived. Merlin had warned me of my mortal sister's treachery, but I would not listen.' His gaze returned to Gareth. 'And you must hold nothing against him, either,' he said. 'Now please find my friend a horse. And you, my good Accolon,' he continued to the knight. 'You shall be my Champion and bear Excalibur emblazoned on a shield *clean* of any blood …'

When Amyas found a drier ascending path to follow, he brought everyone out through the side of mound into the sunlight of an early afternoon beside the Weir River. They then saw the reason for the Underway's wetness. Something was damming the river, which had risen halfway up the bank.

Before they entered the forest, Accolon heard Arthur counselling Gareth to warn the Kindred to say nothing to the Weirdfolk about the cruelties of Mortleroy. He thought he understood why when, riding ahead with Arthur and Mildgyth, Amyas and Nemway, he was the first of those new to the faerie kingdom of Weir Forest to meet its long hidden inhabitants, and his eyes grew round in wonder. Even among the Kin of Beauty, he had never seen the kind of exquisite loveliness and perfection of form as exhibited by the Weirdfolk. Nor had he ever met with such a collective innocence as shone from these fae; their faces alight with joy and happiness as they came to meet the cavalcade. After the knight's experience, lying so long trapped and injured in the half-lit gloom of the underpass, it was like being born again; his eyes awakening to a whole new world which he drank in thirstily. These delightful fae around him might know nothing about their host of new visitors, but Arthur was their focal point. And here he was leading Windflame

– who carried a strange but beautiful lady in plain grey. She was never out of Arthur's adoring and worshipful gaze for long. The Weirdfolk, dancing and clapping their hands like children, followed behind and lead the way ahead in a colourful and variegated procession of welcome for them all. Accolon had seen nothing like it in his life before, nor was he prepared for the beauty and simplicity of the Queen or the imposing presence of two scintillating figures, one of iridescent black at her right hand the other in brilliant white at her left, and both flanked by other court officials.

*

White Wand's eyes were on Gwen as the Queen rose to her feet at Arthur's appearance. News of his arrival had come long before any sight of him, but Stella knew it had failed to prepare Gwen for a home-coming like this; her son in such strange clothes at the head of a small army – to say nothing of the nun-like fay he was leading towards her.

The gathering, all ready agog with excitement went wild with delight to see the pair walking hand in hand for Arthur to present her to the Queen.

'Mother, this is Mildgyth. She has consented to be my bride and future queen.'

Gwen embraced the fay lovingly and welcomed her among them with a kiss. The mild reproach over her son's absence, so often voiced to White Wand when she had tried to comfort the Queen, left unspoken but Arthur knew.

'Dearest Mother,' he said, kissing her in turn. 'The Lady Nemway has told me how grieved you were over Our absence and We apologise. We had no idea it would take so long. But now We are of age it is necessary to be about the business of Our Kingdom. And We're safely back,' he reminded her, 'thanks to Nemway, Amyas, and Gareth – and, of course, Am-mar-el-lin. There is also much to do.'

He turned and beckoned several knights to his side as Gwen took her seat again. 'Allow us to present our Champion Sir Accolon, and Our Kindred of the Grail knights: Sirs Jessant de Lys, Hugh de Brett …'

Stella wasn't surprised that Gwen seemed to find it quite bewildering as her hand was taken and kissed by each in turn before their introduction to White Wand and her partner, Redweird. Her alarmed eyes sought Stella's in silent pleading: *What do we do with such a large company? How shall all these to be assimilated into the life of the Weirdfolk?*

The Wych smiled back reassuringly. *Not your problem, dear Gwen*, was the message it returned. *Leave it to Arthur. He knows what he's doing.*

And, watching Arthur, Gwen's expression became wistful when he drew Mildgyth to his side and kissed her, then beckoned Redweird, Nemway, Amyas and Omric to say something in a low voice that made Omric gesture in the direction of the Gnomes' Mansion.

Arthur turned back to his mother. 'I will not be long,' he said quietly. 'But I need my court to hear what Nemway, Amyas, and Sirs Gareth, Accolon and the Kindred's Commanders can tell us about the state of things outside this forest. It needs to be in private and as soon as possible without disturbing our people.' He looked across at Stella. 'White Wand, I should have liked to have had you also with us, but you know how much I need you here for the fae and for my mother and Mildgyth. I shall charge Redweird with acquainting you with all that is said …'

CHAPTER 19

COMMANDING THE WIND

Accolon tried to react alertly to the small gathering in the Gnomes' Mansion, but gazed spellbound instead at the splendour of the Great Hall; its walls covered in scintillating tapestries. One in particular, behind the Master's golden chair which Omric now offered Arthur, showed a cascading mountain stream. The light, sparkling from water depicted in diamonds, had shadows of aquamarines that made it appear to actually flow. Brown rocks of cairngorm overlaid with a lichen of turquoise, garnet and kunzite gleamed blue, dark green and lavender. Topaz and chrysobel formed the banks, and in the background jade, emerald and malachite depicted trees, and bushes with trunks of cairngorm and amber, all quivering, somehow, in sunlight.

'Accolon …?' It was Arthur's voice summoning him back from his absorption.

Dragging his eyes away, he looked askance. 'Sire …?'

'What have you to say?'

'To what, Sire?'

'Haven't you been listening?'

'Sire,' Accolon gestured an appeal at their surrounds, and shook his head, 'I've never seen anything like this before.'

Arthur shook his head with a sigh, dismissing the matter of the knight's inattention with a resigned gesture. 'And now,' he went on to the Wychies, Omric and his Officials. 'Our forest has to become a place of healing and refuge.'

'But my liege!' exclaimed Redweird, 'The forest itself is doomed! We have been waiting for an escort from The Son of Nudd to guard and guide us from here to a place of safety–'

Nemway leant forward to interrupt: 'I understand from Gwyn himself that he sent an Owl with a rather different message to the one that was received via the Dove,

'A Dove?' asked Accolon, now giving his full attention. 'Are you sure it was the Dove of the Weirdfolk?'

'I was there,' said Nemway. 'It spoke by the power of the three Wands. Why do you ask?'

'For a time, I was in charge of the detail guarding one of the great Dragons in the dungeon at Glastonbury, and imprisoned with it ...' Accolon paused, looking around at them in discomfort and embarrassment, '... was the White Dove of the Weirdfolk.'

Gareth was indignant. 'So, the Dove was real but its message was meant to lead us into ambush!'

Nemway turned a rueful face to Arthur 'And I was made to doubt the Otter of the Denefolk.' she said. 'Now I know that the Sage, my son, sent you true greetings, Sire. Just now, when I needed to know where I could find you, he told me, or we'd be searching for you yet.'

Accolon looked at her with surprise and then at Arthur with concern. 'Sire, you cannot trust the Denefolk,' he said, shocked. 'It is well known that all lying originates from them. They send false dreams and whisper all kind of vile mischief on the wind, *and* poison the waters with their contrary ... magic ...' he faltered to a stop aware that Nemway had stiffened angrily, and Arthur was shaking his head at him.

'Accolon, Accolon, if you had been listening, you would understand. Now as you love me, love these Our people also.'

Accolon subsided in confusion wondering what he

meant, whilst Arthur went on to Redweird: 'Please, if you have the refugees I sent on Windflame, I will show you what I mean, and they will need clothing ...'

Redweird hurried away for his charges, and Omric sent a gnome for the troll they had adopted and dressed. When the gnome returned with his charge, Accolon stared in horror at the squat, hideous form that he was being asked to love with its purple-black face covered with warts, long yellow overhanging teeth and dull, squinting, red-rimmed eyes. And this, he knew, was better looking than most – but love ...!

When he then saw Gawain rise from his seat with a cry of anguished recognition: 'Raglan, my love! My beautiful, beautiful wife!' Accolon hardly knew whether to laugh outright, or cry in pity for a knight gone mad.

Gawain turned in appeal to Arthur. 'Sire, please, may I?' and held out his hand for the Cup.

Arthur handed it to him with a affectionate smile. The knight knelt holding the chalice gently to the lips of the nightmare which drank and as it did so seemed as if to wake from a long, long deep unconsciousness; stretching and yawning, shedding its clothes and changing before their eyes until, quite suddenly, they realised a revelation of willowy loveliness knelt in tears at Gawain's feet. She hardly needed the cloak that Gawain took from the Chamberlain to place around her shoulders. But he held her close, kissing her as he drew her long hair over its top to flow down around her.

The action broke their spell-bound witness. Nemway clapping her hands with undisguised delight at the miracle and Accolon closing his gaping mouth with the realisation that he must have missed something terribly important when he hadn't been listening – although what it could have been, he still couldn't begin to imagine.

Like a spell broken, Percivale started to Gawain's side. 'Mother!' he cried.

Gawain looked astonished. Raglan touched Gawain's face. 'My love, our mortal son. I couldn't stay with you and watch him grow up in the arts of war so alien to my nature in Arthur's mortal court–'

Gawain looked at Percivale. 'Why didn't you tell me who you were back then?'

Raglan hung her head. 'I made him promise not to reveal himself.'

'Apart from Mother, I'd never met a living soul until I was fifteen,' Percivale said with a laugh. 'When I saw Launcelot with four of his knights in our deep forest in Wales why, with their jingling armour and the bridles of their horses ringing like silver bells, I thought they were the very angels that Mother had told me served the King of Heaven. Launcelot said that he did indeed serve the King of Heaven, but that I should go to His appointed Ruler on earth, King Arthur at Caerleon and become a knight at his great Table.'

'Gawain, I wept,' Raglan pleaded. 'But in the end I had to let him go. I told him you were the best and bravest of all Arthur's knights, but not to tell you who he was.'

'But how did you know the troll was Mother?' Percivale asked his father. 'I had no idea until she changed.'

'I didn't. What I said simply sprang to mind from what I saw which was so like Raglan's appearance when I first met her. She had been spelled by Morgan le Fay to catch Arthur out and get him killed.'

Arthur leaned forward. 'And would have succeeded but for you, my friend,' he said, going on to Percivale: 'Your mortal father honoured his word to the knight of Taren Wathelyne, that he would marry the Lady Raglan if she gave him the answer to his riddle. I begged him not to – it was a terrible sacrifice–'

'Which I gladly made, Sire,' Gawain interrupted. 'And see how wonderfully we were each rewarded. And you,' he went on, clapping Percivale on the shoulder. 'Through your mother, you became one of the noblest of all the Knights of the Round Table. Just think,' he went on to marvel: 'We rode together, you and I, and I never knew you were my mortal son.'

Gareth nodded. 'And now I know how you won your title: "The Fair Unknown",' he said with a grin.

By the time the Wychy had returned with a mung who took on his true form as a mabyn, and a cave-wight and wellsprite that also turned into Denefolk. It all became too much for Accolon.

He rose and went to fling himself on his knees before Arthur. 'I have been prideful, ignorant and self-serving to have chosen Mortleroy as liege,' he confessed. 'I thought I knew it all – and now I have so much to learn.'

'Accolon, you know now what my Wychies, Counsellors, and Officers also needed to see and hear. This is what Mortleroy – King Death has done. And to see how much he so especially hated the Kin of Beauty and the Denefolk that he made their enslavements the most ugly and unloveliest of all.'

'But why these and not us?' Accolon asked, still unable to take in the whole implication of what he was being told.

Arthur replied gently. 'There are only four great divisions of the faerie in Brython,' he said drawing the shamed knight to his feet. 'Where is his sport if King Death can't set you one against the other?'

'You mean …?

'Yes,' Arthur nodded gravely. 'You are as indoctrinated as much as ever your Kins are malformed.'

Accolon was shocked. 'Sire, that makes *us* worse. We persecute and hound them wherever they are.' He hung his head. 'Sire, I am ashamed and sorry.'

'You are not to blame. But you are now a witness, you must tell your companions what you have seen.'

'My liege,' said Redweird, 'we have not yet heard anything that Sir Accolon could probably tell of things we need to know.'

Arthur nodded. 'Thank you, my Wychy; indeed.' Seated around the Master's table, Arthur began by asking the knight everything he could of the deployment and strength of the enemy forces. He then laid down the rules of engagement under which they would assault the Citadel of Reading. Amyas could knock down as many walls as he liked – Mortleroy needed to be shown – and Nemway would rebuild them.

Here Arthur looked at Nemway with a twinkle in his eye. '… That is, my Lady, I hope you will?' he said. 'I know you have the gift.'

'My liege, it is yours,' she said without hesitation.

'But,' Arthur turned back to Amyas with a warning: 'have a care that no life is taken. There will be so very little time. When We have been received in Reading, We shall need you to go immediately to open an underpass to the Kindred's Stronghold by the Chapel of Blue Fountains and to open again the entrance within it that you found there to Weir Forest. We shall need you to garrison each of these Underways for all who will be using them. '

Amyas inclined his head. Kye then learned the vital role that he as Royal Herald had to play in announcing what was and would be happening. 'Kindred of the Grail,' Arthur continued, addressing their Knight Commanders. 'We shall need each of you also to act with utmost speed. Sir Jessant and his Company to search out and escort the Mung gathering in the woods at Cyngsfold to your Stronghold. Mildgyth will be there ready to administer the Cup of Healing. Then you must guide your charges back here to Weir Forest. I charge Sir Geraint to do the same with the Wellsprite. The Lady Nemway has spoken to the Sage of all the Seers who will see

you are guided to where you will find them, even as Sir Hugh
de Bret will be led to wait for Hugh ap Gwyn who will be
bringing the Cave-wight up from their holes and burrows,
and similarly escort him and them. He turned to Redweird.
'My Wychy, even as you provide clothing for the Weirdfolk
when they return here, will you – can you provide these in
sufficient quantity for my brother Amyas to take with him
to clothe my people who will be naked? And not only that,
but find and bring home all those Weirdfolk now alive as
mortals without destroying their mortal form?'

Redweird responded promptly: 'My Liege, consider it
done.'

Amyas and Omric both looked at each other and then at
Arthur with a frown.

'Sire,' Amyas said, 'And where and when shall we expect
to see *you*?'

'You shall see me return with Mildgyth, Gareth, Gawain,
Percivale – and many others,' he was assured. 'Then you
will close all those entrances behind us that you will have
held open.'

It looked as if the conference was at an end, but Arthur
had one more request. 'We need a messenger,' he said quietly.
'Who will go for us?'

They all looked at each other willing to volunteer but
wondering how they could fit it in on top of everything
else they were being asked to do, when Gareth rose and
came round to place a fae-sized dove – no larger than a
mortal house fly – on the table before him, saying: 'The lady
Mildgyth gave me this, and words to say: "If Arthur needs
a messenger then give him this – my heart. It will fly to the
ends of the earth should he so desire.".'

Arthur's face lit with a smile of almost boyish relief.
'Thank you, thank you!' he said before looking around at
them all saying firmly: 'And now rejoice! Whatever you see

or hear, We tell you now, all will be well, and you shall see all manner of things *made* well ...'

*

Nemway received her instructions in private. Arthur would ride at the head of his army clad in the shining armour she had brought him, girded with Omric's sword. As soon as they had gained the Citadel, however, she was to have charge of his armour again, and take it secretly to the Chapel of Blue Fountains. She must then return to Reading with Omric's sword keeping it hidden from sight until she knew when the time had come to reveal it. '... You will do this?' he asked.

'I will, my liege,' she promised with a sigh, 'although it sounds most strange ...'

*

At a wave of his Wand, Redweird could supply all the clothing Amyas would need to take with him. Reclaiming Weirdfolk, however, without the death of their mortal bodies, was something else. His predecessor had not left him entirely unprepared, however. One of the last entries in his book of wisdom read:

... Attend well, Wychy. You, once Edward We'ard and mortal Guardian of this Forest of Weir for seventy years, are now the last to hold this Office of Black Wand and *may have need to continue* the work of rescuing the fae scattered in the surrounding villages and even further afield if all have not yet been recovered in time.

It is normal for those returning to do so at the end of their natural mortal lives (or accidently ingesting Wizard's Woe!). However, to avoid panic among mortals with any spate of untimely 'deaths', know that the addition of Stillbind in proportion of two to one of the former, will preserve the mortal body but liberate the wraith within, thus: when the fever induced by the 'Woe' reaches a certain height, thereby detaching the wraith, the antidote Stillbind will act so that the patient will recover from what will appear to have been a twenty-four hour attack of influenza and be none the worse for the experience. And, as in the majority of these cases he or she would never have suspected any radical difference between themselves and other people, they will also be none the wiser…

Redweird had had little or no inclination to act on this advice, until he knew the right time had come.

And that time had come, he reflected – but the logistics were intimidating. They made it a problem he needed to share with his Wych; two heads being better than one.

Stella welcomed him into the privacy of her Retreat with a delighted smile, and listened attentively as he outlined the difficulties of complying with Arthur's wishes.

'… I have the means,' he ended. 'But not the 'how' of *where* to find and reach each fae. They could be scattered to the four winds from here.'

'I can help you with the *where* – because it is given to me to know where our people are in mortality,' she said, 'even as it is given to you to know the *when* to welcome them on their return here. I can willingly help you prepare the dosage here, in my Retreat, where we may work together, and give you the name and whereabouts of every fae still missing from my Roll. But how you will reach them I can only guess.' Stella ran her Wand over the runic tapestries of her predecessor. 'White Wand-that-was records that when Merlyn's Heir went to find a translation of his Assyrian title he travelled, unbeknown to you, with you by car because you knew where to find the person who could do it.' Finding what she was looking for she went on: 'I can give you names of those who are still in Three Weirs and the surrounding towns and villages. If you can remember where those villages are, a driver might be wandled into taking you. But one as far away as Southampton and even in France, Germany and Italy …?'

Although she left the question hanging, she had given Redweird enough to see his way forward. Just how long it would all take was something he could worry about later. For the moment, he would simply enjoy her offer of help with preparing the dosages. And working alongside his Wych in this way was a whole new experience for them both. Her helpful and intelligent suggestions revealing a hidden side he had never had the opportunity of appreciating until then. Doing so in the privacy of her Retreat, made him yearn to put work aside and simply enjoy the time she was allowing him to share her space. He couldn't help but marvel. A Wych without doubt was the loveliest of all her wiccies *And to be so close …*

He knew she sensed his thought as she touched his Weird, her fingers gentle. 'Beloved, I wish I could come with you.'

He smiled. 'Shall I not have you with me in my heart, my love? There has to be one of us here – and who better than you to welcome those I shall be sending home.'

Stella's expression became wistful. 'I remember my return – High Moon it was and such a celebration …' she paused a slight frown creasing her brow. ' … So long ago, now. But the Royal Vintner, himself, dear old 'Rosynose' – as we used to call Rozyn-who-Knows –welcomed me and brought me across the Crystal Bridge on his dray. He called me 'Our Star Maiden' and, because of a vision, I was able to announce the coming of Royal Arthur.'

'Which goes to show how truly wyché you are, my love,' he said, his voice tender as he drew her to him.

She melted into him. 'Beloved Redweird, you have so much strength and patience, I love you. Go carefully this night. It is a perilous thing you are doing.'

'I would say more miraculous than perilous, my love! No mortal thing can hurt me. I have my Wand and my will – and if ever the wandling of mortals could be justified, surely tonight's errand will make it so? Yet, even as Arthur has said: "all will be well, and you shall see all manner of things *made* well." ...'

*

Darkness had fallen by the time Redweird set off and the weather, never a problem normally, became one when he reached the road. Wind and rain might not worry him – picking up every reflection of light, the rain danced in the wind like cascading jewels to his elfin eyes – but it concerned human beings quite a lot when he needed transport. The first car he jumped on had its windows closed, so he had to leap off again. The next vehicle, a MG sports model which had seen better days in those pre-MOT years, had a leaky hood, no windows and the young fellow driving it seemed sufficiently mellow not to mind the inconvenience. Redweird leapt aboard, perched on his shoulder, pointed his Wand of Office and ordered him to a garage to fill up on petrol. They had a long way ahead of them, he therefore had two spare cans of it put on board and the garage owner appeared not to mind the lack of any payment. It seemed the best Redweird could offer in exchange for the amount of time he would need chauffeuring around. He deplored the absurd necessity of having to wandle a mortal to get him from A to B and all places necessary in between, and felt concern for a driver who would no doubt worry himself to death over what would appear a huge lapse of memory.

On the other hand it would be a bonus if it helped the young man to give up drink driving in the future!

Even with transport, progress seemed slow – as if hindered in some way by an invisible presence that pushed and pulled at him from another direction. He had to keep urging the driver to put his foot down. There were so many to reach: Three Weirs village held the most, then Hurstlea and Corsham before reaching out to more remote places and scattered cottages in the surrounding area, with an isolation hospital in Southampton listed as his final destination. He despaired over the continent; it seemed well out of the equation.

In the small hours of the morning, he was at last able to direct his driver to take the road to Southampton. '… as fast as you can,' he mistakenly added. The sudden spurt on a straight road with nothing else in sight, the car took off with a loud bang from somewhere in the rear. The driver wrestled madly with the wheel while the car rocked and bounced all over the place before, turning around, it plunged across the verge into a wooden fence.

By the time Redweird had to desert the driver, because the approaching headlights of a large truck summoned him with the promise of another lift, he gathered it had been a burst tyre.

As he stepped into the blaze of light, however, he found himself confronted by a ghostly figure, its willowy shape outlined by the streaming rain's rich colour of bouncing gems that ran to join the streams of silver in the cambered road.

It spoke in a sigh: 'You travel a strange and tortuous way, wizard.'

The veiled accusation prickled. 'It's the best I know how!' Redweird answered. 'I haven't much time and I need to get to a place known among mortals as Southampton.'

'Then allow me …' And, as the lorry rumbled to a halt by the stranded car, Redweird found himself seized and lifted as if by a strong wind while the apparition continued soughing beside him: 'There are paths unknown to men by which we travel, yet for a wizard you seem strangely ignorant of them.'

'Then I hope you will also return me to the place known to men as Three Weirs when I have done what I am sent to do in Southampton?'

'I will wait for you.'

'Who are you, and who sent you?'

'I am Huw of the Denefolk, and the Sage of all the Seers who is my father sent me to help you fulfil Royal Arthur's will. Your haste and determination has not made it easy.'

And Redweird remembered his sense of an invisible presence with a pang of guilt. What an enormous amount of time he had wasted – quite apart from wrecking the young man's car.

'I have so much to learn,' he said, his tone apologetic.

Huw took him where he needed to be – even to France, Germany and Italy – and deposited him back at Weir Forest by dawn.

Redweird gave him his grateful appreciation. 'Before you leave,' he said, 'may I – could I ask for the safe and speedy return of all the fae that have been released?'

Huw's simple assurance: 'We serve,' sighed away as he disappeared.

*

Stella received her Partner with wonder. 'O incomparable Wychy,' she whispered into his Weird. 'Bless you, thank you. Every fae accounted for and safe– ' She stopped his lips with a finger. 'Don't rob me of my gratitude to you *whatever* help you say you had. *You* did this–'

'Nevertheless,' he said firmly, 'Who else but Royal Arthur can command the wind …?'

CHAPTER 20

HANNIBAL

Reports of Nemway's sudden disappearance so puzzled Myrddin that he felt he really had to investigate for himself. If she had gone into hiding to distract him it was possible he might stand every chance of catching her when she surfaced again.

Taking off as a mortal sized Royal Falcon, he plummeted down every now and then to inspect any adjacent cover enroute until the sun's glitter on a fast moving cavalcade caught his attention. At the same time, something else caught his eye: two fae-sized black falcons were scouting ahead of it in wide reconnoitring circles. He should have anticipated such a meeting, but hadn't and, although his disguise might deceive others, it certainly wouldn't deceive them.

Even as he spotted them, one wheeled sharply in his direction, blowing itself up to his mortal sized falcon and dived straight for him. He dropped into a grove, morphed into the nine-inch-high black armoured Lord of the Grail and waited for the bird's arrival. He had a score to settle with it and the remainder of its kind, anyway.

The falcon's instinct appeared miraculous. It plunged into the grove and came straight for him. Then, apparently surprised at not finding a bird but a well armoured knight, it checked and landed a few inches away staring at him with its photographic eyes recording every detail of Myrddin's appearance for its master.

The wizard knew it would be off in a split second at any hostile move, and he wanted to keep its attention. Moving casually, and taking a seat on a small branchlet lying on the ground, he began rummaging plasma from some overhead fronds growing within reach. Carefully positioning himself where the falcon was able to see what he was doing; he smoothed a wafer thin portion into a sheet on which he began writing. With its head on one side and its sharp bright eyes attentively following his every move, Myrddin's assurance grew that each detail was noted. The bird, obviously familiar with scrolls, wasn't going to leave without this one.

Myrddin scrawled rapidly, then carefully rolled the sheet up, fashioned a piece of wax and sealed it firmly with his sceptre. Reaching out, he lay the tiny roll carefully on the ground between them as if offering it to be taken; then stood haughtily, even backing off a step, to wait.

The falcon looked from him to the rolled sheet and back again, patently tempted but suspicious. When it moved at last, it did so cautiously, never removing its eyes from Myrddin's until within reach of the parchment. There it paused but the magician remained immobile with an air of indifference until, when the bird made a lightning change back to a fae-size messenger that could deliver the scroll to his master's wrist and seized the missive in its beak, Myrddin's sceptre descended in a sharp chop across the back of its skull knocking it senseless.

Changing to a mortal sized falcon himself, Myrddin proceeded to devour the creature and take in any message it might be carrying. He found it impressed with the same vision of the lean dark visage that he had seen once before when he had caught and devoured the first of them.

'You will fly in company with my High Constable, O scavenger of the skies, and shall be to him for this time only as his own hawk to his wrist instead of mine. You shall scour the heavens before him, and seek out a certain witch armed with a Whip, and

guide my High Constable to meet her. Seek diligently also for a certain magician from foreign parts, a Saracen entitled the Prince of Damascus. When you find him be dutiful and courteous, and convey to him thus, that my majesty is deeply beholden to him for the salvation of my ancient Citadel of Reading. Charge him not to delay his coming to me that I may suitably reward him with such poor means as lie in my power.'

In one sense, it left a sour taste on Myrddin's tongue. If he had kept his previous costume, the bird would have straightaway carried any message he wanted to send Mortleroy to his, Myrddin's, own advantage. However, it seemed that the usurper still had some urgent need of his prowess despite the war being as good as over.

He remembered the other falcon, still likely to be hanging around waiting for the first which gave him an idea. Flying out of the grove, still fae-sized, he located it and sped straight for it. At once the other checked its circling and winged towards him, evidently thinking it was its companion was inviting it to come-see. Myrddin turned back, hovered a moment over the grove, then plunged into it.

Up to a point, he repeated his previous tactics. Changing back to the Lord of the Grail with his visor down to hide his features, he presented the scroll and knocked the creature insensible. Only this time, instead of eating it, he stayed as he was and performed what amounted to an astral lobotomy; removing the bird's brain and inserting a new one of his own making. After its restoration to consciousness, Myrddin programmed it to his will in much the same way as had previously been done by Mortleroy.

From his earlier kills, Myrddin knew that each falcon had its own secret name between itself and its Master; and this one's he had learnt was 'Hannibal'.

He ordered it to depart at last with the misinformation that, having found the Lady of the Lake and her charges had detoured from their approach, she was now five miles behind the High Constable. The other sight impressed on the bird was Myrddin's appearance as the Prince of Damascus.

He watched from above as Hannibal returned to the High Constable. It pleased him greatly to see the huge cavalcade halt, reverse direction and head off back to Glastonbury the way it had come. The falcon then flew off in the direction of Glastonbury itself to deliver its second piece of news, while Myrddin resumed his hunt for Nemway. It seemed to him that the sooner he got his hands on the newborn Yathra, the better. Under his tutelage – perhaps his regency – who knew? – but that he, the Lord of the Grail, could turn the entire resources of Britain towards the rescue of the Weirdfolk from the doomed Forest of Weir.

Sometime later, with still no sign of Nemway, Myrddin was impatiently wondering where Hannibal had got to. The brainwashed bird had been instructed fly from the High Constable straight to the King with the apparent sighting of the Prince of Damascus and to fly back again with anything Mortleroy might have told it. Myrddin considered it should have shown up long since unless Mortleroy had somehow divined his interference.

In an effort to find out what might be going on, he caught and ate a passing hawk and found that it held an astonishing vision of the Earl of Reading at the head of a small army tearing due west towards him with Peredur's party racing some miles in his wake to catch up.

Quickly catching and digesting another fae-sized spy-hawk made him increasingly uneasy to find news of other Mortleroy partisans riding hard for the same destination.

Disregarding a paranoid notion that Mortleroy could be summoning all of them to catch whoever was responsible for messing with his Royal Falcon, the only logical alternative that presented itself was a sudden need to augment the defence of Glastonbury. Yet Ranulph had told him that Mortleroy had declared he had been successful on all fronts and that Gwyn's discomforted forces had retired into oblivion. So of what nature and from what quarter was Mortleroy expecting new trouble?

It all made waiting for Hannibal doubly frustrating. When the bird finally appeared, Myrddin learnt that it had spent the intervening time conveying urgent orders here, there and everywhere calling for further reinforcements from quite different strongholds. Hannibal's final mission then was to find the elusive Prince of Damascus and impart the most flowery inducements the usurper had ever transmitted to anyone.

Stripped of verbiage and reading behind the words, it told Myrddin that Mortleroy felt cornered and was offering half his kingdom to anyone who could preserve him from utter defeat. Contrary to the King's previous bulletin, his war with the underground rebels was by no means over. Gwyn's forces had suddenly reappeared from all directions riding hard for Avalon. The Mabyns had also broken out of their ancient fortresses in the Gogmagog Hills and were appearing in the open from time to time out of unexpected Underways north, west and south of London. And, as if this were not enough, there had appeared from nowhere a large force of warriors bearing the insignia of the Grail who, in company with the Rebels, had inflicted a crushing local defeat in Sussex. Almost as an afterthought, the message mentioned that the long promised infant Yathra, spirited away by the Lady of the Lake, had disappeared. If the mighty Prince of Damascus who had so ably manifested his goodwill towards his brother monarch of Britain by preserving the impregnability of his favoured Citadel of Reading, would come at once ... etcetera, etcetera, etcetera.

Myrddin's anger at Gareth's audacity in deploying the newly formed Knights of the Grail had to go on hold while he considered the other implications of the message; one being that Mortleroy did *not* have the royal babe – which was a relief. On the other hand, it also made it a logical deduction that Nemway's disappearance tied in with Cousin Gwyn's reappearance. The Lady had gone, or been taken underground, which boded ill for Yathra with Gwyn's record of accomplishments. When he considered the position of Mortleroy, it was plain that King Death's survival was now in the balance. Only similar or greater magic than Algaric's could possibly serve to hold him and his kingdom together; especially the most important symbol of that kingdom which was the sacred fastness of Glastonbury, where the old Arthurian legend centred on ancient Avalon.

It was this above all which determined Myrddin to accept the invitation immediately. Avalon was the focal point in a wonderful history, and it was only from there that Myrddin could hope to control the present alarming situation – provided of course that he got there first. Once installed he should be able, with the help of the usurper's legions, to hold the place against all comers – including a loose cannon named Gwyn.

Naturally, this meant making a short-term ally of Mortleroy but, after sorting Gwyn, there would be plenty of time to decide how to liquidate the usurper.

The real concern at the back of his mind, however, was that if he, Myrddin, had not contrived to produce Yathra before the Weirdfolk came out of the Forest, the first in the field would capture popular imagination, which meant everyone would accept the bogus Arthur. He wondered if he shouldn't warn Mortleroy and have him put *his* people on the hunt for the missing youth.

He winged resolutely on until noon when, on one of Hannibal's returns, he had them both descend into a nearby wood.

He took in all his dupe could tell him and then dictated the following message: 'Fly to the King of Brython, bird of my belonging. Say to him that the Prince and Magician of Damascus approaches and will begin an ascent to the Tower soon. Say he shall be recognised by a mighty jewel of the orient that blazes from his green and yellow turban and by the ring of fire that shall surround him when he swings his mighty mace three times ...'

CHAPTER 21

MORTLEROY

Mortleroy licked his lips, his forked tongue flickering too fast even for a fae to see. The constant need to check his surrounds had grown in the past few years. Mortleroy had felt threatened ever since his quarrel with Algaric had left him without a magician. Anyone suspecting their King's real nature could not fail to betray it, they would be shaking in their shoes – and there *was* a trace of abnormal fear somewhere, but so faint as to be barely discernible, masked as it was by the heavy threat from Gwyn that hung everywhere like a pall of thick red smoke. Another search and – *yes, there it was!* Someone *had* discovered him. But who and where? He sat back, eyes closed, tongue tasting the ether, thin nostrils stretched wide and twitching, every nerve extended – and was overwhelmed by a new and closer scent. It wasn't what he had expected yet the bouquet of aromas that had just arrived for his attention in the depths below made him drool. Everything else could go on hold. This delectable feast had to be enjoyed while warm and still fresh.

*

As the rim of the moon rose above the horizon in the outside world, Mortleroy stood hidden in the shadows of the dimly lit vault to watch Avellane, Gaheris, and Edric returning to consciousness.

Gaheris, the first to move; raised himself on an elbow to peer into the gloom with a frown. 'Where on earth are we?' he asked, climbing to his feet 'I thought we were dead after that encounter with Edric.'

Avellane rose with rather more alacrity. 'Ugh, the place is crawling!' he exclaimed, scrubbing the back of his hand down his side.

'Where? I can't see anything.'

'Something slithered over my hand. There!' he said, pointing. 'A snake! And look at those walls – they're green and dripping with slime!'

'I know what's happened,' Gaheris said, sounding confident. 'We're ghosts and this is purgatory.'

'Ghosts can't feel, and *I* can,' Avellane told him firmly. 'And anyway I've never believed–'

'How do you know ghosts can't feel– '

'Where's my helmet!' The angry roar made them glance round. A murderous looking Edric had clambered to his feet and was glaring at them, a badly damaged sword arm swinging uselessly while a deep black cut showed in his side. 'Which one of you has taken my helmet?'

Avellane and Gaheris both reached for their swords and found them gone. Edric's wounded state made them look down at themselves, then at each other and Avellane's eyes widened.

'You *should* be dead,' he whispered in awed tones.

'*You* should speak for yourself!' Gaheris said with spirit. 'Nothing wrong with me. But it's evident *you* were riddled with arrows!'

Mortleroy stepped forward with a mirthless chuckle. 'Gentlemen, gentlemen! I can assure you that this is neither the time nor place–'

Edric fell on his knee. 'My Lord, you are here! How wonderful! Thank you! You see I have brought you Avellane – Gaheris–'

Mortleroy silenced him with a voice like ice: 'You have brought me nothing! *I* had you brought here. This is where every one of my subjects ends up – and that includes those who fancy their allegiance is to Gwyn ap Nudd!' This came with a sneer at Avellane and Gaheris. 'I *am* King Death and all are subject to me.'

Edric objected: 'We're not dead. We're alive.'

'Fools! You only thought yourselves dead. But now you *really* die – slowly and in the most exquisite agony that will give me the utmost pleasure to watch and savour.'

'But I am not your enemy!' Edric cried in horror. 'I have served you well? Here are your enemies – Avellane and Gaheris–'

'You served no one but yourself, Edric. But now, here in *my* kingdom, you shall truly serve me and I shall give you your proper reward. You shall be first – the others can watch. The Kin of Beauty are the most sensitive of fae – apart from the Weirdfolk I am told but have never had the pleasure of watching one of them feel another's pain.' He beckoned into the darkness beyond them to bring forward six black robed, masked and hooded figures. They placed two crates which they carried between them gently on the floor before him.

'My 'specials',' Mortleroy said; greeting Avellane's cold, proud, gaze with a thin smile. 'Resistance is useless,' he said. 'You'll find my guards stronger than you are – much stronger.' This Knight of Beauty's pride and sensitivity delighted him. It made the prospect of having him watch Edric's reduction to a terrified scrap of screaming jelly even more pleasurable. He nodded the guards: 'Strip him.' He noted Gaheris flinch as the armour was torn roughly from the Constable's useless arm, and then his look of astonishment at seeing the limb whole and the wound in his side apparently healed. 'You are surprised, Gaheris?' Mortleroy taunted with a thin smile. 'I told you, you only *think* yourself dead. Wounds have no meaning here – but these that you shall see

– and feel – and fear, do.' He motioned one of the keepers and pointed. 'Open that box.'

When obeyed, Mortleroy reached in and drew out a small scaly reptilian looking creature with scalpel like claws. 'Meet Sweetly,' he said softly, and placed the thing on Edric's now naked form spread-eagled on the floor with four guards each holding his arms and legs apart between them.

Gaheris started forward, struggling against his captors' hold. 'You can't do this–'

Mortleroy laughed. 'But I can – and do. Sweetly is one of many, and Edric's remains will then be fed to my other pets – serpents that swallow their remains and go among my people to spit their captured spirits out to incarnate and live and grow and return to *me* again and again and again providing renewed and even greater pleasure every time.'

'You are evil!' Avellane spat, his jaw tightening and balling his hands into fists as the creature made a delicate incision in the Constable's groin. Edric's body arched, striving to escape the vice-like grip of his captors.

Mortleroy rubbed his hands together watching Edric while keeping an eye on Avellane and his subordinate. 'You have *no* idea how good this feels–' and broke off. A tiny sound had escaped the rictal stretch of Edric's bared teeth. Mortleroy gestured a guard. 'Any moment now and he's going to scream. Another – quick, quick – I can't wait!' Then tensed, waiting for the tortured knight to break and when he did, let his prisoners see the piercing screams sending him rigid in ecstasy. It ended when one of the creatures, attracted by the noise, scuttling up to Edric's open mouth where it cut out his tongue and disappeared down the abruptly choking and retching throat of a convulsing body.

Mortleroy then set the creatures to search, probe deep to bring out fresh and delicious morsels for him to sample, before relaxing back with a sigh of satisfaction. 'A pity all good things have to come to an end, but I still have you two

– and an even greater delight reserved especially for the Kin of Beauty. When I have finished with the delectable contents of your brains, you shall each end up a mindless troll.' He almost doubled up with howls of laughter at their dismayed and horrified expressions. Oh, the enjoyment he could now expect from Avellane's revulsion and agony over the torture and suffering of his second-in-command. It was too much to resist any longer. He nodded to the two attendants holding Gaheris: 'Next–' and broke off. An imminent arrival summoning his attention in the upper world, made him groan with vexation before taking leave of his 'specials' – he really wanted to kiss the little reptiles, but they were too dangerous even for him. He had to content himself with praise: 'Sweet, oh sweet, my little sweetlies. That was *so* exquisitely done, my little beautifuls!' He left with a promise to the two knights. 'I shall be back.' And now they knew what was coming to them, the anticipation became even more delectable …

*

The build-up of the opposing forces impressed Myrddin more and more as he detoured to by-pass their hurrying hundreds. It was the same with Gwyn's army, which had sprouted magically back into the open in surprisingly large units. After that, he flew on alone, ducking and weaving according to his immediate observations, until he arrived in sight of the tall, grass-grown Tor where St Michael's Tower reared its lonely head on its crest. He had learnt from Hannibal that the remnants of a crypt, long closed to human eyes, lay in its foundations. Ranulph had said Mortleroy held court here during residence, when he also conducted the age-old Ceremony of the Skull.

Myrddin dropped into cover, reconstituted himself as the Prince of Damascus, and brought out *Earthshaker*.

Providing himself with a snow white mount, he rode towards the Tor noting the Tower's commanding situation above him. No rider, let alone a belligerent force, could scale it without detection for there was not a shred of cover on any side. He looked at the man-made serpentine path winding to the summit and decided it was not for him. He needed an impressive approach.

On a lower western slope of the Tor's east-west aspect, he found the way. Broken fragments of an old megalith lay scattered over the ground. The largest, even when on its side as this was, loomed hugely above him, alive with power. He knew the splintered rock meant a misalignment of the earth's current that made his intention a dangerous exercise – if he failed to control it properly …

He prepared himself carefully, however, rehearsing his mind in every manoeuvre he needed to take at exactly the right moment. He then retreated the necessary distance to give his horse speed and space for the jump. Urging it forward at a gallop, he brought it up in a leap to land foursquare on the surface of the rock.

Instantly, the tight spiral of energy caught him and spun him off at a tangent to the summit. His sudden and dramatic appearance there, like some mounted whirling dervish, visibly stunned the small mounted force led by a Constable and Herald awaiting his arrival.

Myrddin allowed them to trot forward until they were a mortal yard or so from him before he unloosed *Earthshaker*. Three times, he whirled it above his head like a flaming Catherine wheel before, stilling it with his hand, he calmly hooked the mace back on his saddle-bow as if he had done nothing extraordinary and waited motionless while the shaken Constable approached. The officer greeted him in awe and in the name of the King of Brython.

The wizard responded briefly and they escorted him inside.

He found the stern: 'Peace or death in the name of the King,' that came from the midst of a line of lances and drawn bows inside the railings around the tower, answered –unsurprisingly – with the password: 'Damascus'.

His derisive thought nevertheless triggered a warning. Playing with fire was hazardous. Mortleroy was something more than another Ranulph who could be intimidated or browbeaten. *But that doesn't mean I can't make a damn good entrance …!*

He followed his escort on down to a skilfully disguised hole in the Tower's foundations which bored at an angle through the masonry for several mortal yards before it narrowed abruptly to an opening just large enough to admit one rider at a time. Passing through in turn, he found himself in the vastness of an arched and columned crypt.

The restraining hand of a knight on his steed's bridle went unnoticed while he looked from the great throng of assembled courtiers stretching away on either side towards a remote tableau. A golden throne surrounded by banners depicting the four protective Dragons of the Faerie drew his eyes to its occupant and a face he recognised at once as the instructor of the Royal Falcons.

Magnificently double crowned by a central golden skull, its eye-sockets inlaid with ruby, surrounded by an outer coronet of gold set with jewels, his form concealed by voluminous robes of purple, Mortleroy's deep set eyes returned Myrddin's dark-grey gaze with probing intensity.

Like the meeting of two keen rapiers, both sought instant advantage of the other. They held this searching regard without blinking while the herald stepped forward and after a vigorous fanfare recited the King's titles, naming him Lord of the Over-world and King of all the Ancient Isles of Brython; Lion of Realms beyond the Seas, Father of the Five Peoples, Victor of Lyonesse, Tamer of Dragons, Guardian of the Holy Skull and Lord Warden of the Isle of Avalon.

The list terminated with a jubilant fanfare which, to Myrddin's ear, sounded a challenge to put up claims even half as impressive and he rose to it. When the herald approached and enquired what his manner of announcement should, Myrddin didn't even answer. With his eyes on Mortleroy, he drew his sceptre from the folds of his gown, laid its point on the shoulder of the trumpeter's embroidered tabard and signalled him to open with a fanfare which, controlled by the magician's wand, shook the crypt with deafening notes. It was so long and varied, it made the previous effort seem no more than an overture to a full length opera, but not monotonously so. No, the paralysed hearers were thunderstruck. Even Mortleroy blinked once or twice as if ridding himself of some hypnotic influence. Nor did it rest there; still under Myrddin's control, the herald then reeled off title after title in honour of the distinguished visitor, and scribes who were present to record the exact notations might well have suffered from the fae equivalent of writer's cramp before the recitation ended:

'... The most puissant potentate Am-Mar-El-Lyn, Eternal Prince and Royal Mage of Damascus; Wielder of an Hundred Thousand Swords; Heir of Merlyn, Lord of the Stars, Seer of the Secret Heavens; Brother of the Sun; Husband of the Moon; Reader of the Royal Stars of Persia; Prince of all Enchantments; Lord of the Seven Thousand Holy Salamanders by whom the Element of Fire is ever at his command; Master of Djinns and Effreets; Imperator of Imps, Director of Devils; Shaker of Mountains and Stiller of Waters; Tyrant of Tempests, Raiser of Storms; Devourer of Dragons; Render of Rocs; Conqueror of Beelzebub, Behemoth and Baphomet; Ravisher of Isis, Astarte and Ashtoreth; Subduer of Shaitan; Slayer of Set; Caliph of every Sacred City of the East; Conqueror of Cathay; Arbiter of India; Supreme Satrap of Egypt; Overthrower of the Pyramids; Binder of Babylon, Scatterer of the Legions of Nineveh; Raiser of the Dead, Lord of the Living; Consort of Ten Thousand Concubines, Sire of a Thousand, Thousand Deathless Sons ...'

Would the recitation ever end? Mortleroy's bored expression spoke for itself that it was pure show.

But could he expect anything less from the colourful personality he had heard about from Ranulph? Myrddin reflected, aware of the King's thin, impatient fingers tapping the arms of his throne, whilst the narrowed eyes continued to appraise him as the recital continued. Even so, Myrddin hoped that, making allowances for the poetic and flowery images traditionally employed by Easterners, Mortleroy might yet begin to feel that if the turbaned magnificence at the other end of his court could do even half of what Ranulph claimed, he could be backing a winner after all and making his crown secure. On the face of it, half a kingdom was a reasonable reward for services rendered – if he survived to give it or the Prince of Damascus ever lived to enjoy it.

When the titles ended, the King's lips tightened again as he steeled himself against yet another excruciatingly long fanfare.

Myrddin considered it only politic to yield to protocol at the end when the High Constable whispered a little unsteadily that all visitors, whatever their rank, dismounted in the presence of the King of all Brython. All the same, he unhooked his magic mace and took it with him as he began to walk the long avenue of awed and bewildered courtiers.

The swiftly veiled look of wary apprehension that lit Mortleroy's eyes at his advance might have vanished the next moment but showed the King had seen the power of the mace, and that the moment now approaching him held every suggestion of an instant incineration. The wizard was therefore impressed when Mortleroy rose slowly, unarmed and impassive to stand with his arms crossed for the few moments before his possible nemesis arrived at the dais.

The move was imposing because it conveyed so much. The magician came to an unexpected stop, thereby bringing the High Constable escorting him also to a halt.

Turning to the official, with the mace held out across his hands, he said: 'I would not meet so great a monarch with the discourtesy being thus armed. I place this in your charge until I take it again.'

As the High Constable received it on his knee, Myrddin hoped Mortleroy would find the act difficult to credit. He doubted the King owned a weapon like it but if he did, would anything have induced him to hand it to a complete stranger? He noted the look of instant irritation that crossed his face at the murmur of admiration going around the assembly. Myrddin imagined it was unlikely any other personality before had been permitted – let alone had the audacity – to assume such a bearing in the least comparable with the usurper and it clearly rankled. It looked as if Mortleroy might be having second thoughts on whether he had been wise in welcoming such a powerful personage into the heart of his kingdom. The wizard realised that had the future not appeared so uncertain, Mortleroy might well have signalled the High Constable to slay the intimidating Prince with his own weapon and so dispose of the problem on the spot.

Chuckling inwardly at the prospect of the game of Beggar-My-Neighbour that was still to come, Myrddin began solemnly: 'I have travelled far to consult with you, Brother of Brython, for I found it written in the stars that you alone can interpret a most mysterious vision.'

'Brother of Damascus,' replied Mortleroy, in equally dulcet tones, 'your nobility overwhelms me as much as your obvious prowess, but hospitality demands I first regale you after your long and perilous journey to these shores. Come, Chamberlain, lead us into the banquet that I ordered to be prepared in honour of my royal guest. See to it also that the *servants* of this most puissant Prince are given all that is needful for their welfare.'

The sneer that accompanied the words made it an intentional insult – since Myrddin was clearly alone. He met it with a disarming smile. 'Brother of England, I have no necessity for visible retinue, my needs are amply met in other ways …' Again, he drew his sceptre, this time waving it airily and beside them stood a towering jinni wreathed in a coiling spiral of smoke, '… Behold!' he exclaimed.

Mortleroy, looking somewhat shaken, did then take a step back at the unexpected and forbidding apparition.

Myrddin felt he could now count on the other's ban on all further sarcasm for the duration; especially when he went on to address the jinni wrathfully: 'O unmannerly fiend from hell! On your knees this instant and bow yourself three times before my host – no, grovel at his feet and plant kisses on his toes in token of my deep displeasure with you!' Myrddin smiled inwardly at the slavish obeisance which followed. He guessed Mortleroy would willingly have done without and, equally imagined, the touch of the evil-looking creature's lips going through the royal slippers with a feeling not unlike that of having thorns inserted beneath each toenail.

Myrddin hardly knew how he had managed it, but mentally shrugged. He *was* Merlyn's Heir and it seemed he was growing in magic without even realising it. He continued to the jinni: 'Now lay before my Brother of England, the poor treasures I commanded you to summon from the guardians of my royal vaults in far Damascus.'

From out of nowhere a shower of blazing gems descended into the jinni's hands and, from there, poured into an enormous pile before the King's feet. The hoard, so large that all gasped as it became a glittering mound so high that both Myrddin and Mortleroy had to both move aside.

But Myrddin's intention to make the demonstration not only startling but acutely embarrassing didn't have *quite* the effect he was after.

Surveying it, the King turned to him with a raised eyebrow and waving a hand at the mound said quietly: 'The magnificence of your gift impoverishes me, wizard. I would have to ransack the resources of half my realm to equal even a tithe of it!'

This turned the whole thing back on the Prince of Damascus by revealing the intentional effect. With a flick of his sceptre, he bade the jinni disappear.

'It is nothing, O King. Truly a trifle that has no need of acknowledgement but which I nevertheless hope you will accept.'

Mortleroy inclined his head, awarding him a thin smile.

Touché Myrddin echoed in silence – and there still remained the disturbing future to consider.

Destiny allowed little time for that however. They were about to leave the hall at the head of a marvelling procession to enjoy the banquet when a knight hurried in and with bare formality cried: 'My liege! My liege! A messenger from the underground Rebels approaches with a flag of truce!'

CHAPTER 22

A BLAZE OF TRUTH

When Gwyn Son of Gwyn Son of Nudd rode up the Tor disguised in the armour and bearing the device of one of his most famous knights, he knew exactly how far he was stretching his neck. However, under a flag of truce he should at least be given the opportunity to say what he had come to say – although Mortleroy was apt to react rather inconsiderately if the content of such a message overstepped the limits of his temper. This was one of two reasons why Gwyn had chivalrously undertaken the task himself; the other was to see the expression on his arch-enemy's face when he was given an ultimatum designed to send him paralytic.

Although Gwyn was not mailed in the overall green armour in which prophecy said he was doomed to die, a safe get away could still be difficult. But Gwyn had once held Glastonbury himself and knew its secrets. He also knew that if his followers should prove slow in opening the Underway from Annwyn which led directly to a corner of the Tower's foundations or, on arrival there, find that time had dislodged or seized up the mechanism operating the small innocent looking slab leading into the crypt, then he could be in trouble. Then again, if they didn't get the signal which would bring them pouring out into the midst of their enemy, he would be done for. Previously, he had always scorned to use the stratagem because it would end the blissful centuries of war. But times were changing …

*

As soon as the announcement was made, Mortleroy was almost apologetic: 'It is customary to hear this news, Brother of Damascus.'

'The custom is universal,' agreed Myrddin diplomatically. 'Perchance the Rebel sues for peace, or at least a truce?'

'More like, it covers some treacherous plot to his advantage,' Mortleroy answered, his expression dark.

'But you will admit him?' Myrddin probed, intensely curious to hear it for himself.

'I shall indeed. And for his own sake, his words had best be fair, or I swear his head will roll …' Mortleroy paused before adding with venomous intent, '… down the Tor until it comes to rest in Chalice Well.'

'You are well named King Death,' Myrddin said sarcastically.

'You know my secret name?' hissed the King.

'You say it yourself, Mortleroy. But we have not yet heard what this truce-bearer has to say. And I will know if he speaks truth – or lies.'

The King's expression of dislike for his disturbing guest increased, along with one of resignation that beggars couldn't be choosers. He ordered the mound of treasure to remain untouched and that a second throne – only less elevated – for the Prince of Damascus to be set beside his own then signalled for the messenger to be admitted.

If Mortleroy wanted to surprise his enemy's envoy – announced as Sir AEdwold of the Ravine – he was not disappointed.

The way that the pile of treasure registered with their visitor with a blink and abruptly narrowed eyes and pursed lips that twisted in a calculating look, Myrddin knew it had been earmarked as legitimate loot to the Kin of Beauty as soon as ever the lapsed tenancy of the Tower was regained.

Mortleroy addressed his herald: 'Inform the messenger that We …' he paused to emphasise the plural pronoun,

'… that We, the Lord of the Over-world and the Prince of Damascus command him speak such servile message as his cowardly master–'

'To whomsoever is appointed to hear them,' he was interrupted in a voice which carried the length of the hall, 'Hear then these words of Gwyn ap Gwyn ap Nudd, Lord of Annwyn and Lord of Doom. That I have lately taken into my royal keeping the person of a child born to the Lady Margaret of Eden's Ford that is the predicted incarnation of the Great King of ancient time, namely Yathra the Lord and Self-Inheritor of this ancient realm. I call upon you to surrender to him forthwith the crown, powers and all entitlements that are truly his. Obey, and I, Regent of the Royal Child, will spare you the slaughter which will be inevitable if you dare defy your heavenly King-to-be.'

The news and impudent challenge rocked his hearers visibly – even if for different reasons. The collective gasp of horror from the assemblage at the kidnapping itself was enough to remind them all that the traditional belief that Arthur would come again and rule over his ancient domain once more lay deeply embedded. Mortleroy, himself, had already injudiciously published the arrival of the Child-King and could not now deny it. Many knew that the belief had been deliberately fostered in the sure knowledge – at any rate while Algaric had been with them – that the magical Ceremony of the Skull would prevent any such happening. So of course, with Algaric gone, Yathra had duly appeared.

Myrddin received the news as a direct threat to his own ambitions. A quick glance aside affirmed a raised eyebrow of askance that Mortleroy had shot at him which meant the wizard had made enough of an impact for the other to be prepared to take a lead on the kind of answer he should return to Gwyn and, left to Mortleroy, Myrddin guessed that he would no doubt have sent it in the form of the messenger's head, but even King Death realised the damage *that* would do in his followers' eyes.

'Make no reply in haste or anger,' Myrddin mouthed under his breath. 'Better to invite the messenger to your banquet, while we think of the best way to outwit his insolent master.'

The crafty suggestion met with immediate approval and Mortleroy instructed the herald to convey his pleasure to Sir AEdwold of the Ravine, requesting his presence at their table.

*

Gwyn listened, aware that the invitation meant his two hosts were stalling. Had he not been keenly interested in finding out more about this new personality styling himself the Prince of Damascus he would not have agreed to any kind of dalliance; but it's an asset to know how one's adversary ticks. To everyone's relief, he therefore answered he would spare his hosts one hour of hospitality, at the end of which, message or no message, he must return to his liege.

The banquet hall was long and filled by a single broad table that ran almost its entire length. The width at its upper end was sufficient for several banqueters, usually the King flanked by his favourites of the day. On this occasion, it was limited to himself and to the Prince of Damascus. The envoy was given a seat at the far end. This allowed Myrddin and Mortleroy to speak privately while studying the new arrival who met their intent looks just as boldly, but found the Easterner's gaze, in particular, unreadable.

*

Speaking from the side of his mouth, Mortleroy asked: 'What plan have you in mind, Brother of Damascus?'

'One that I alone can perform, Brother of Britain,' Myrddin whispered, and warned: 'Watch, and do not betray *any* surprise.'

Myrddin had made up his mind to return guile with guile by scaring the messenger with such a show of magic that he would return to his master in a state of quivering fear if the Rebels persisted with their challenge. He knew whatever he did, the report had to be impressive or Gwyn, who was also a Lord of Fire, might not be sufficiently stupefied.

His first revelation was to cause a loaded plate to rise from a servant's hands of its own accord and settle on the table before him. He then carved delicate slices with an invisible knife.

While he continued to gaze unwinkingly at Sir Ædwold, a portion conveyed itself unaided to the King's open jaws at his side.

Respect showed in the messenger's eyes. Mortleroy looked elated, although he tried to conceal it. He let his appreciation be known, however, by ordering a loving cup to be filled and set between himself and the Prince of Damascus. None had ever seen anyone so honoured before and a sense of drama began to build – even before the tense sequel that followed.

The Royal Butler at once presented Mortleroy with an ornately chased and ceremoniously filled cup. Mortleroy took it, held it high, invoking the blessing of the Sacred Skull, before handing it courteously to his fellow dignitary for the unprecedented privilege of the first sip – or half its contents at most. Everyone looked stupefied to see the princely magician's head go back and back and the cup upturned nearly vertically until the last drop disappeared down his working throat.

Of itself, it was guaranteed to stretch the goodwill of Mortleroy and his followers to breaking-point and it was evident that only the belief that habits in the East must be rather different to those in the West prevented any expression of feeling. Nevertheless, when the Prince's hand came slowly down and upturned the cup, setting it rim down in front of the King, the action constituted the deadliest of insults. Hands flew to sword hilts, and Mortleroy half rose with a surge of anger – yet paused as the Prince checked him:

'Turn it upright and raise it again, Brother of Britain,' he said fiercely in a low voice, 'or you and I are both undone.'

With a hand that almost trembled, Mortleroy obeyed and was incredulous. Full to the brim, drops spilled as he conveyed the goblet to his mouth – even more while he drank deeply in his eagerness to make it appear that his guest's astonishing behaviour was quite in order.

Applause and cries of admiration took the place of momentary dismay, and all eyes turned to see what the effect had been on Sir AEdwold.

*

Gwyn's mounting respect for Myrddin's feat with the carving was only because he had never thought of doing anything similar himself. However, his astonishment grew to see his new adversary's sleight of hand and mind with the wine. The way the droplets bounced from the King's robe and spattered like jewels on the table, for instance, was evidence of masterly artistry. What else had he to learn from this Mage from the East?

He soon learnt. A great Boar's head, placed on the board before the King and the Prince, abruptly burst into flames at a pass from the latter's sceptre. It burned and spluttered as much as any mortal one might have done roasting in its own fat, and revealed to Gwyn that this magician was, like himself, a Lord of Fire. Be that as it may, nothing prepared him for what followed.

The Prince reached out, lifted the blazing mass from the huge dish, then slowly and deliberately pressed it down over his jewelled turban until it rested lifelike on his shoulders.

Gwyn hardly heard the cries of horror, dismay and wonder that greeted the phenomenal act as he stared transfixed at the frightful apparition. Nor did his amazement end there, for the boar-headed prince called loudly through the flaming jaws for another filling of the loving cup. The butler obeyed with wavering hands and, when full, Myrddin took it and rose.

'Watch and tremble, AEdwold of the Ravine,' he said. 'Watch, tremble and remember; for thus did the magic of Am-Mar-El-Lyn quench the fireballs your rebel master wanted to rain on Reading's Walls.'

The ugly jaws of the awesome head opened upwards, the loving cup rose and tilted steeply … the flames went out, the superimposed head vanished and left Gwyn staring into the mocking eyes of the royal guest.

The whole thing had truly staggered the Lord of Annwyn. There were features about the trick which even he, a Lord of Fire, would have hesitated to imitate. There was more to it than that, though. By quenching the astral flames with wine, the wizard had revealed himself as master of yet another element – water. Gwyn well knew that only a practitioner of proven genius could ever aspire to the mastery of one element. To achieve mastery of two was rare; to be a master of three rarer still; while to have mastery of all four elements was almost, although not quite, beyond comprehension, and no known magician had ever succeeded Great Merlyn to that pre-eminence.

However, the Prince's words about quenching the fireballs of Reading had sparked a memory of something that Nemway had said when she had explained how the treachery of a magician of the Weirdfolk, now long gone, had caused her to hoax the death of the Green Dragon of the

South. She had also told him that Lady Margaret's infant was no more Royal Arthur than he was himself, which mattered nothing to Gwyn. It was Lady Margaret's conviction that had convinced Mortleroy, and that was good enough for Gwyn to seize the King of Brython by the short hairs and bring him to his knees – the prospect of which did a lot to make up for the fiasco of Reading. By now, though, he had had enough of play acting and anger made him spring to his feet.

Pointing a furious finger at his tormentor, he cried out: 'I demand that you, Lord of Two Elements, say who you truly are.' And before Myrddin could reply, Gwyn seized a goblet of wine himself, and hurled its contents on the board causing a pillar of fire to leap up in its wake, bringing knights and ladies leaping to their feet to back away with cries of consternation.

Gwyn's voice rose and challenged his adversary above the commotion: 'By the presence of this holy Element of Life and Power whose sovereignty makes equals of us both, I exhort you reveal your truth, O Brother in Fire.'

With a look of surprise, the Prince responded by dashing the contents of his own cup down his end of the board to result in a similar fire. 'Reveal who *you* are yourself, AEdwold of the Ravine!' he called mockingly. And blew on the fire he had made to speed it menacingly down the board.

Recognising the test, Gwyn at once blew quickly on the column of fire he had caused which sped to meet the other and, where the two mingled, there rose in an even greater conflagration in the centre of the board.

'So we are declared to be one, fellow Lord of Fire,' he said, adding swiftly. 'Yes, I am Gwyn ap Gwyn ap Nudd, King of the People of Beauty, Lord of Annwyn and Lord of Doom. Now say *who* you are, or let the fire between us return and consume you utterly.

*

It was a soul-searching moment for Myrddin. He knew, as Gwyn did, that to speak any lie in the united presence of the fire between them would allow his opponent's power to triumph and place him at his mercy.

He therefore replied with truthful care: 'I am Great Merlyn's Heir who, by virtue of this inheritance, do take my right to his titles in heaven and his treasures on earth. Therefore am I known as The Lord of the Heavens – Am-Mar-El-Lyn!'

The announcement had his hearers stupefied; even Gwyn apparently, for he took a keen look at the fire between them. The spoken words were true. Myrddin gave him no time to marvel for long however for, like a skilled general, he followed up his initial advantage by putting his adversary on the spot. 'Yes, it was I, Lord of the Heavens, who routed your arts at Reading, and feel no shame for doing so. Shame on *you*, Gwyn ap Gwyn ap Nudd for invoking the fire of heaven upon antagonists unskilled and unprepared.'

It could be seen that the bolt went home as Gwyn hurried to excuse his action. 'The intention was ill-advised, Heir of Merlyn,' he said, his tone reflecting his discomfort. 'But not altogether evil of itself. She who called herself Mergyn, Queen of the Weirdfolk, broadcast the news everywhere that Royal Arthur would be born again of her. As all know, I never was in vassalage to Arthur, but Mergyn requested my help. I therefore promised safe refuge to the Queen, her child and all her people in Annwyn. But, as Reading commands the southern terrain of Britain, I had to deal with the problem urgently ...'

'To Annwyn?' interrupted Myrddin. 'But the sacred Dove of the Weirdfolk spoke only of Avalon. Its words were ' ...Go to Avalon, most blessed of Queens; to the nearest of your kind, the Kin of Beauty that dwell in Glastonbury's Tor–'

'My message was otherwise, and would have been delivered by an Owl after my own likeness,' thundered Gwyn. 'And may the holy fire consume me if I lie ...'

*

Seeing the fire had not altered, Myrddin stared wrathfully at Mortleroy.

The usurper, who had begun edging away at these words, raised dissenting hands: 'Don't listen to his lies, Great Prince. The Rebel King has great mastery over *all* the birds of the air–'

'The fire says otherwise,' interrupted Myrddin curtly. 'What mystery is here?'

'This is no mystery!' Gwyn roared heatedly. 'It's malfeasance! The whole world knows that this Overlord of Evil captured the Dove of the Weirdfolk the very day Great Merlyn disappeared. Algaric enslaved it and held it captive here in Glastonbury ever since. The fire bears witness.'

For a moment, Myrddin's anger knew no bounds when he thought of all the countless errors and confusions into which the Dove's misleading message had led him. But now was not the time to voice his rage.

'What say the stars in this matter of Royal Arthur?' he asked, abruptly dowsing the huge flame between them. This engulfed them all in darkness and caused people to stumble this way and that until Gwyn made a sweeping gesture with his hand that lit the hall with the brilliance of myriads of stars.

'If you are familiar with the Royal Stars that govern the destinies of Kings and Princes–'

'I know them,' he was told briefly.

'Then witness the track of that–' Gwyn was cut short by a commotion at the hall's entrance and a soughing of wings.

'What devil's trick is this?' said Gwyn angrily sweeping the stars away and restoring the hall to normal light.

It was a fae-sized Hannibal coming to rest on the table before Mortleroy and Myrddin where it gazed from one to the other in confusion, but with eyes that mirrored the Citadel of Reading under fierce assault.

CHAPTER 23

MY ENEMY'S ENEMY

From what he was seeing, Myrddin realised that Mortleroy must have sent Hannibal straight out again on another tour of inspection after receiving news of the wizard's impending arrival and now the confused bird stood with its head cocking from one to the other of its masters.

Mortleroy looked around in surprise when the Prince of Damascus made a shielding gesture, and retreated behind him. 'There's nothing to fear,' he said disdainfully

He was not to know that while he looked long and searchingly into Hannibal's eyes, Merlyn's Heir was doing the same over his shoulder and, as they gazed, it was a moot point which of the two was the most staggered by what they saw. Every detail was graphic. The Citadel of Reading was under assault. From the depths of the waterless moat, showers of stones were being hurled against the ramparts bringing down masonry which in turn brought up surging clouds of dust from below through which now and then, armoured forms of a vanguard could be seen. With only a spiky ball attached by a chain to their wrists, they were flailing the walls and holes were beginning to appear in the foundations threatening the towers above.

'The Mabyn!' the King said in a whisper.

Myrddin hardly heard him. Before the Great Gate of the Citadel, a well known figure riding a white unicorn was delivering even greater blows. All were scornful of the boulders that came crashing down on them from the battlements. A mabyn knocked over here, a mabyn there, but seldom more than one at a time for their weapons' range meant keeping a respectful distance from each other. Then arrows flying in sheaves from the ramparts led his eyes down to the most incredible sight of all. Three companies of the Knights of the Grail, a company of gnomes, the self-appointed bodyguard of Arthur with the Master of Gnomes at their head, along with Gareth and Accolon, flanked a figure in gold and silver armour whose shield bore the garlanded sword and crown of Royal Arthur.

'It's impossible!' the wizard cried out illogically. 'The wretched bird is hood-winked by some contrary magic.'

'My Royal Falcons never lie,' hissed Mortleroy before realising what was going on behind him he tried to shield the creature's gaze but Myrddin seized his wrist in an iron-like grip.

Mortleroy, infuriated as much by the grip as by what he was seeing, repeated that his messenger could not lie. 'By the Skull!' he swore. 'What you see by magic is no more than what its eyes have seen.'

'Of that, I'll be judge,' growled Gwyn who had come striding up from the opposite end of the table and now sprang to seize the other wrist. 'There is no fowl of the air that can lie to me.'

The spectacle of the King pinioned by his royal guests brought his attendant knights starting forward in alarm and rage – the High Constable drawing his sword.

Hurling a bolt of fire at his feet with his sceptre, Myrddin barked an authoritative: 'Begone!'

'And who is this that wears Arthur's magic mail?' demanded Gwyn, staring into the bird's lucid eyes.

'Mad Mergyn's brat!' his fellow magician spat with bitterness. 'I *made* the fellow with my own hands. But don't blame me for the armour. That witch of the Whip who claims kin with you, she gave him that!'

'And those others – the ones the arrows don't seem to pierce?'

'Erstwhile Mung and Gnome, and Mabyn of the Forest enslaved by Algaric at the will of this evil wretch we hold here between us–'

'By the Skull,' Mortleroy swore again, struggling wrathfully between them, 'I am beset by friend and foe alike. 'To me! To me all loyal knights–!'

'Silence!' Myrddin snarled, glaring back at the faltering knights who had started forward. 'Stand off if you don't want to see this miscreant's bowels sheared with gouts of fire.'

'… And I his balls with incisors of the same,' Gwyn promised almost as an aside, for his eyes were held fixedly by the swiftly moving scene that he continued to watch. 'See there, Merlyn's Heir! The King of the Mabyn has breached both wall and gate and your 'Arthur' spurs in to attack.'

The three stared spellbound as Hannibal's eyes showed them what followed as Arthur and the gnomes with lances levelled had charged down into the moat bed and up again through the shattered drawbridge and portcullis through clouds of dust that hid them for a moment from the defenders who were few. Ranulph had taken the majority of his army with him to answer his King's call to defend Glastonbury.

Yet there was little or no fighting. As Arthur's Herald sounded a fanfare, runners were crying through the streets that their besieger was none other than Arthur-come-again whom they had so long expected.

And Myrddin watched aghast as arms began to be laid down in wonder, and homage paid to their deliverer.

Mortleroy raved, swore and struggled at the searing sight. But not until Arthur's standard appeared on the walls was he released and allowed to vent his wrath on his attendants for their cowardice at not coming to his rescue.

Myrddin turned away with black recriminations in his heart. He himself had demonstrated the vulnerability of the Citadel's walls to Ranulph, yet instead of strengthening them, the vainglorious idiot had spent the time preparing for a gala!

'What counsel have you now, O Merlyn's Heir?' Gwyn demanded harshly. 'It's plain enough the three of us are finished if this goes on. What happens now?'

Myrddin could understand Gwyn's feelings; they were as personal as his own. For a thousand years and more, the People of Beauty's King must have had dreamed that he would be the one to take this prized jewel from the enemy's crown.

'We fight. What else?' the wizard answered rounding on him. 'The Kingdom is threatened by an even greater evil than the present.'

Mortleroy's narrowed eyes darted to and fro the pair of them, revealing him as alarmed and frustrated as any who were listening.

'I wish the Fates had led the Weirdfolk to Annwyn before such trouble came,' owned Gwyn lugubriously. 'I swear by the Wonderful Head, I'd have held this Dupe of Mergyn's in thrall a thousand years–'

Mortleroy cut him short vengefully: 'Just as *you* hold Dame Margaret and her child Yathra this very moment!' adding softly, his eyes still going from one to other. 'It seems we could be all of a single mind, O Masters of Many Elements?'

'That will never be, O Master of Too Many Minds!' Myrddin said with a sneer, and went on to Gwyn. 'For myself, I will bow the knee to none but Yathra.'

'And I to neither true nor false,' Gwyn declared punctiliously. 'My sires never celebrated a suzerain and neither shall I. I therefore fight this wretched oaf that has stolen Reading from me.'

'Then I say again that we are all of one mind,' Mortleroy insisted. 'I would rather have surrendered this most precious jewel of my crown to you Gwyn ap Nudd, than have it crushed beneath the heel of this unlawful wretch. Come, Lord of Annwyn and Merlyn's Heir, let us speak in private ...'

And at the end of that conversation, Mortleroy had contracted an alliance with his two worst enemies, each with their own private agenda, but united in bringing about Arthur's downfall.

It seemed everything had started to fall into place for Myrddin when he realised how the way lay suddenly open to delete the phantom image of Arthur and eliminate Mortleroy at a single stroke. But he had to move quickly. The Denefolk would be spreading the news of Arthur's victory everywhere to the outcast and hunted faerie who so longed to believe their rightful King had come again. Myrddin could imagine the news already singing in the soughing of leaves and carried in the ripples of running water, tempting even the timid Well Sprite from their stony depths to dance around them, believing they would be unmolested by the wolves which they would think had slunk away to their holes.

In the end, after telling Mortleroy and Gwyn to 'Hurry up and get on with it, if they wanted Reading back.' Myrddin took his leave with a promise to Mortleroy: '... And I shall return with something greater than Reading to give *you*.' And, leaving the two to argue, haggle and bargain with the other other as to what numbers each would put in the field, he flew for the Chapel of the Blue Fountains.

*

Peredur's son, Osric sat in the bay of his bedroom window. His parents had apartments in one of the towers on the battlements at the summit of Dome Hill facing east. Sun and moon being the centre of Osric's existence, his window gave him his favourite view of the sun's first long fingers stretching out across the landscape to create shining paths of light.

A wistful thought had just come into his mind: *Wouldn't it be wonderful if–* when a massive crash of falling masonry startled him. *What …? Where …? Why …?* Springing to his to his feet, he ran from the room to join a crowd of servants and fae-at-arms all hurrying to gather around an opposite look-out in time to see a another great hole appear in the citadel's west wall.

Reading under attack! But wasn't the Prince of Damascus supposed to have defeated Gwyn? So who …? He fled the embrasure and pounded down the stairs to the great square below. Townsfolk were pouring into it from every quarter as more of the outer walls crumbled under the thunderous assault – even the great Gate! Fear and hope struggled together in Osric's breast. Either Mortleroy had found them out in some great misdemeanour – Ranulph had revolted at last. Or had someone greater arrived to free them?

A fanfare sounded from a splendid looking herald who had somehow appeared on the ramparts drawing people's attention with a cry: 'Arthur lives! He is come again! He says "Lift up your heads, my people! Your deliverance is near!"'

'It's Arthur!' cried a voice near him. 'It's Arthur-come-again!'

Then forerunners who had leapt through the shattered gate were shouting: 'Peace! Peace! It is Arthur-come-again. He is here! The message he brings is peace. Hear him! None shall die. You are immortal, you cannot die …!'

And terror seized Osric. This 'Arthur' sounded even worse than Mortleroy! At least those who did not know their king's true nature lived with the comfort of believing they *did* die; unlike himself who knew they went on living to suffer unspeakable torment in unknown depths below at Mortleroy's pleasure.

Did Arthur know what lay beneath his feet? he wondered. He knew himself. He had always loved the moon and once, as a child, had seen her reflection in the water of a well. Laughing, he had reached for her and toppled in. *My first lesson in immortality*, he remembered with a shiver. He couldn't drown. He wished he had. A wellsprite had caught his foot and drawn him down. Fight and struggle as he might, his childish strength had been no match for the sprite's remorselessness. Reaching bottom at last it dragged him along and up again to another place above water level and left him in the gloom of a green and slimy tunnel. There were voices somewhere – he had crawled upwards towards them. What he saw over a ledge above him seared him forever. It mightn't have been so bad if it had been strangers, but Mortleroy and Algaric were no strangers. His young life had beheld the King's magician as a favourite 'Uncle' figure who, whenever he came to Reading, visited his parents and delighted to enchant Peredur's son with little magical things; who had assured him that he had it within himself to do the same and even encouraged him in small attempts as any fond adult might encourage a child to copy an easy example. It had been fun. Osric had succeeded in the simple exercises he had been given. But *never* again – not after seeing 'Uncle' Algaric like this – engrossed with Mortleroy in taunting and tormenting wretched souls screaming and sobbing for mercy and finding none. If that was what magicians did, he wanted none of it. And then the Prince of Damascus had arrived and somehow seemed a *different* kind of magician, prompting Osric to dare question him. But that had been a long time after he had escaped from what had happened in his childhood. When Algaric had glanced up and seen him, Osric's legs, giving way under him, he slid back down the way he had so laboriously crawled. He had had no idea how he was to escape the terrifying labyrinth except the dumb and spidery wellsprite who had seized him lay in wait to take him back to the surface via the same well he had fallen into. He had fled to his room, quaking. He knew he had been somewhere and seen something that he shouldn't, even if it wasn't his fault, and retribution usually arrived quickly. But nothing happened, nor had he ever seen Algaric again after that. He overheard later in a whispered conversation that the magician was rumoured to have been poisoned. Osric wondered whether he too had descended into that same hell that no-one knew about yet lay beneath everyone's feet. Guilt haunted him at being too frightened to ever breathe a word of what he had seen.

Now he watched from a distance as this new King dismounted in the city square. A party of jubilant citizens had appeared carrying a podium between them; the crowd clearing a way for them to rush it forward for a radiant looking Arthur to mount and address them, while his followers all gathered to one side.

Osric's eyes widened at the calm way in which the youth, who looked little older than himself, yet possessed such unmistakeable bearing and authority and spoke directly to the point without shouting and everyone could hear him clearly.

'Knights, ladies, citizens and servants of Reading,' he began. 'Are any injured? They shall be healed. These walls that have been broken down shall be rebuilt. But time is short ...' And from there Arthur went on to outline all that they would find immediately happening. Contrary to the usual practice for defeated knights to be sent in shame and in shackles to their new ruler, he told them that any one of Reading's defenders, who wished to leave, could to do so and be personally escorted by his Champion, Sir Accolon to Arthur's own hidden kingdom in the Forest of Weir. All prisoners would be freed and likewise escorted by the Kindred of the Grail to the same place. Once again he stressed the importance of immediacy. Now was the time to make up their minds, he said. These measures needed to be implemented at once for their safety and protection.

Osric could hardly believe his ears. It seemed this new King would be leaving the Citadel intact and unguarded; everyone was so busy carrying out his directions: 'do this', 'do that',' escort these', 'escort those', no one appeared to notice he was disarming himself until he was left with no more than a few knights who refused to leave him. Osric watched them kneel before him, saying:

'We served you in mortality – we know you, we love you, we stay with you. Let it be with us whatever befalls you …'

What kind of King are you? The youth wondered in shocked and silent amazement.

And while the citizens, so busy sorting out who was staying or going didn't even hear, Osric listened to a new magic. It came from the Lady Nemway, a quiet, pulsating hum that brought the walls and gate somehow together again – whole and solid – all by themselves! They only noticed the marvel when the Lady Nemway had gone and his father, Peredur arrived and set up camp the other side of the moat to lay siege.

CHAPTER 24

THE RE-TAKING
OF READING

Far behind Ranulph's party travelling west, Peredur had received the Earl's hawk and turned back at once. He had difficulty believing his eyes when confronted with an undamaged Citadel.

'No!' he exclaimed in fury when his second in command queried the lack of any visible damage. 'What's happened is that someone has betrayed the Earl's secret tunnel! But see, we have a party of truce.'

Four knights accompanied by Osric, a square of white fluttering from his lance, came to a halt before them. Three of them, bearing the emblazonment of a Golden Cup, he recognised with amazement as erstwhile comrades, Gawain, Percivale and Gareth. The fourth showing the embattled Tower of Glastonbury, revealed the garrison's Commander, Damas who had been left in charge of the Citadel's defences.

'So who's the traitor who revealed the tunnel?' Peredur demanded.

'No one,' Damas said quietly. 'The walls were flattened by the Mabyn King with his magic weapon *Moldwarp*.'

Peredur, remembering how the Prince of Damascus had actually forecast such a disaster, wondered why nothing had been done about it. 'Who repaired them?' he asked bluntly, staring up at the Citadel in disbelief.

Osric spoke up, although looking at Peredur as if he didn't expect to be believed: 'Father, the Lady Nemway *sang* them back into place and order.'

But Peredur eyed him without surprise. He had heard of the Lady's powers and now it appeared she was on Arthur's side. He turned back to Damas. 'So what's the position now – and why do you come to me under a flag of truce? Would *I* have killed you if you had come alone?'

'I wasn't taking the chance,' Damas said cheerfully. 'Anyway, when Gareth, Gawain and Percivale heard that you out here, they were anxious to meet you. Your son also wanted to come.'

'And why isn't he at home, having care of his mother?'

'Because there's no need,' Percivale answered for the youth. 'Arthur wanted no one slain–'

'And his numbers far outweighed ours, anyway,' Damas cut back in. 'The place is practically half empty now. Only a few knights who refused to leave and enough civilians to keep the Citadel in good order are left. No trolls though and the dungeons are empty. You are at liberty to enter and be welcomed peacefully anytime you like.'

If Peredur had known what it meant to be 'saved by the bell' he would have recognised it as more than appropriate to that moment, coinciding as it did with Ranulph's appearance. It thankfully meant he could hand the whole crazy situation over to his superior without a qualm.

Ranulph, who had kept his force hidden among the trees down the hill, had come riding up to hear the truce party's terms for himself; first calling Damas and Peredur aside.

'*We* take the tunnel,' was his instant decision when he heard what Damas had to say. 'But those three,' he pointed towards Percivale, Gawain and Gareth, 'Stay out here with you Peredur, until I've seen what the position is for myself.'

Peredur protested: 'They carry a flag of truce! I'm not making them prisoner.'

'They either stay out here, or come with us blindfold,' Ranulph ruled. 'They certainly don't go in and warn everyone of our numbers!' And he rode over to state his terms.

'Fine,' Percivale accepted with a shrug. 'Gareth, Gawain and I have no objection to staying here with Peredur.'

When Ranulph and Damas had left with their own and Peredur's smaller force, Peredur dismounted. 'You three should leave now,' he told them. 'Ranulph will have you all imprisoned.'

Percivale laughed, swinging down from his mount. 'Then we'd better take the chance while we still have it to bring *you* up to date.'

'Peredur we have truly seen Arthur. He's in there now,' Gawain nodded the Citadel, as he and Gareth followed suit to join them on the ground. 'We're not leaving him and we'd like you to join us.'

'It's good to see you all, but I can't leave Ranulph.'

'It would be nice to think he'll join us when he's seen Arthur.'

'Come,' Gawain said firmly, beckoning each of them. 'Let us pray.' And the watching Osric saw them draw together, arms across each other's shoulders, their heads bowed.

*

Myrddin arrived at the Chapel of Blue Fountains to find Mildgyth with an overjoyed Faith who couldn't wait to tell the news of Arthur's arrival at the Chapel with Gareth and the Knights of the Grail, Nemway and Amyas; to relate the rescue of Accolon, and of everyone's subsequent departure en masse to Weir Forest the previous day. When she went on to extol Arthur and explain why Gareth and the Kindred had gone with them, the wizard realised it was no more

Gareth's fault than his own for making 'Arthur' so well that his workmanship was fooling everyone.

'But you didn't go with them?'

'Lord Am-Mar-El-Lin, am I not your squire?' she asked, her tone earnest, her eyes anxious.

Mildgyth, standing by, joined in with the practicable observation that it had also been necessary to have someone to Ward the place in her absence: '... I went with Arthur with the Cup to heal those he had sent ahead of him on Windflame.' She gave him a gentle smile and went on: 'Arthur said the Cup properly belonged with the Weirdfolk, but asked me to bring it back here for all those who will be arriving soon and will need it.'

'And Royal Arthur thought it only right and proper that I should be the one to wait for you.' Faith assured him. 'I chose it an honour.' she added quickly when she saw his lips tighten and his eyes darken at the words 'Royal Arthur'. 'Your strongbox was also left in my care ...' and she hurried off to bring the thing to him.

*

While Myrddin waited alone in the Chapel garden, one of the messenger hawks he had made for the Kindred returned to its perch. Idly wondering what information it carried, it staggered him to learn it came from Gareth with a report for Faith that Ranulph had retaken Reading in a surprise attack, and that Arthur was now his prisoner ...!

In part the news came as a relief. It dealt with the problem of exposing 'Arthur' as a fraud. But what of his, Myrddin's, own beloved Knights of the Grail? What had happened to them? It was hard to imagine they had been defeated – unless they had been metaphorically caught with their pants down – again! Grief, worry and anger made him send the hawk with his own message to Ranulph that the Prince of Damascus would be arriving shortly in person.

With Faith leading a pack-animal laden with his box of possessions from the Chapel, Myrddin undertook his return to Reading by horse along the same fae-path that had been used by Avellane as well as Peredur. Once more in the guise of the Prince of Damascus, he rode up to the Citadel and paused in astonishment. The walls stood solid, the moat restored, the drawbridge down – and Ranulph and Osric waiting to greet him.

'Welcome, most honoured and beloved of Princes,' the Earl cried, evidently feeling that this reunion had made his day except that the din of jubilant cheering that broke out on each side of them made further talk impossible until they reached the privacy of Ranulph's apartments.

'So how did you do it, beloved Earl – to take the Citadel so soon and have it repaired so quickly?' Myrddin was able to ask politely at last as Ranulph signed Osric to present the magician with a goblet of wine.

'In the first place, we were drawn away from the Citadel with orders from the King that we should all ride for Avalon to protect his stronghold from the Mabyn–' the Earl began.

'–*and* from these mysterious Kindred of the Grail which have suddenly appeared in the realm,' Osric reminded him quickly.

'Yes, yes,' the Earl said, eager to recite his version of what had happened. 'We had scarce ridden a dozen leagues, when news came that my beloved Reading was under attack by the hosts of this pretender Arthur and his pagan followers ...' And he went on to tell how he had at once turned back, had ridden in through his secret underground passage and taken the invaders unawares. '... Not even the churlish knights who surrendered the Citadel to this 'Arthur' had thought to betray its existence!' he exalted. 'So we entered secretly and broke in on a High Council of War being held by the Pretender. We took them all by surprise. I had seized Arthur with my dagger at his throat before his companions could get to their weapons. I talked with them while my knights fell to slaying all they encountered – which was not difficult since they were in the main dallying with the ladies of my court. But I was able to make what terms I could with those who trembled for the safety of their so called King whose life I was holding at knife point.' Ranulph beamed. 'The ruse succeeded and it was agreed that all slaying would cease if Arthur surrendered to us, and his adherents took themselves off and never again imperil this Citadel.' Here the Earl paused and looked pensive. 'I tell you, though, never have I captured a youth so fair either in looks or manner. I have to confess in all honesty 't'was *he*, rather than I, who reasoned with his followers and persuaded them to agree with my terms. He actually *begged* them to leave him; assured them that he was all that Mortleroy wanted, and promised them that all would be well. He told them to return to their forest where he would see them again shortly.' Ranulph spread his hands eloquently: 'I ask you?'

Myrddin hardly heard. He was cursing himself for having forgotten the secret passage and his respect grew for Ranulph and his impudent stratagem. 'So you now hold the Pretender here as hostage?'

'Indeed he is in a dungeon, along with those that are left of the traitorous miscreants who surrendered my Citadel to him.' And the Earl nodded benignly. 'I am minded that they shall hang from the walls this very night in greeting to our sovereign King, and in celebration of such a victory.'

'You are too kind, dear Earl,' murmured the wizard, concealing his revulsion. 'And Arthur?'

'He will await Mortleroy's judgement, of course. Only he can say what form of sweet vengeance he shall have executed upon such presumption.'

True but galling, Myrddin reflected with vexation. This Arthur was his own creation, and the idea of Mortleroy having such a masterpiece in his power for even a short space of time was deeply irritating – and all Nemway's doing. Believing the Pretender to be the true Arthur, she had obviously persuaded him to launch an attack that had inevitably ended the way it had because the youth *didn't* have Excalibur.

The wizard had no idea where the true sword was, but knew he was in possession of the trick one that she had tried to plant on Arthur but which Myrddin had spotted in time to make another.

Now that the trick one spelt the end for Mortleroy, a grim smile of satisfaction lit his features at the thought that it also meant he would be returning a duly chastened Arthur to the Forest and instructing him to stay there while he, Myrddin went to rescue Yathra from Gwyn. Given the way things were working out, he might even bring himself to thank Nemway rather than blame her. He had waited long enough to put the young upstart in his place and events were combining perfectly for the opportunity.

Yes, Myrddin deliberated. *This spell in the dungeons at Ranulph's expense will do the young upstart a power of good. And I shall take my proper and unquestioned place as Yathra's Regent* ... He brought his attention back to Ranulph, and wondered at his askance expression.

'You are silent, great prince,' Ranulph said, looking anxious when he saw he had the wizard's attention again. 'Is something amiss?'

Remembering what the Earl intended for his prisoners, Myrddin said: 'My dear Ranulph, I was thinking. Wouldn't it be wiser to leave the criminals who betrayed you, to the King's justice, also? After all, those who betrayed you, betrayed him also, and Mortleroy might well desire a form of his own devising for vengeance – he might consider boiling alive in oil to be too good for them.'

Ranulph beamed his relief. 'Once again you save me from myself, dear Prince. You are so right and there still remains much to be done if all is to be in place for our Sovereign's arrival.'

'I am truly amazed at how much you have all ready repaired – the walls, the moat …?'

'Trolls, dear Prince, trolls. They work so hard and, fortunately, are such mindless creatures they hadn't the sense to understand they had all been freed and could leave like the rest of the captives – which means those will all have to be caught again for the King's entertainment tomorrow. Not all bad, though. Other entertainers; acrobats, mummers and the like, they're still here.' He paused, looking at Myrddin hopefully. 'I *had* wondered if you might care to provide a drag –' and corrected himself quickly '– a lion or some such other fabulous beast to … chase the trolls … around …?' He faltered to a stop at the distinct look of distaste beginning to cloud his guest's face, and gave up 'I suppose not. But,' he said, becoming businesslike; 'I must be about the rest of the arrangements. The King ordered staging and stands be erected in the main square when he heard of Arthur's capture. You will excuse me?'

The idea of such a public arrangement came as a pleasant surprise to Myrddin. It promised that his planned dénouement would be even better than he had hoped. Not just the king's courtiers, but the whole city would witness the unseemly struggle Mortleroy would have in trying to remove the sword from its sheath. It would make the usurper a laughing stock. Thankfully Myrddin had it with him in his box.

*

Osric's world, which had started to turn topsy-turvy with the arrival of Arthur that morning, finished on its head by the afternoon when he listened in bewilderment to Ranulph's account of how he had re-taken the Citadel.

There had been no 'slaying', 'no dallying with the ladies'. There here had been no time; Osric had watched Arthur systematically divesting himself of all protection. Amyas had taken the Mabyn and gnomes and gone. The Kindred of the Grail likewise – apart from three knights who insisted on remaining. It was true that Arthur had not resisted and had insisted that the few knights who were with him be spared, Ranulph had agreed, but later still had them thrown in the dungeons anyway, and called for a feast to celebrate his so called 'Victory', even though there were so few servants left to prepare and cook for it, Osric's mother and other ladies of the Court themselves had to take a hand in its organisation – with Osric standing in as butler. Then there was Arthur himself …

How could anyone sit so calmly; alone and unafraid as he had, waiting for Ranulph and Peredur to become their unresisting prisoner?

And his father, Peredur, had actually asked Ranulph to allow Gareth, Percivale and Gawain to sit at table with them as guests of honour that night – until the Earl heard Mortleroy was at the gate and had them hurriedly thrown in the dungeons as well.

'See you, brother,' the three called back as they were taken away, and Osric felt for his father who looked bereft.

'Father–' he started.

'You don't know, son. You don't know,' he said, wiping his mouth and coming to some decision.

And neither do you, father. Neither do you.

Peredur addressed Ranulph: 'My Lord …?'

Ranulph looked surprised. 'You're very formal, Peredur?'

'I have to ask to be allowed to join my friends …'

*

As soon as he could, Osric slipped away to visit the dungeons. None of the usual torches were in their sconces to light the way around the labyrinthine passages. He had to feel along the walls until his eyes got used to the dimness. The imprisoned knights, their eyes already used to the gloom, could see him though.

A voice in the dark asked if he had come to release them.

'I have no keys,' he whispered back. 'I'm looking for Arthur.'

Peredur's voice came from another cell. 'Osric, you shouldn't be down here. Get back at once before you are missed.'

'Mortleroy has arrived, I want to tell Arthur.'

'He's the next level down then. Keep left and you'll come to the stairs. Be careful.'

When Osric found the stairs and saw a soft illumination ahead as he rounded the next corner at the bottom, he made for it quickly and his eyes widened. The light came from the knobbed tip of a staff held by a strange figure wearing a long dark blue tunic with a wide square neck richly embroidered with strange designs. On a broad belt around the stranger's waist, there hung scrip and pouches. On his brow, above kindly and commanding features, there gleamed a broad circlet of gold. The stranger was knelt before Arthur, saying: 'Your message was received. I am Dian Cécht.'

Osric frowned over a name that sounded like 'Djien Chaist'. He had never heard of it, but the visitor said: 'I am of the Sons of Danu, and am sent at Argetlam's command from the Fields of the Blest. He received your Dove and sends me to your aid. I am to tell you that he also sends Manawydan's *Wave Sweeper*.'

'Thank you. And now – you know what has to be done and how to do it?'

'Indeed. Are you prepared?'

'We are prepared,' Arthur replied, rising to his feet to kneel before the other who had risen to his own. The stranger paused a moment as if gathering strength, then struck Arthur lightly on the head.

Osric gaped to see the King fall apart into two bodies; one still in rags, the other in a white tunic.

The one in white rose and embraced Dian Cécht, saying softly: 'Father of Healing, I thank you. Please, convey my gratitude to my brother Argetlam.' He then lifted the other of himself to his feet to address him in tender tones: 'Bless you, Wychy-that-was, and thank you for your unwitting gift. You shall be re-united with Jack in union with the Christ, his anointed one for His *entire* creation, both mortal and immortal.

Arthur then walked through the wall of his cell to where Osric stood.

'Have you come to be my squire?' he asked.

Osric had to close his still open mouth to be able speak: 'Sire, you have just split in two and walked through a solid wall! Are you a magician like Gwyn ap Nudd?'

Arthur looked amused. 'Not I,' he said. 'But I need one. Do you know where I can find one?'

'There's the Lady Nemway,' Osric said eagerly. 'She knows how to sing walls back into being! How *did* you walk through that one?'

'It's only your imagination that keeps you from doing the same.'

'Why are there two of you?'

'If *you* had to be in two places at the same time, don't you think it would help?'

'Well, yes,' Osric agreed with a nod. 'That makes sense.'

'Now you must return – and *whatever* you see, don't be frightened.'

'But, Sire, if I am your squire, I want to – I want to be with you. You need me.'

Arthur smiled. 'I *need* you to take a message from me to the Lady Nemway …'

CHAPTER 25

A SWORD UNSHEATHED

Curious to see what kind of fay it was that could inspire such an attack on the Citadel – and deciding it was too dangerous to have the young Pretender brought before him at Glastonbury – Mortleroy could not wait to get to Reading. Apart from which, Ranulph deserved the honour of a visit – even if the Earl was being given little time to prepare for it.

For his part, Ranulph couldn't wait to introduce the Prince of Damascus.

'We have met,' Mortleroy told him tersely, before greeting the wizard with a sly smile of triumph: 'It seems my good Ranulph, here, was ahead of you, Enchanter.'

'Ah, but *I* promised you a greater prize than Reading,' Myrddin returned equably. 'And when it comes to it, where better to demonstrate it than on this platform with all to witness.' However, he declined the other's offer to share his interrogation of Ranulph's prisoner.

Mortleroy had Arthur brought up from the dungeons to stand in chains before him, and was astonished. One searching glance into the cool, fearless grey eyes that locked onto his own told him this was undeniably Arthur-come-again. Heaven knew what Gwyn thought he had kidnapped. Here before him was purity, innocence, and calmness, wisdom and understanding – and he hated it. However unbelievable, the youth lay now undeniably within his power to destroy as he had done before.

His thin lips curled derisively. *Was Arthur thinking he was going to be delivered in some kind of divine manner in the nick of time!* He sneered aloud: 'So, you are the stripling who dares to challenge me?'

'Your mistreatment of my People has come to an end,' his prisoner answered with authority.

'And you are?'

'You know who I am.'

'And if *I* know who you are – which *my* subjects might find difficult to believe seeing you thus in rags and shackles – what is to prevent me from having you slain where you stand?'

'Nothing at all – but I *shall* come back.'

Mortleroy dismissed the idea with contemptuous wave of his hand. 'I think I can live with waiting *another* thousand years for *that* to happen.' Then gestured his Court's attention to his prisoner. 'Behold, 'King Arthur',' he mocked. 'Yes, believe it or not this is the youth who claims to be King of all Brython.' He waited until the nervous laughter died to a titter, and changed his manner abruptly. With a grim and humourless face in which his eyes glittered like black ice, he said venomously: 'Tomorrow, I shall have you beaten publicly to a pulp – and I mean a pulp. Your remains will then be chopped into pieces small enough to be distributed to the four points of the compass ...' he spat: '... and *then* let us see how quickly you manage to come back from *that*!'

*

In retrospect, Nemway decided that Arthur had known what was going to happen – and not only known but even directed the sequence of events himself. After handing his horse, and armour to her to take to the Chapel of Blue

Fountains, he had also given Omric's sword into her charge. '… You will find Mildgyth is expecting you.' he said.

*

She found Mildgyth at prayer in the Chapel. The afternoon had been busy receiving the Kindred. They had started bringing back their charges to whom she administered the Cup before they went on to Weir Forest under gnome escort and the Kindred went out again to look for more. Nemway spent some time with her before returning to the Citadel with the sword hidden under her cloak. Neither of them had had any inkling of what had happened in her absence, but Mildgyth had felt uneasy. Nemway had done her best to comfort her, painting a picture of how easily the Citadel had fallen without bloodshed and how Arthur had been received by Ranulph's knights and Peredur.

As soon as she saw Mortleroy's Royal Standard flying from the ramparts, Nemway realised just how warranted Mildgyth's fears had been. Wondering at what could possibly have happened in her absence, she quickened Windfleet's pace.

Ranulph met her in the square where a number of trolls were slaving away erecting scaffolding for a large and ominous looking platform. Nowhere were Mabyn or Gnome to be seen, or any Kindred of the Grail – only Ranulph's own knights, plus those of Mortleroy who were everywhere.

The Earl beamed his pleasure from ear to ear. 'Lady Nemway! His Majesty will be pleased to see you …'

And the usurper indeed greeted her with a delighted smile, declaring to her horror: 'Dear Lady of the Lake! You arrive not a moment too soon to witness a most fortunate occasion. Would you believe it, Arthur – no less – has presented his head to me on a plate? Come, even as you have slain the Green Dragon of the South, you shall witness the destruction of this ridiculous young upstart. My only lament is not to be able to keep him alive while I have him tortured and publicly beaten each and every day – but someone might rescue him. No, he has to be eradicated quickly and completely. I promise you some *eminently* satisfying entertainment. He'll not come back from this in a hurry ...'

*

Myrddin had wondered at the size of platform being raised in the square; far larger than was necessary for an execution. It became clear, however, that with the inclusion of a dais, Mortleroy himself intended to be the executioner. Clearly, the satisfaction of dealing the death blow himself was too much to be handed to a menial.

And what was the point of being all-powerful if you couldn't have and do things the way you wanted them? he thought. He wondered, too, if it wasn't some personal dig at himself. He had told Mortleroy that he had made the youth with his own hands as a babe, and the usurper would give a lot to have one over him. Destroying his creation would provide some kind of twisted happiness, he supposed, although not if he got in first with Nemway's trick sword.

*

Nemway could hardly believe her eyes when she saw the Prince of Damascus drawing Excalibur from beneath his cloak and offering it to Mortleroy. *Arthur knew!* was her instant reaction. *And that's why he instructed me to bring Omric's sword!*

Myrddin's look of triumph at her expression of consternation told her that he thought he was presenting a 'trick' sword to Mortleroy and, thereby, fancying he was hoisting her with her own petard. *He'll therefore believe that*

I'm offering Excalibur when I present Omric's sword. She drew it quickly, inwardly praying Mortleroy would take it. 'Majesty, *this* is Excalibur!'

Mortleroy's eyes flicked between them. 'Which of you do I trust?' To Myrddin he said: 'My faithful Ranulph won Reading back for me and delivered Arthur into my hands; not you. All you did was to try and bankrupt me and plot with Gwyn ap Nudd.' His eyes went to Nemway. 'But you, my Lady of the Lake, are my proven friend despite our previous misunderstandings, and have slain the great Dragon of the South.'

He beckoned the Seneschal forward. 'Draw that sword,' he said indicating the one in Nemway's hands.

He drew it easily. Nemway saw Myrddin's jaw drop.

'Now that one,' he said pointing to the one in the wizard's hands.

When the steward failed, Mortleroy took the sword. 'I misjudged you, great prince. I thank you; you have indeed given me a greater gift than Reading!' And, laying his hand on the hilt, drew the blade without effort and it left its scabbard with a scythe-like scream …

*

The wounding sound penetrated the ears of every faerie being in the realm – in the depths, the heights and beyond. In the Forest, its keen vibration seared the Wychies – who also tensed at feeling the remnants of Dragga hiss, heave, and boil; alarming both of them when they sensed a thousand saw-toothed reeds dragged from their beds for the swirling current to sweep away through his cavern. In the deepest dungeons beneath the fastnesses of Reading, Warwick and Glastonbury, three great dragons roared as they hurled themselves against walls that had then become eternal seals of imprisonment.

The remaining Mung still waiting in their trees for their deliverance, clung to each other convinced they were about to be cast to the forbidden ground below. The bewildered Wellsprite heard it in the gush of water that flushed them out of their dank, dark homes into the light of day. The dumb Troll screamed aloud and tore distractedly at the misshapen forms from which there could be now no deliverance. The Cave-wight would have shrunk into their fissures against an enemy from which there was no hiding, but Hugh knew he had heard the sound he had been told to wait for so gathered them quickly together to lead them to the Cyngsfold woods.

In Stygian blackness in the depths below Reading, an oubliette swung gently with the movement of a figure that lifted its hands in thankful praise for a resonance that promised a long prayed for deliverance.

Nor did it stop there. In the Halls of Annwyn, the piercing sound snapped the strings of the sacred harp of Llyr and these, falling loosely on the Wonderful Head below, awoke it so that it bowed three times and uttered a cry so awful that its four perpetual guardians fell to their knees and broke their swords across their thighs in token that their vigil was at an end.

The great Mac Oc leapt awake in the depths of his palace in the Boyne to find the sword of Nuada had fallen from his silver hand and the living Spear of Lugh raised from its drowsy bed of poppy leaves that had kept it asleep so long.

Alarmed, the Hero hurled it towards the heavens crying: 'Fly then, you fury of blood and fire, and our Mother Danu guide you swiftly to the destruction of our enemy.'

Yet, released from his hand, the Spear sank back to its scented poppy-bed causing the Mac Oc to exclaim in amazement. 'What! Do *all* the treasures of the Tuatha De Dannan forswear their ancient destinies? Come Cuchulain and wield these failing weapons of our Kin!'

Cuchulain came at once and hurled the Spear and it succeeded in leaving his hand.

'See, it speeds beyond these shores towards the alien land of Britain.' cried the Mac Oc in triumph.

'Yet has no spirit,' replied Cuchulain. 'See how slow it flies, like a bee over-laden with honey. 'I smell the coming of the last of all our dooms ...'

*

Myrddin stood in a daze of horrified disbelief. *How had it happened?* Somehow, he must have confused the swords. Yet the fact that the Seneschal had drawn the other with ease belied that. *So what had gone wrong?* More importantly, what was he to do about it? But, what could he do? He had handed the rightful Kingship of all Faedom to its worst enemy, Black sourness engulfed him. *It's all the fault of that witch Nemway. She's tricked and confused me – again!* It was she who had sealed Excalibur against him – against any – except Mortleroy. *After all, the blessed thing had been drawn and wielded well enough by Accolon, as all know.* Equally, everyone knew it was the Sword in the Stone that had been the one that could only be drawn by Arthur. Full of shock and anger, Myrddin, said: 'Slay Arthur as you will, but I promise you that all you will have is the death of a foolish half-wit youth!' which was true in its way and Mortleroy's triumphant laugh reason enough to ram it home, although it felt like a betrayal of 'Impy' and the wise and kindly Wychy who had been before Myrddin. Now he had to leave Reading at once if he was to rescue Yathra ...

With as much dignity as he could muster, he inclined his head in a short acknowledgement of Mortleroy, saying: 'Excuse me, Majesty, I have to go.'

'But you can't – I need you.'

'You have Excalibur. What else *is* there that I – or anyone

– can give you now?' he said harshly and turning on his heel strode quickly away.

*

Back on the great pile of scaffolding erected for Arthur's execution, Mortleroy turned on Nemway. 'You presented me with a *false* sword!' he accused.

'I could not believe he could possibly be offering you the real thing!' she answered with such patent truthfulness that she knew he believed her. 'I thought it could be a trick – a sword made of one piece that *nobody* could draw. I had only hoped to save you from such an embarrassment by giving you one that you *could* unsheathe.'

He smiled magnanimously. 'I am indebted to you, dear Lady, I truly am. I confess I also had my doubts. But you gave me a fair opportunity to choose the right one. And now …'

He walked over to Arthur and, with one massive blow, struck the youth's head from his shoulders; it bounced off the scaffolding onto the ground below where it rolled to Osric's feet.

Osric picked it up in tears.

On the scaffold above him, Nemway begged sweetly 'Your Majesty, the boon you promised?' She felt sure that neither Accolon nor Sir Edric had mentioned the ones she had asked of them. Mortleroy had already told her in gloating detail the purpose of the four horsemen below who had begun looping the arms and legs of the headless youth thrown down to them to tie to their saddles.

'That is true, Lady Nemway,' he said, dragging half his attention away from a spectacle he was clearly enjoying. 'Whatever it is that you crave, dear lady, it is yours.'

'That I might have his head, Majesty?' she whispered as winsomely as she could. It was as much as she dare ask;

given that Mortleroy's sole purpose was to make certain his rival would never rise again.

For a moment, it seemed Mortleroy had a struggle to answer. Then: 'And why not?' he said. 'I already drink from the shrunken astral of his human skull. It shall be my unbounded pleasure to present it to *you*, my Lady Nemway.' He stood at the edge of the platform where Osric could be seen holding it, and shouted: 'You, boy! Bring that up here.'

Nemway cried tears of joy; an emotional show that apparently assured Mortleroy she was overwhelmed at having such proof of her enemy's death in her hands. Except Nemway wept with relief because if he had kept it as a trophy for himself, she believed no one would ever see Arthur alive again.

'Now I shall ride to show it to the King of the Mabyns and dash his hopes forever,' she said, sobbing happily.

'But Lady, you've only just got here, and I want you to stay,' said Mortleroy, looking surprised and disappointed. 'I have been looking forward to your company for a long time.'

Nemway pouted like a spoilt woman. 'Your Majesty! You said I could have anything I wanted, and I've been looking forward so much to wiping the smile from that bumptious Mabyn's face.' She smiled at him teasingly: 'Now, when I get back, who's to say I won't stay as long as you care to have me – and I *might* even have the terrible *Moldwarp* with me to present to you …?'

When Osric stood before her with the head, he whispered urgently: 'Lady Nemway, I have a message from Arthur for you. He said: "*Gather the pieces*" And to ask you to ask the Sage to please direct the Prince of Damascus to Yathra.'

Nemway looked at him in surprise. 'When did you have opportunity to speak with him?'

But Mortleroy was looking back at her, impatience edging his tone as he demanded: 'Aren't you coming to see this?'

'Of course, your Majesty,' she said, rising at once. 'I wouldn't miss it for the world!' And went to join him.

At his signal, the four horsemen ripped the body apart, to be followed by trolls who hacked the remains into fragments between them. 'Now bag the lot up,' he ordered. 'And you,' he pointed at the horsemen, 'scatter them to the four winds.' He chuckled mirthlessly. '*Now* we'll wait to see how long it takes him to get back from that …!'

*

Mortleroy watched Nemway leave, still suffused with the intense pleasure it had given him to see Arthur torn limb from limb. *Pity the upstart hadn't been* alive *to feel it for himself.* He made up for that slight displeasure, however, by revelling in the anticipation of Nemway's promised return. To have such a magician – albeit it with different abilities to Algaric – but necessary. With the Lady of the Lake and the Prince of Damascus, Mortleroy was once again safe from attack. He really must think of some suitable reward to keep the Prince on side. He didn't like the way he had stormed off. *What was it he had said? 'You have Excalibur. What else is there that I – or anyone – can give you now?'* Perhaps his huff could be mollified by introducing him to his underground delights. Algaric had enjoyed them – even providing his own new and always exquisite novelties for both of them to enjoy. Yes, he would offer the Prince of Damascus a special titbit in appreciation of his gift. It would not do to have made an enemy of him.

Fully satisfied that he had the situation under control, Mortleroy relaxed and imagined the pleasure of sinking himself into the hot sweet honey pot that would be his fulfilment in Nemway. Yes, it had been a Good Day. A very, very Good Day, indeed.

Now to pay a little visit to Algaric …

CHAPTER 26

RESTORATION

Nemway shouldn't have been surprised to find the Sage of all the Seers had pre-empted her. He sounded patient enough, however, to forgive her thoughtlessness, even going to an unusual length of answer when she asked for his help.

'Mother, who else but my people, the Readers and Knowers would hear the words that Osric son of Peredur spoke to you and therefore follow and collect from the four winds the remains he seeks. He already has them but awaits his head ...'

Nemway sped for the Chapel of Blue Fountains. She had asked Mortleroy for Arthur's head feeling sure that, having a mouth into which she could pour water from the Cup of Healing, he would be restored.

When she entered the Chapel, however, she froze.

Not only was the figure that had been on the Cross lying shattered on the floor, but the lifeless form of Mildgyth herself lay in disarray before it and Nemway believed the worst of sacrileges had been committed. Fury consumed her. *Another result of that black-hearted warlock's handing of Excalibur to Mortleroy!*

Devastated with sorrow, she pulled herself together, set her burden on the floor and hurried to raise the nun's head. Even as she touched her, however, Mildgyth's eyes opened.

They stared abstractedly into Nemway's own and then her hands came up to grasp at her in thankful recognition and relief: 'Oh Nemway, dearest sister – how wonderful to see you!' she said – and burst into tears.

Nemway held her closely, calming her emotion until the sobbing ceased, although the nun still trembled within her protective arms.

'Dearest Mildgyth, try and tell me what happened? Who was the robber who violated this place – and yourself?'

'Robber?' the nun asked her eyes bewildered. 'There was no robber. It was when this happened that I was left bereft'

It was Nemway's turn to frown. 'When what happened?'

'This morning, while I still prayed, a most alarming wizardry – a terrible sound. It pierced me like a sword. And, look–' she gestured the broken pieces around them: 'the image of the Saviour fallen – wrecked! I fainted at the sight.'

Almost laughing with relief, Nemway held her tightly. 'Dearest Mildgyth, it's only an *image*. The real Arthur is–'

'Here, Mildgyth!' Arthur's voice from behind them, finishing her sentence as if on cue. 'I am here.'

'My Lord!' Mildgyth's glad cry and struggle to free herself from Nemway's arms made the other abruptly aware that in her astonishment she was holding on to the nun instead of letting her go.

'Arthur!' she cried; her gaze flying from him to the bundle she had laid on the floor when she had lifted Mildgyth. 'But I have only just gathered … I thought …' and tailed off as he shook his head, smiling.

'Don't you remember?' he asked. 'Didn't Merlyn's Heir make unwitting provision for me against this time?'

And Nemway's mind flew back to the morning of Arthur's birth, and White Wand telling her how her partner Black Wand had been so against Mergyn, he could not believe she had conceived any child, and therefore fashioned a babe himself in order that the little people shouldn't be disappointed. '… The Queen and I then witnessed another miracle …!' the White One had continued, for, when they placed it beside the real one, wonder of wonders, the two had merged into one being! The Queen had been fearful of what it meant, but Ann had comforted her; reminding her how protective Black Wand always was and ever had been and that this, although her Brother Wand might not realise it, was surely a most fortunate provision for Arthur's future safety.

Nemway had answered thoughtfully herself: 'That may well be true, dear Wych. The babe *does* possess a shell with mortal link.'

It had filled Ann with wonder. 'Then prophecy is truly fulfilled – mortal *and* immortal both!' she cried.

How the pair of them had wept and laughed together, filled with joy and wonder. Where before Nemway had nearly wrecked the day in her anger, Ann's words had enabled her to hold out her hands and say: 'Come, sister, let us return at once and make the day rejoice for our infant King …'

She saw Arthur incline his head at the light of recollection in her eyes. 'Merlyn's Heir always works for the best as he sees and believes to be true,' he said. 'Just as all things work together for good for those who believe in my coming. He is not the first, nor the last, to be so blind as to when it happened.'

Mildgyth, who had lifted herself from Nemway's arms, now stood. 'I was so afraid …' she faltered. 'I thought something terrible had happened to you – when …' and she indicated the empty cross.

He held out his arms. 'What – the moment of my release?' he asked gently, taking her to him as she ran to his embrace.

It sounded almost a tease to Nemway, until she realised that Mildgyth would have no idea of what had happened.

The nun was simply thinking Arthur was the same as she had last seen him – which was when Nemway also realised that Mildgyth had always seen Arthur as he was now, different. It was Arthur, but not quite the same as he had been. Still on her knees, Nemway met his eyes and silently gestured the bundle beside her on the floor.

Over Mildgyth's shoulder, he gave the barest shake of his head but with a smile said gratefully: 'Nemway, I thank you that what you have won for me can now be restored whence it was taken …'

*

Jack Hundell's cheerful 'Morning, Nan!' spun his grandmother round to stare at him in astonishment. He had never, ever greeted her in such a way before. Not that he wasn't always bright-eyed and cheerful with her; he was. Yet this morning he seemed – somehow – changed. And then it struck her – he was awake; not just ordinarily so but alertly as if from some long, deep sleep.

'Morning, luvvy. You slept well?'

'I did that, and I've something to tell you, Nan – he said I should.'

'Who said you should what, luvvy?'

'Jesus. He were there in my room last night – like you said he always were – only this time, I could see him an' he were just like me! And he says "Jack, what would you wish for most in all the world." And I just stares at him, 'cause I couldn't think. So he says, "Would you like to be what people call 'normal'?" And I says "No," to that at once – 'cause normal's hurtful. Then I says, "But I would *like* to be someone who could *stop* people hurting each other." He looks a bit sad then, and says he couldn't do that. "Everyone's got free will to choose to love or hate for themselves, Jack. But I can give you love, and wisdom and understanding that will help *you* to heal them." And then, Nan, he touched me here,' and Jack indicated his heart, 'and my head. And he says "Be born again, Jack Hundell, in the Name of the Father, Son and Holy Spirit. Now, tell no one," he says. "Only your grandmother. She will know what to do and how to help and protect you.".'

And his grandmother felt she knew exactly what had been meant by those words. She had always held a profound belief that ever since Joseph and Mary had found Jesus in the Temple, his parents hadn't understood but his mother had been reminded of the wonders of his birth which she treasured in her heart. It might well have been then that over the following 'hidden' years, little things – or something big even – could have sparked a growing understanding between Jesus and Mary that, having brought his attention to a neighbour's trouble, hurt or illness and learning of his love for his neighbour, that Jesus would never refuse her plea for help for them. That, swearing his mother to secrecy, he had always known how, where and when to direct her to what would help the situation and, however strange his instructions might have been, they had always worked. How else were Mary's words to the servants at the Wedding at Cana, to be interpreted? To Margaret they shone with a revelation of Mary's relationship with her son; the hidden understanding between them that dismissed his apparently unkind reply: 'Woman, what has that to do with me? My time is not yet come,'[1] like water off a duck's back. She had simply told the servants to do *exactly* whatever he told them. The manner of his reply, however, had told Mary that this miracle was the last of the private ones. Such requests had to come to an end now with the commencement of his public ministry.

---

1 John 2:4

Margaret Hundell met her grandson's clear, un-complicated gaze with a smile and kissed him. He would indeed need protecting. 'We won't tell a soul, luvvy. You just go on being you, the way you are, and I'll see that whatever you tell me you'd like me to do, I'll see it's done ...'

*

Gaheris stared aghast at what looked like a ghostly horde of shining-faced avenging angels rising up from some unknown depths below. When they began advancing on him in the green gloom of the cavern, he turned to run. He had already had more than enough of the place as he could take but Avellane, catching his shoulder, held him fast.

'Wait!' he said, pointing. 'Look, there's Gars and not a scratch on him – and you saw me lance *him* through, yourself. But that one in front next to the one carrying a staff of light – he's got a head on his shoulders – but he's also carrying it *under* his arm. *And* he's whole – yet looks in pieces!'

A reluctant Gaheris looked back. It was true. There was nothing odd about anyone else among the stranger's white clothed followers. And now that Gaheris was looking, he began recognising friend and foe alike – all that he knew for certain had been killed.

An already surreal world became even more surreal for him when their leader reached them and said: 'I am Arthur-come-again. I am come to show you that you cannot die. You are alive and whole–'

Gaheris' couldn't help a stab of ironic humour. 'It comes to mind to say: "Physician, heal thyself",' he said, pointing to the severed head.

'That is my witness,' Arthur said. 'Who would believe me, else?'

Gaheris pointed to Edric. 'Try him.'

He watched Arthur kneel beside the naked fay as

Avellane started talking eagerly to Gars. 'How come – what happened …?'

The kneeling figure beside Edric had placed a hand the Constable's chest, saying: 'Edric, wake up! You are alive – free and whole. There is nothing wrong with you or binding you.'

Edric opened his eyes. But–' he began, and Gaheris saw him cringe and knew he remembered how he had been rendered dumb.

'Come!' Arthur spoke with authority; rising and holding out his hand. 'Rise!'

The knight groaned. 'Save me – I can't – I *cannot* go through all that *again*.'

'Edric, I am Arthur-come-again. Come with me and you will never go through that again. I am here to rescue you. I am not dead. I do not die.'

Still groaning and sounding far from convinced, the Constable said wearily: 'So this is life, is it? To live Mortleroy's torments over and over again for all eternity?'

'Not in my Kingdom. Death has no more power over you than what you give it to either hurt or destroy. You are immortal, so why believe in death? You are alive –*be* alive – and come with me and these others.'

Edric gave in: 'Lord, *you* touch me, and I shall be whole.'

And Arthur did – drawing him to his feet. Here,' he said, taking a white tunic from a pile carried by one of his followers, clothing Edric and embracing him. 'Be whole, my friend. Be unafraid.'

And Gaheris began to believe then. Edric not only revealed himself without a mark on him, but somehow even *looked* different – although still recognisably himself – but no longer belligerent or even so wide as he had been.

And so it went on; Arthur's growing company searching out and recovering the lost and freeing the damned from the cages of their eternal tortures until one last thing remained.

Arthur had them all to grip each other's hands, then told them to shut their eyes as he described the appearance of a chapel with a cascade of blue water each side of the door. This was where they would find themselves when they heard him say they could open their eyes – and it was so.

Of course, Edric recognised where he was immediately and turned to Arthur. 'Sire, please, I beg leave to see my wife and son. I need to know they are safe. My wife was told that you had been born of her – Yathra will therefore be in terrible danger from the King.'

'Gwyn ap Nudd has your son, Edric. Go to him; speak with your wife. Tell her all that has happened to you. Tell Gwyn also of Avellane and Gaheris–'

'Sire!' Avellane said. 'Please, let us go and witness to Gwyn ourselves?'

Peredur wanted to collect his wife and Osric. Arthur assented, also to others who wanted to go straight away to tell their friends what had happened. He agreed to all, and instructed they should return quickly with any who would come with them of their own free wills – there must be no coercion. 'Speak your truth firmly but gently,' he said. 'If your hearers choose not to hear, that is their choice. They may not be forced.' Then gestured to where Nemway stood waiting at an entrance into a mound. 'In there you will find a way to my Kingdom. It cannot remain open long ...'

*

The tiny slab of rock hanging from the over-arching roof above a depthless chasm needed no walls to imprison Algaric, but had given him time to reflect and repent of his relationship with Mortleroy. He couldn't remember, or maybe didn't want to think, when or how his relationship with the King had turned sour. Certainly Mortleroy's insatiable appetite had begun pall and sicken Algaric until the day when everything had culminated with seeing the terror-stricken eyes of Peredur's young son – who was in fact Algaric's own. There had been no need to wonder how the boy had come to be there. It didn't take much to imagine some malicious wellsprite who had witnessed his dalliance in the court-yard with Peredur's wife, and simply bided its time to drag the unsuspecting child into the depths to see the real nature of his loving 'Uncle'. The shamed magician had at once shielded the child from being seen or sensed by Mortleroy and, from then on, refused to have anything more to do with the King.

Since neither had power over the other and Algaric had chosen his own way of cutting himself off, Mortleroy could come and rant and rave all he liked about the Skull.

'... Without you to fill it with blood, the way lies open for Arthur's return. What about that? It'll be the end.' Without the satisfaction of answer or comment, however, the King eventually gave up coming and left the magician to rot in the oblivion he had chosen. There wasn't even a way of getting him forcibly removed from it. Algaric had magically sealed off any way of reaching him.

Since time had long lost all meaning in the black void around him, Algaric had no idea what aeons he had spent there before he heard the answer to his prayers in the sound of Excalibur's unsheathing.

It wasn't long after that he saw a soft light lit an opening in the side of the rock wall which revealed Arthur with another holding aloft a staff of light.

'Algaric, you have been heard, and I have come,' he said. 'Will you now come with me?'

'Tell me how I may command the Green Dragon, my Liege, then leave me here where I may serve you best.'

'There is a price,' Arthur said, a note of sadness in his voice.

'I know, my Liege, and I am more than willing – even as you were for me.'

'Dian Cécht will tell you how it may be done ...'

Sometime later the bright flicker of a torch illumining the same opening in the rock wall heralded Mortleroy's approach. 'I have Excalibur!' he exulted.

'I know – I heard.'

'Now you have to obey me!'

'I can't leave here; I've thrown away the key. You should go to Glastonbury. Gwyn will attack it your absence. You have summoned the giants, but I will send you the Green Dragon.'

'The Lady Nemway has slain it.'

'Then the Lady Nemway must have been fooled.'

'You weren't able to chain it last time. What's different now?'

'Time,' Algaric said. He added nothing more.

When he was alone again, he climbed one of the three chains holding his platform to a grill now visible above him, unlocked it and pulled himself up into a narrow passageway ...

*

In the Forest of Weir, Algaric stood hardly visible in his long green robes against the vegetation on the brink of Dragga's dark swirling waters opposite The Wandle.

'I who imprisoned your brothers have freed them,' he said. 'Now I come to free you,'

An answer rose out of the depths like a voiceless ghost: *One has already saved eight of my roots to do that.*

'Great Merlyn bound you to those roots. Fill me with your remaining essence, and I will free you from these bonds.'

Why would you want to do that?

Algaric spread his hands. 'Trust me,' he invited. 'I am a vessel you can break at any moment – all I ask is that it will be a moment of my own choosing and I will give you meat …'

*

Despite Arthur's words to the effect that it was helpful to have two bodies when he needed to be in two places at the same time, it didn't help Osric to weather the shock of seeing him beheaded. The fact that his head then rolled to his feet rather than anyone else's was what made him cry. Its silent and helpless appeal for him to be the one pick it up, and the relief he felt at being the one ordered to bring it up and give to Nemway, all answered the question of how and when he was ever going to get near her to give her his message. Nemway's startled look at hearing his words and her question, made him wish he could have explained. There was no time for that though. His own safety and that of his mother were his next priority. He didn't know what was going to happen to his father – he had heard the Prince of Damascus suggest that Mortleroy might consider boiling alive in oil to be too good for him. He had to get his mother away. Neither of them was safe with Mortleroy now on the rampage. He knew where they had to go. His father had said 'Go to the Forest of Weir, tell them what happened here'.

His mother didn't make it easy. Peredur's arrest and Arthur's beheading had taken all the stuffing out of her. She sat crying most of the time. Osric wondered what Arthur would have done, and his words came back to him: 'It's only your imagination stopping you.' But Algaric had encouraged him to use his imagination practicing the little things of magic that he had been teaching him and which Osric had wanted nothing more to do with. Yet Nemway had used magic to build the walls – and she was good, he knew that instinctively. How he wished she was there with him now. Use his imagination …

'Come on, Mother,' he said cheerfully. 'We're going for a little walk; it'll help you feel a bit better.'

Imagine, imagine, imagine he kept concentrating as they walked. He kept his eyes shut, too, fixing his mind on going through the wall, down a flight of steps, through the great protecting outer wall onto the hill and into the trees …

'Where are we, darling?' asked his mother a little anxiously. He opened his eyes. Everything he had seen so clearly had happened. They were in the trees and over his shoulder he could just see the top of the Citadel's walls …

They were found by Peredur, Gawain and Percivale who were on their way to Reading; Peredur to rescue his wife and son, his companions to persuade Ranulph to join them.

It made sense that Peredur should turn back with his family. 'If Ranulph is with us, we will bring him,' they said. 'If not, there would have been little sense in your coming. If they had still been there, he would have used them as hostage.' And they both looked at Osric as if curious to know how he had got away.

Osric found it a relief to hand over to his father. The strain on finding his way in unknown territory had begun to tell.

They arrived in the forest just before the catastrophe; so Osric had been able to see and marvel at the Crystal Bridge, but above all, when he had crossed it, to find Arthur alive and well.

'It was just like you said, Sire,' was his modest answer when Arthur asked how he had left. 'I just used my imagination.'

Arthur at once turned to Nemway. 'My lady, may I present you with an apprentice?' And that was how he came to be there and to see what happened.

CHAPTER 27

MYRDDIN BATTLES FOR YATHRA

To find Yathra, Myrddin had to find Gwyn. But how do you find someone who lives and travels mainly underground? One thing he knew Gwyn would be unable to resist would be a challenge to fight but how and where to send it? Unable to look Faith in the eye after his fiasco with Excalibur, Myrddin had left her in Reading. He didn't want to call Hannibal – the falcon would take news of his whereabouts to Mortleroy – but he had brought his hawk and Gwyn had an affinity with birds. The hawk returned almost immediately with an acceptance of the unknown Lord of the Grail's challenge and directions as to where the King would be found.

*

A surrounding number of spectators and pavilions made a colourful setting for the arena in which they were to duel. Gwyn had ordered a plain straight course rather than a list where the barrier would have been an obstacle when both contestants needed as much manoeuvring space as possible for fighting on horse and on foot.

There were few preliminaries. Gwyn appeared mailed head to foot in green armour, reputed to be the only suit in which he was vulnerable, bearing a shield of the same colour emblazoned with a crowned white owl.

Opposing him at the other end of the course, the Lord of the Grail glittered in black from his tall plumed helmet down to the hooves of his sable steed, his breastplate marked with a chalice of gold, and his buckler with a golden eagle. But Myrddin was not happy with Gwyn. He judged him to be as hot tempered as ever; careless of his unknown challenger's strength and impatient to have done with him, while Myrddin wanted a fair fight and for it to be recognised as such.

'The contest is ill-matched,' he called out, just as the judges were about to give the order to let battle begin. 'My arms are Wayland made, and those of the King of Annwyn are not. Give me arms tempered to those of the King of the People of Beauty.' And threw his lance to the ground, followed by sword and dagger.

It was difficult to hear the Judges' reply above the immediate hubbub, and they had to wait for the crowd to quieten sufficiently before announcing that such chivalrous consideration being without lawful precedent, the objector must remain at liberty to wield the arms that were his, however powerful they were.

When Myrddin again refused, saying: 'Nevertheless, I would rather meet the Lord of Annwyn without them.'

The crowd was in riot with admiration.

'By the Wonderful Head,' Bras-de-Fer was heard to say. 'I swear if Gwyn brings him low, I will avenge him upon the person of the King myself.'

Myrddin appreciated that Gwyn would feel needled to the core and look on the offer as an insult to his courage but gave an inward shrug. *I've done my best, so be it.*

Sure enough the King demanded that battle begin, calling on all to witness that he was the scion of the Houser of Llyr. Who was there alive that dare defy his right to uphold the glory of his heaven-born line? Saying which, he flung down his own lance, sword and dagger, and spurred his horse. 'Á

Gwyn. Á Gwyn.' he roared and charged like a bolt towards Myrddin with shield held high, plainly intent on crushing him with that piece alone.

Pricking his horse forward, Myrddin jerked his animal to the left at the last moment so as not to clash shield to shield and too late for Gwyn to change his own to his right arm to make an effective stroke.

Gwyn swore loudly, hurled his steed to the right and cannoned into his adversary instead. Taken off guard like that and with such force, Myrddin and his mount crashed to the ground.

Scrambling to his feet and helping his horse to rise, the wizard was surprised to see Gwyn already bearing down on him for a second time and had dealt him a thunderous blow on his helmet before he could remount. It laid flat him on the ground again only more hurt in dignity than in fact. It made him get to his feet with alacrity, however, and had nearly settled in his saddle when the whirlwind passed yet again with Gwyn dealing him the equivalent of a karate chop with the edge of his shield. Toppled to the ground for the third time, Myrddin struggled erect as quickly as he could, smarting that Gwyn should make such a fool of him without a shred of chivalrous consideration. But then no one had told the wizard that in combat á l'outrance there were no rules. He had no chance of remounting in time to counter the menace once more bearing down on him. Apparently unaware, or uncaring of the dents in the front and along one edge of his shield, the Lord of Annwyn was coming in for the kill and Myrddin had no choice but to defend himself while still on foot with the face of his shield before mounting his charger again to face his tormentor on horseback.

Although it seemed to be dawning on Gwyn that something had gone badly wrong with his unusual weapon, which had now buckled inwards on both sides and had a deep indent down the centre so that its shape resembled a kind of thin fish with a broad fantail uppermost, he didn't act as if perturbed by it. But it enabled Myrddin to brush what amounted to a fistful of scrap metal in the King's grasp, effortlessly aside. Determined to put an end the fight as soon as possible now. He mounted, turned and careered quickly after Gwyn's plunging horse. He was in full spate by the time the other wheeled for his return. What happened next came out of the blue for both of them.

Aware that to use the edge of his shield as Gwyn had done, would cut through mail and body alike, Myrddin held it at arm's length by one of the arm-holds; ready to swing it face down to deflect Gwyn's aim. The moment they clashed however, a flaming spear came out of nowhere; hit the wizard's shield a glancing blow which deflected it on to Gwyn like a bludgeon. It struck the Lord of Annwyn simultaneously on the shoulder and helmet. With a shower of sparks, the spear then shot slowly into the air again leaving Gwyn to fall to the ground like a log.

While astonished eyes followed the fiery flight of the spear into the distance, Myrddin's immediate thought was for the King. He had spun around, returned and dismounted before any marshal arrived and what he saw dismayed him. The mailed shoulder was mangled out of all recognition and the side of the helmet crushed inward. He knelt, tore away the bars of the helmet, and gazed appalled. He was still staring at the frightful wounds when Bras-de-Fer came up and spoke to him.

He looked down at the wrecked body of his king, and said: 'My Lord of the Grail, the judges concur that the stroke was fairly aimed, and that you are not to blame for the phenomenon of the spear.' He drew his dagger and presented it hilt foremost. 'A mere formality, the King is doubtless already dead, but the law of mortal combat demands–'

'Never!' Myrddin cried springing to his feet. 'Your King is immortal, he cannot die! He lives!'

'Nevertheless, it is the law–'

'Not in *my* book, it isn't,' Myrddin said in fury. 'Take him to his couch and watch him well, for I shall return with healing – and woe betide you if I find *any* who administered him differently. Now take me to meet Dame Margaret and her son, Yathra.'

Myrddin knew he had to ride fast to get the Chalice, but could the widow and her son ride with him as quickly? Then he remembered the speed at which Nemway had flown with them, so judged it was enough when it came to assuring Yathra's safety.

Bras-de-Fer took him to a ringside seat where the widow had watched the duel with the sleeping babe. The company around them, still buzzing more over the wonder of the spear than any concern for Gwyn, began to quieten as Myrddin explained his intentions, and the need for speed.

The Dame at once appealed to Bras-de-Fer. 'Sir Knight, who is this Lord of the Grail and what does he mean by saying I must ride with him to this Forest of Weir? The Lord of Annwyn himself assured me that I am being taken to my Sovereign, King Mortleroy, who even now waits to receive me and my child into his protection at Reading?'

Bras-de-Fer, looking as if he had become more than a little weary of Dame Margaret's airs and graces, did his best. 'Lady, the People of Beauty owe Mortleroy no allegiance,' he said. 'Our own King lies at death's door. We wait here for this good Lord of the Grail's return with the healing he has promised. You are not safe waiting with us and this fair Lord has promised to see you into safe refuge. I therefore beg you. Lady, go with him now and with all speed–' he broke off, mouth agape distracted by a commotion at the arrival of three white-clothed figures who were being greeted with cries of amazement and shouts of:

'Avellane!'

'Gaheris!'

'Excuse me, my lady,' Bras-de-Fer said absently, his gaze fixed on them. 'This I must attend.'

Edric passed him in a hurry to see his wife. 'Margaret!' he cried. 'Arthur has come! Give me our son and make yourself ready. We leave for Weir Forest at once. Mortleroy has Excalibur–!' Edric's urgency and Margaret's shock at seeing him alive made it difficult for Myrddin to get a word in with their immediate demand to account for each other.

When he managed at last, Myrddin's tone was sharp: 'Edric, listen, please! Your son, Yathra *is* Arthur-come-again. The Arthur *you're* talking about was killed in Reading – Mortleroy struck his head from his body–'

Comprehension lit Edric's eyes. 'Ah – so *that*'s why he was carrying it!' he exclaimed and, in answer to their quick looks of confused askance, said: 'Arthur is *not* dead, he's alive! He brought us up from hell.' He looked at his wife. 'I came immediately to take you and Yathra to him, my love. We must hurry. Mortleroy has Excalibur and prepares to undo all that Arthur has accomplished unless he can get everyone away in time. Give me Yathra and make yourself ready.'

'Edric, didn't you hear what I said?' Myrddin asked in frustration.

Margaret, a little querulous and more than doubtful, handed the babe to her husband, saying: 'Are you sure about this? The Angel said–' she was cut short by Avellane's arrival at Edric's side with Gaheris. The Commander's bearing no longer cold or aloof but looking despondent.

'We've been to see Gwyn,' Avellane told him. 'He doesn't hear us.'

'I'm hardly surprised,' Myrddin said, his lips curving in a dry smile. 'Bras-de-Fer wanted me to finish him off completely. I'm *trying* to get away to bring back the Cup of Healing.'

Avellane nodded. 'So Bras-de-Fer said. He told us everything's that happened and what you said – which are the very words Arthur spoke to us! "You are immortal," he said. "Live!" But Gwyn doesn't hear us.'

Myrddin looked at the babe stirring awake in Edric's hold, the little arms pushing aside the shawl in their struggle. He hadn't seen the child properly before that moment. The clash of difference between this one's still dazed half-asleep eyes and his memory of the miracle he had seen in Arthur's alert grey ones at the same stage of development and had not recognised, caused an involuntary cry of shock and anguish to escape him: 'This *isn't* Arthur-come-again!'

'No,' agreed Edric at once with a fond, proud grin. 'This is my son. Isn't he wonderful?'

Appalled and horrified, Myrddin stared at him without comprehension. Time vanished as his mind reeled. The impact of everything he had done to deny the reality of the one person he should have been serving rose in front of him in a nightmarish reality. Nor could he blame it any of it on Nemway. The witch he had so convinced himself to be in league with Mortleroy had been constantly faithful to someone he had just as consistently betrayed – even to death. What he was to do now? How was he to – how could he even begin to make amends …? The sound of Avellane's voice addressing a crowd that had gathered around himself and Gaheris began to penetrate Myrddin's mind and he found himself reaching for the words like a drowning man offered a lifeline.

'… I tell you all,' the knight was saying. 'Arthur showed me – us – that he – that we – are immortal. We cannot die. But we have a choice. We can choose to go on living as we did as mortals, or live with him instead, beyond the reach of being subject to what we imagined to be the same here as it was there …' And Myrddin realised with a jolt that he had fallen into the same trap. It wasn't the Cup of Healing that

Gwyn needed; it was what he had needed himself: a large dose – a very large dose – of plain common sense …

He grabbed hold of Bras de Fer. 'Take me to Gwyn!' he said his tone urgent,

*

At the foot of the couch on which Gwyn lay, Myrddin drew himself together and, in a loud voice, cried: 'Gwyn ap Gwyn son of Nudd, Wake up!'

'Who calls?' the faint voice sounded thin and somehow disembodied.

'Your immortality.'

The voice grew a little stronger with fretfulness. 'I'm dying.'

'Impossible! You are immortal.'

'I don't *feel* immortal.'

Myrddin moved to his side laying his hands on the ruined features, working at them hard. 'You *feel* my hands,' he said harshly. 'But immortality is not a feeling, it's a fact,' 'You *are* alive *and* you live. Therefore *be* alive! Be whole!' And slowly, to his relief as he watched, Gwyn's battered features began reforming themselves, coming back to normal under his hands.

Gwyn opened his eyes. 'You – Lord of the Grail,' he said on seeing the black armoured figure still wearing a closed helm standing at his side. '*Who* are you?'

'Your fellow magician,' Myrddin said, lifting his visor. 'But I have not saved you by magic. Look …' and he indicated the listening and watching Avellane and Gaheris who had followed Bras de Fer. 'They can tell you better than I.'

Gwyn swung his legs to the floor and sat up: 'I was told you two were dead,' he said in astonishment.

'We thought so too – when we woke in hell with Mortleroy in charge,' Avellane agreed with feeling.

'–But Arthur freed us and everyone else there and brought us up out of it.' Gaheris added. 'There is so much to tell you, Gwyn, but we need to get to Weir Forest – Mortleroy has Excalibur and you were hit by the Spear of Lugh.'

'That's impossible!' Gwyn exploded. 'Llyr is my ancestor; the spear could never be used against me.'

'I told you, Mortleroy has Excalibur. It commands the Spear–'

'Again I say, impossible,' Gwyn insisted, dismissing the news with a gesture of contempt. 'Excalibur cannot command the Spear–'

'The Spear was not aimed at Gwyn ap Gwyn,' Myrddin interrupted. 'It was aimed at me – I was fighting him. I deflected it, it bludgeoned Gwyn ap Gwyn.'

'There you are!' Gwyn cried. 'I tell you this, also. It's legend that gives the Sword its power. I'll fight Mortleroy any day – and in green!'

Avellane sighed. 'Gwyn, if the Lord of the Grail hadn't brought you back to consciousness, you *would* have been taken as you were to the same place where *we* found ourselves. Mortleroy would have had a field day with you. Imagine, *you* his greatest enemy, at his mercy! But that's all changed now. We're finished with the old ways, Gaheris and I. Arthur promises a place in his Kingdom for all who want to come.'

'I am your King!' Gwyn said in outrage. 'You swore fealty to me!'

But the two knights were adamant. 'There's a saying in the mortal world that death cancels all contracts,' said Gaheris. 'Well, we've been through everything that amounts to *that*, and were saved by Arthur. That's all we've come back to tell you – and whoever else will listen.'

While Myrddin stood with Bras-de-Fer listening to them and pondering the change in manner and bearing of the two knights, he wondered: *How am I ever going to face Arthur?* It was tempting to think he *could* remain concealed behind his visor, a black armoured figure of mystery; far better than revealing himself as the witless magician who had handed Excalibur to Mortleroy – except it wouldn't fool Arthur, and nor did Myrddin want to. He owed Arthur-come-again a very deep and very personal apology which he couldn't begin to think how to phrase or what amends he could possibly make.

Something then occurred to Bras-de-Fer causing him to leave them. Myrddin addressed Avellane. 'You remember me?'

'We both do, Am-mar-el-lyn. And owe you an apology for the way you were treated. I should never have behaved the way I did that day.'

'Avellane, I assure you it's forgotten. I have done something far, far worse. I need to go to Weir Forest, also. If I may ride with you, I would like you to tell me everything of how you met Arthur?'

Gwyn rose to his feet. 'Then I return to Annwyn and muster all who yet remain loyal to me and lay siege to Glastonbury …'

'He'll learn,' Avellane said to Gaheris. 'Remember what Arthur said? No coercion. If he won't hear, that's his choice. He can't be forced.'

They found Bras-de-Fer with a number of knights waiting for them when they emerged from Gwyn's pavilion with their King.

'Bras-de-Fer has told us told what he has seen and heard. We want to return home and fetch our families and go with Avellane and Gaheris to Arthur's Kingdom,' their spokesman said.

'I'm your King,' Gwyn said, and Myrddin felt the weight increase on his shoulders.

'They have a right–' Bras-de-Fer began just as a white owl appeared and came to the fist that was held out to it by Gwyn. From its perch it stared fixedly at its master.

Gwyn looked stunned at what he studied in the bird's eyes. 'This is terrible,' he whispered. 'The Formor and the Firbolg have been summoned to burn and lay waste our valley of beauty beyond the Western Gates.'

A cry of dismay went up from his knights. The Valley of Beauty – home to the Tylwyth Teg; an Arcady so secret that it was never guarded for fear that the presence of mailed knights and warriors would have drawn Mortleroy's attention to it. In ancient days its one mighty safeguard had been the Great Red Dragon of the West.

Avellane spoke first and in a heavy voice said: 'Now I will go with you Gwyn – but as Arthur's knight.'

Gaheris said something to him in a low voice that made Avellane nod and add: 'And all who follow you, Gwyn, will need training and practice in overcoming the wounds they receive. While Mortleroy holds Excalibur, he still has his dungeons and his scavengers.'

Myrddin turned to Edric. 'You have a wife and child to protect, I will go with you.'

'You are welcome, Sir Knight. I shall go via the Chapel of Blue Fountains …'

CHAPTER 28

FIRE IN THE FOREST

What had already started off as a wonderful day with Arthur's return and the multitude he brought with him, became even more so when the magic of the Weirdfolk's Wychies brought the Crystal Bridge into being at noontide. Not one of them had ever seen it other than at High Moon, when the delicate star-silvered structure lit the only way from the Weal to The Wandle. The sun-sparkling formation appeared so different to the way it looked in moonlight; the novelty nearly caused them to miss the approach of the Royal barges down King's Weird.

In the first, cloaked in a blazing mantle of gold and wearing the crown of the Weirdfolk's Ruler, Gwen sat bearing the gold Wand of Office. At her side were Nemway and Mildgyth; the former in blue and silver, the latter in a white gown fastened with a golden girdle and wearing a wimple. Two wiccies-in-waiting accompanied her, together with the Royal Chamberlain and Kye, the Royal Herald.

The second gleaming barge carried Arthur, plainly clad in a white tunic but having a mantle about his shoulders of crimson, gold and purple quartered with the four dragons of his kingdom with his brow encircled by a thin band of gold. With him were Amyas and the Master of Gnomes both mailed and armed in their different fashions and a company of gnomes mailed cap-a-pie, bearing across their breasts the Green Dragon surmounted by the plain gold ring of Arthur's crown.

The crowded glowing mass of colour that looped to and fro across the face of Wandleside erupted in a frenzy of singing, cheering and clapping; redoubling in sound when Arthur responded with a raised hand acknowledging their joy and happiness.

The significance of it all dawned as they came ashore. Kye, the Queen's Herald greeted them as guests of the Queen of the Weirdfolk, and not the Weirdfolk's especial rulers as Alder and Gwen had been.

In the Circle of Rejoicing, Gwen took centre place on the Crystal Throne between Arthur and Mildgyth who sat in equally majestic chairs either side of her, and either side of them were Nemway, Amyas and the Master of Gnomes.

The jubilant throng settled into its usual places – with the exception of the host of newcomers, whom the Lord Chamberlain marshalled into different parties.

Another fanfare from Kye, and the Chamberlain beckoned all the newly returned little people of the Weirdfolk forward to present them first to Gwen as their immediate Queen, and then to Arthur. In the second group all those of the Kin of Beauty; the Mabyn and Denefolk who had returned, knelt to Arthur as their Liege Lord.

Arthur then wed Mildgyth. The ceremony proceeded by the ancient custom of public avowal on both sides. He took the wimple from her head with his own hands, crowning her his Queen with a replica of his own simple circlet of gold, and presented Mildgyth to his people as their undoubted Queen of all Faedom.

*

Redweird could not have said was it was that made him leave the gathering, except a feeling of unease about the high water level of the Weird. He had noticed it when he and White Wand were welcoming the royal party ashore.

Remembering how he and Stella had sensed the end of Dragga, he sped off quickly to the southern end of the Wandle to check the water level there, while Nyzor dispensed his barrels of specifics. Yes, the Spinner was rising and water had started creeping over the strand below Wandleside. It appeared the remains of Dragga were blocking the Woe's outlet into the Spinner causing the waters to rise in the other two Weirds.

He hurried back to the Circle of Rejoicing where everyone was still happily dancing the hours away, and found the Royal Pilot already reporting to Gwen, unnoticed by the rest of the rioting fae. Loy had also been to check on the barges, having noticed the rising water.

'… some magic stems the outlet from the lower reaches, Majesty, your Barges already float nearly level with the Wandle banks–'

Loy, like everyone came to a frozen stop where they were as a flash and a roaring sound of what seemed to be continuous lightening started flickering through the sky beyond the Wandle.

While those in charge calmed the fae, Redweird hurried away to Weirdsmeet to see what was happening.

To his dismay, The Crystal Bridge had disappeared, effectively marooning the Weirdfolk despite the two empty barges which lay juddering by the bank. The gems encrusting their hulls were emitting flashes that reflected a growing fire in the Forest. A flaming Spear had arrived that had begun rushing from end to end of the Weal and back again slaking itself in a growing holocaust of fire.

It was no time to wonder *why* it had happened. He was on his way back to Arthur, thankful he could at least tell him the cause of it and was met by a rush of excited fae coming to see the fire.

White Wand's guardianship had already turned their terror into wonder.

'The White One says it is a mighty sign that Sunne and Mona sends to honour our King and Queen!' they cried to Redweird.

How well the magician knew it was because Stella had said it, they believed it and were running to gape and gasp at the awesome spectacle that was fast destroying the loveliness of their forest home. With their fear turning to cries of wonder and admiration at the scene, however, Redweird gave Stella full marks for quick thinking.

'This is no honour from on high,' said Arthur in a low voice, when the Weirdfolk's Wychy reached his side.

'My Liege, it is good that our People are not afraid, but better perhaps if you could ask Queen Gwen to direct them back here to the Circle of Rejoicing? The Wandle will soon be flooded, and there is urgent need to find the best way out of it with your counsellors.'

While the two Wands worked hard to distract the happy fae from anything but gleeful excitement, Arthur urged a simple plan on Amyas; Nemway; the Master, and Loy – Captain of the Queen's barge.

'Redweird tells me that this fire is astral as well as physical, so we cannot go through it,' he began. 'But let all the fae be evacuated via the Royal Barges straight away to the Mansion of the Gnomes where the ground is higher and, because of the surrounding barrenness will be unaffected by the fire. It will require several journeys, but unless someone else has a better idea …?'

'Sire, the Weird is long,' said Loy. 'It will be hard rowing against the current on our return for the next lot, and if the waters rise swiftly–'

'Let the Weirdfolk go first,' said Arthur, 'and let relays of gnomes, Mabyn and others share the rowing.'

'The journey needn't be tedious nor long,' said Redweird. 'If we all go to the southern tip of the Wandle, we can cross and re-cross quickly near the entrance to the Spinner.'

'The current there will be fierce in such a narrow channel,' objected Loy, 'but if the Master can lash a good strong cable between both banks and we use the barges as ferries–'

'No need,' cut in Amyas. 'Let us go to the point that your Black One suggests, and I will build a bridge that will span the river in no time.'

'Dear Amyas,' Redweird said. 'If you are thinking the Wands can rebuild their Crystal Bridge there – they can't. It's been destroyed.'

'Black One,' said Amyas with a rare smile. '*I* will build the bridge.' And whirled *Moldwarp* in his hand. 'What is one tree felled when all are done for?'

And that was how it was done.

It needed many blows. But at last, a bank-side spruce toppled and fell, making an accurate span across the Spinner and the brambles to the Wynn's steeper bank. Another tree was needed to bridge the Brook of Wynn also but no shortage of willing gnomes; mabyns and knights available to carry it forward.

Nemway went to rescue the horses from the Royal Stede. And, since both Wands had records and belongings to salvage from their Retreats, they put Wendy and Baddenham in charge of leading the Weirdfolk safely across the surging flood. Accolon came with the main body of knights and Kindred of the Grail with Nyzor bringing up the rear on his dray.

After Nyzor had deposited the contents of the dray safely in the Mansion, the Master of Gnomes worked with the Vintner to transport his vats and stills, and the two containers that held Dragga's roots.

White Wand did not leave via the felled trees. The royal thrones, the Oracle, together with the Wychies' possessions, and Nemway with Windfleet and Windflame were all loaded on the Barges in which Gwen and her household, and Arthur and Mildgyth with attendant gnomes would be the last to leave with their crews.

Wychies' Weird flowed like a river of molten fire beneath the rowers; a scintillating reflection of the sparks from the bursting trees high above them, but threatened danger from flaming branches that fell and bounced down Wandleside to plunge hissing into the muddy water at its foot.

Simmonds, at the tiller of the Queen's Barge, looked back and with eyes nearly as round as Smye's, called excitedly to Loy positioned behind the Queen, her Wychies, and Nemway:

'Captain, the waters are rushing in upon the Wandle. The three Weirds are fast becoming one …'

'Eyes for'ard, Helmsman,' Loy barked. 'We're heading too close to the bank. Look back again, and I'll fling you in the Weird myself–'

'Look, there's Dreadful,' cried Gareth from among Arthur's guard. He was pointing to the tops of the trees that flamed above Wandleside. But Loy and Simmonds dare not take their eyes from where they were going to see their dragon enjoying the time of its life.

*

Being a creature of fire, Dreadful was in his heaven, roaring and blasting away to his heart's content among the trees. Fortunately, by this time the astral element of the flames had dissolved itself leaving only the physical to which he was impervious; so that he gambolled blissfully among them for a long time. It was a fire bath never to be forgotten, the kind of heavenly experience which an aged dragon might tell his envious grandchildren about time and time again and still have them snorting to hear it re-told to them before they went to bed. Here he was lord and king with no magicians to command him do this; do that, or endearing little people to take advantage of his good nature. Here he could roar and flare away to his heart's content; rolling himself in fire-dust to send it flying with his wings in a glittering cascade that also rolled down the cliff's side and threatened to spread through the air to the barges.

'Wychies, pray bring that dragon under control!' Arthur said.

The over-intoxicated Dreadful could have found himself doused in the river, but was impelled away to Wychies' Lane to discover a more tangible enemy to fight. Mortals had invaded the forest!

And what an invading force it was; dismayed men from near and far were trying to bring the inferno under control. Villagers with sticks and scythes and pitchforks beat vainly at the flames. Dreadful blew himself up to his enormous green fighting stature and launched himself at them. But although he hurled himself against them one after another, they neither saw nor noticed. It was a great fight though, a mad fight that went on and on for more than an hour during which reinforcements arrived in blue and yellow suits wearing helmets and riding great red monsters that roared and smoked along the lane. These he attacked with a vengeance when they stopped and men ran hoses into the river to send huge jets of water into the fire, but to no avail.

He could not harm them and they could not harm him, so his assaults became more sporadic as it eventually dawned on him that mortals were off the menu. There was nothing for it but to turn back for his home in the forest. And this was when his take off run skidded to a halt before a brown-robed beggar in sandals, carrying a staff.

Whatever guise Myrddin might adopt, Dreadful always recognised his creator.

*

When Myrddin and Edric, with wife and babe, reached the Chapel they found Amyas still garrisoning the Kindred's underground Stronghold, waiting for the return of other knights who, like Edric, who had gone in search of family and friends to tell the good news of Arthur's coming and the invitation to his Kingdom. Some of those who had already returned, reported the word was spreading; but attitudes hardening. If Mortleroy had been able to draw Excalibur, it had to mean he was their rightful king. The very fact that he had been able to invoke the Spear of Lugh against Gwyn went to prove it. Some argued that that was nonsense, so confusion reigned.

Amyas, who looked impressed on seeing the Lord of the Grail, was astonished to learn who wore such mail and amazed that the wizard should want to leave it in the Chapel, said: 'Armour like that can't be left unworn at a time like this.'

'Amyas, I have to see Arthur. I've made the biggest and worst mistake anyone possibly could make, and I can't go armoured like this, nor in anything less than sack-cloth. All I have any legitimate right to as Merlyn's heir is his guise as a beggar – and to a certain command of magic.'

'You will find no one in the Chapel,' Amyas told him. 'Mildgyth returned with Arthur via the Underway I'm guarding here for the return of Arthur's knights. Do you want to leave it here …?'

*

If he hadn't heard Avellane's account for the Spear of Lugh, Myrddin would have wondered at the phenomenon of the weapon he found rushing to and fro across the forest like a wild thing. As it was, it told him that he hadn't been the prime target. It had been aimed at the Weirdfolk as a whole and he was an incidental on the way as one of them large enough to be noticed because he was attacking Gwyn! The Spear had taken him by surprise then but now he knew what it was and what to do, he raised his staff – and the Spear plunged down to bury itself head first into the ground. Again with his staff he then magnified the firemen's efforts and aided them further by calling on the Sage of All the Sages for rain – and received a deluge.

There was a slight difficulty persuading Dame Margaret onto Dreadful's back but, with her husband helping, it was managed.

Myrddin smiled to himself a little wryly at a memory it roused from what seemed an eon ago when he had first found himself in the forest entertaining the little people with his stories of Hellbane Harry 'So ... Dreadful set off through the howling storm, flying high above the tops of the trees, with the two familiars clinging perilously to the spikes on his spine. The thunder rolled in volleys of sound that rocked the valleys below–'

'But August, you said they were flying over trees ...'

CHAPTER 29

NEMESIS

The huge number that had gathered in the safety of the Gnomes' Mansion revealed it had a capacity far in excess of anything that anyone who wasn't a gnome had ever imagined. The Master had a whole complex of halls opened up to accommodate the different kins. His admiration for the way Ann and Redweird conjured some wonderful illusions to help soften the realities of underground living for beings designed to delight in life above it, knew no bounds. There was no escaping the fact, however, that the Desolation had struck and the Forest destroyed. Even if mortal hands were already relieving the flood by removing the blockage, the Weirdfolk and their next-of-kins could not go on living in the Mansion of the Gnomes for long. But Arthur knew that.

Gathered in the main hall, with the great table drawn to one side, he held court seated in full armour in the Master's gold chair. Mildgyth, in a white and silver robe; its sleeves and hem edged in tiny jewels of blue, green and red scattered here and there with shining jet, sat at his side on another. Together they welcomed a stream of radiant and happy newcomers who praised Arthur and thanked Mildgyth for their deliverance before being conducted by Redweird and Stella to their new living quarters.

'This is a temporary arrangement,' Arthur assured each new influx. 'The spirit of the mighty Manawydan's great ship of old, *Wave Sweeper* will come every High Moon to take all who wish to join with me in our Kingdom of the Blest.'

The willowy form of the Sage of all the Sages was also among those who came to kneel in fealty. But he requested a boon: 'Sire, allow your people the Denefolk to remain here as your eyes and your ears in this mortal world; to whisper on the wind, in grass and leaf to those still to come that they might know to where to wait and watch for *Wave Sweeper*'s return each Moon Day's fullness?'

'Ageless One, it is more than granted,' Arthur said. 'I am grateful, thank you.'

Then came one to whom Arthur rose, his expression relieved and thankful. Taking Mildgyth's hand to bring her to his side so that each held out their other hand in welcome, he cried: 'Myrddin! Myrddin! You are come!' And all heads turned to see the brown robed beggar who had just entered the Great Hall with two others, one holding a baby.

*

Myrddin stared dumbfounded. Where had Arthur ever learned his name? He had never used it except with Merlyn's humanoid appearance outside the forest.

As if reading his thought, the King said: 'I have Jack's memory of hearing you when you formed him. You told him who you were.'

Myrddin bowed his head, his shame enveloping him. 'Oh my Lord, my Liege,' he said brokenly, coming forward to sink on his knee. 'How can I even ask pardon? There is so much. How can I even begin? I was so besotted with my own cleverness—'

But Arthur stopped him; raised him up and said: 'It is enough that you know *now*. And know this also, that if it had not been for your provision, our people's freedom could not have been accomplished, nor would Jack have been restored fourfold in fuller measure than that which you took from him and truly goes on to live with us, even as you intended. Nothing is more needful now than that *you* should be our Great Wychy. Algaric has released the dragons. We are late'

'Now?' Myrddin said, blinking and holding his arms wide to look down at himself: 'Like this, Sire?'

'Yes, just like that,' the King said. 'Come.' Turning to Mildgyth, he kissed her, promising: 'We will be back, my love,' He beckoned Nemway. She rose with a sign to Osric, who had been sitting beside her, to accompany them.

Passing Edric and Margaret where they still stood in the door, Arthur said gravely: 'Welcome, both of you and Yathra to our Kingdom.' Adding with a smile at the Dame: 'It is especially good to see you again, my lady, safe and well with Yathra.'

Margaret, blushing with confusion, curtseyed wordlessly.

*

Jessant de Lys and his companions returning to the Kin's Stronghold in Cyngsfold with another haul of Mung clinging to them like grim death, found themselves one moment in brilliant sunshine, the next in utter blackness with the earth trembling and groaning beneath their horse's feet terrifying the frightened Mung even more.

'Now we're lost!' cried Jessant reaching out blindly to where he had seen Amyas and Omric waiting at the entrance. 'What is this?'

'But this is wonderful,' Amyas' awestruck tones came out of a seeming void. 'This is the way our ancient records say that the Black Dragon of our kind would announce his presence.'

'How can that be? Everyone knows the three Dragons are prisoners of Mortleroy–'

A disquieting rumble from beneath the earth cut him short, and out of the darkness over and around them there formed an even blacker head with huge shining eyes and open jaws pouring out fire above their heads.

The growling earth beneath them seemed to speak: 'Hail Mabyn of Mabyn. Hail Brethren of my ancient Kin. Behold the miracle that is Arthur.' And, as suddenly as the darkness had come, it was gone but flying far above them was an immensity of form that they knew to be the Black Dragon of the North.

*

'Look!' Gwyn cried stabbing his lance at the western sky. Everywhere had flushed blood red in colour, tinting the far off walls and tower of Glastonbury Tor. Even the trees around them seemed alight with the glow of an angry dawn. 'The very heavens pour out their gore in the presence of–!'

He was cut short by a stranger clothed from head to foot in a magician's robe of green. The stranger's staff swept up; the fiery light above and around gathered into a single entity of a immense dragon with wings of flame hovering in flight. 'Behold the liberated Great Dragon of your Kin, Gwyn ap Nudd!' he cried.

The King, exulting and his knights gaping upwards and trembling at the waiting vision which hung above them for a moment; watched as it slowly wheeled around the company of knights as if counting their numbers before it turned and flew away to the west leaving the tops of the trees glowing red in the reflection of its presence.

Gwyn looked back at the stranger; he was gone. 'To the Dragon! To the Dragon!' he cried. The call was taken up as knight after knight spurred his horse and swung away in the direction the dragon had taken with Gwyn at their head until they saw the Red Dragon of the West roar a tongue of fire in greeting towards its great brother of the North. And while they spoke, the Blue Dragon of the east appeared between them also giving praise to Arthur-come-again but speaking in the tongue of dragons, so that no one understood.

*

To mortal eyes St Michael's tower at the top of Glastonbury Tor is roofless. Its wide expanse of space, however, had been magically covered by Gwyn during his occupancy and was one of the reasons the place had been coveted by Mortleroy. Its unrivalled view of the surrounding countryside now gave him a ringside view of the gathering Dragons. The arena was here, the last battle had been called; he waited, also exultant, his grip tightening around Excalibur's hilt. *You old scoundrel! You've provided even better than you promised.* It seemed Algaric had released the Dragons without having to be asked, told or commanded!

In the west, dust, smoke and fire confirmed monsters and giant sized demons laying waste; settling old scores and raping a land that Mortleroy never knew existed until he had drawn Excalibur. The future held the prospect of having the Weirdfolk, too, at last in his dungeons – oh, the delight of it. He could hardly wait. He would soon be refilling the strange emptiness he had found in them. Then smiled. *Of course, Algaric had cleared them out ready to accommodate a whole host of new inmates.* His gaze searched the land again, around and out to the horizon: Now where was the *Green* Dragon ...?

It was something of a shock to turn and find Algaric clothed in a vivid green standing beside him with Nemway and Osric. 'Majesty, it is here,' he said. 'It cannot manifest in sunlight or moonlight; I will therefore command the Black.'

Mortleroy frowned. 'I thought you said–' he began.

Algaric's face contorted in an expression of tiredness and unreadable anguish. 'You wanted the Green Dragon,' he said flatly. 'It is here.'

*

Osric had been petrified when Nemway told him they were meeting with Algaric.

'I thought he had been poisoned,' he said, his knees threatening to give way under him.

She steadied him. 'What *is* this? she said searching his eyes in concern.

He closed them, biting his lips to stop himself bursting into tears. 'I thought–' he began, trying to choke back the bitterness of his disappointment.

'Osric, Osric,' she said, her voice tender as she drew him to her. 'Tell me what happened …' and, bit by bit, she coaxed it out of him. 'If it's any comfort,' she said when she had the whole story. 'Algaric protected you from being seen by Mortleroy that day and from then on has shut himself away from having anything more to do with the King. Arthur found him, and Algaric begged to be allowed to raise the Green Dragon in penance for all the wrong he has done.'

It was something to know but still not entirely encouraging when he found himself face to face with his childhood's nightmare. But Algaric did not even look at him.

How could anyone, least of all Arthur, trust him? Osric wondered, hearing the magician's reply to Mortleroy.

The usurper turned to Osric's companion. 'My Lady Nemway,' he said. 'It is good to see you.'

'Algaric and I are old friends,' she said sweetly.

Algaric touched Mortleroy's arm, regaining his attention and nodding across the huge stretch dwarfing them all, to the other side of the tower's roof. 'Arthur is challenging you to combat–'

'Arthur's dead!' Mortleroy spat the words.

'Apparently not,' Algaric said calmly. 'He tricked you–'

'Tricked!' Mortleroy stepped back staring about him; sounding furious as well as incredulous. 'I *slew* him with Excalibur!'

'Nevertheless …'

Osric had to shade his eyes against the setting sun to see the figure in silver armour standing over there with a beggar at his side.

'He can only be entirely destroyed by the Green Dragon, which is why Great Merlyn bound it. Stand ready to draw Excalibur when the Black settles over us. The Lady Nemway has the Silver Chain of Power which you may use to capture the Dragon again when it has destroyed him.' And so saying he went to the centre of the arena where he stood with bowed head.

At first, Osric couldn't see anything. Complete darkness had descended on them, then he became aware that where Algaric had been standing a phosphorescent green mist was coalescing, thickening and growing into the form of a great hydra, dividing itself into thick coils that grew until they towered above them – poised.

For what? Osric's instinctive alarm made him step back.

Mortleroy drew Excalibur as he had been instructed – and Dragga lunged; a thick mass of swirling coils and a sound like the hissing of a thousand pythons focussing straight for the sword's bright blade. Taken by surprise, Mortleroy slashed out. Lethal strokes split the virulent green mass like lightening yet only for a moment before it reformed with multiplied intensity; the vicious sentient heads spitting or gaping, as they darted, ducked, or feinted, while its tentacles increased their hold, wrapping themselves around Mortleroy's legs, his body – reaching for the sword.

Osric couldn't see Arthur through the solid blaze of green ferocity; so he glanced aside at Nemway instead. She stood with her eyes closed, her hands upraised – *as if sending the Dragon* against *Arthur!* was the thought that occurred to Osric. But no, the thick green phosphorescent tentacles still reached for Excalibur, each head shrieking with triumph as their tentacles tightened around their victim. When Osric, realising what she was doing and added his own imagination to hers, he saw Nemway's right hand suddenly close and, as it did so, one of the tentacles gripped Mortleroy's sword hand. It was trying to wrest the sword from him. With Nemway, Osric concentrated, adding what strength he had to hers. The sword came free. The pair of them together made the action of hurling it away from them towards Arthur. As the sword disappeared, so Mortleroy vanished under the solid green monster that collapsed in on him.

The Black Dragon flying up, revealed Arthur holding Excalibur and Myrddin coming to stab his staff into the suddenly shrinking mass of still virulent looking green. In great a voice, he cried: 'As Great Merlyn bound you, Dragga, so I, his heir, bind your last part, also – so be it!'

Nemway smiled at Osric. 'Now *that's* magic I could never do – which is what, I suppose, I so loved and admired about Merlyn.' She sighed as, much like a golfer picking up his tee before moving on, Myrddin bent and picked up something small and white that lay where the fury of Dragga had roared.

Of Mortleroy or Algaric, nothing remained and in the west, the Red Dragon advanced like a cleansing fire on the swarm of flying, hopping, crawling and jumping monstrosities that began to flee from its fiery breath, and to overcome the strangely formed and huge ogre-like demons that clawed at their throats and fell, choking beneath its onslaught. The Blue followed in its wake restoring peace and harmony to the land, breathing into it the healing powers of a strong and gentler breath …

*

Osric felt the contrast would need a lot of explanation before *he* understood the what and wherefore and how. 'I thought all the Dragons were good,' he said. They were back in the Gnome's Mansion where he stood frowning, trying to puzzle it out.

'Depends which side of the fence you're on,' Nemway said. 'They need to be in balance with each other. That's why Mortleroy never had the Green. Dragga is equal to the other three. Either *they're* manifest, or he is–'

'I know,' Osric interrupted, clicking his fingers. 'Like a black hole in a universe of light – or a white hole in a black universe. But all *four* were there to day – *and* Mortleroy had Excalibur!'

'So?' she said with a smile. 'What happened? Dragga was death to the Weirdfolk but their re-birth into mortal life. Mortleroy was Death. He wanted Dragga and Dragga wanted him – until he had Excalibur. That made a difference. Algaric made a pact with the remnant that was left of Dragga. Algaric to give himself to Dragga if Dragga gave him the opportunity of dealing with Mortleroy. Myrddin has now bound what was left of them. Does that make you feel any better about Algaric?'

'I suppose so,' he said slowly.

'There's something Algaric told Arthur about you, too – and why he encouraged you in the exercise of magic.'

As soon as Nemway said that, Osric knew what it was. He asked heavily: 'He was my father?'

She nodded, reaching out to touch his face. 'It's best you know,' she whispered.

Oh yes, he knew alright. *But, dear God, prevent me from ever mis-using the power I have already felt within me. Make me a healer of Your people, not a devourer.*

*

Myrddin found Arthur looking for him just as he was making his peace with Nemway.

'I confess to some harsh thoughts and words about you,' she said. 'I see now, though, that all you did was meant for good and I have to admire your single-mindedness. So I hope you'll forgive me, too ...?'

The wizard was quick to respond. 'Of course! I would have felt the same–'

'Myrddin,' Arthur drew him aside. 'I have spoken to Redweird, and he understands. I take it from the several guises you have made yourself that it wouldn't be impossible to appear as my Wychy in a black Weird?'

Slightly puzzled, he agreed it wouldn't be difficult.

'Then please do so, and then go and wait by the Brook of Wyn ...'

EPILOGUE

Gwyn judged himself to be the soul of fairness and had the grace to acknowledge when he was beaten. He had seen the Black Dragon enveloping the Tor's lonely tower – and that meant a manifestation of the Green. He had watched it rise and seen the Red and Blue cleanse and heal Tylwyth Teg of all its invaders – and all without his knights being slaughtered which he knew they would have been despite all that Avellane and Gaheris had tried to teach them.

In owl form he flew to Weir Forest. When he saw the devastation, he realised it had to be some celestial fireball to have caused such instant destruction. The vegetation contained no astral likenesses whatever, which meant no wraith could have survived the initial holocaust. He winged his way slowly southward, astonished by the sight of firs growing from the centre of a vast lake of water. Then, turning east over a cliff, he saw the first sign of life. Two tiny cloaked figures had suddenly appeared beneath him out of nowhere and there was no way he could possibly ignore them.

The two wiccies, who appeared relieved and delighted to see him, recognised his name immediately.

'I'm Ann,' one said eagerly. 'I heard your message via our white dove offering help, and guidance and a guard for Arthur and the Weirdfolk to a place of safety at Glastonbury ...'

Once again, Gwyn had to explain the mistake.

'Then you have no idea where our people might have gone?' Ann said with patent disappointment.

'Well, I'm on my way to find Arthur ...?' he offered.

'You are!' she said, plainly astonished. 'Is he not with his people, the Weirdfolk?'

'Apparently he works night and day seeking and rescuing lost fae, commissioning messengers, and sending them out to all parts of the land–'

'And soul by soul and silently, his shining bounds increase.'

Diana's unexpected interruption made Ann look at her askance: 'Pardon?' she said.

'Nothing,' Diana said with a smile. 'Just a line from a hymn we had at my father-in-law's funeral three weeks ago.' She looked at Gwyn. 'I would dearly like to know if my husband is alive.'

'I will fly you wherever you direct me.' Gwyn said, and morphed back into his owl shape which was large enough to carry the pair of them.

*

There was as yet no sign of ambulance or police car. Only the local constable's bicycle propped against the hedge, and the policeman himself slowly and ponderously helping the ashen faced driver, streaked with blood, from the car. Humphrey nodded at the other wreck.

'That rain last night – he must have skidded,' he said. Then, 'My wife, Officer ...?'

Diana touched the owl's head, laying her cheek alongside it. 'Thank you, dear King, it is enough,' she said quietly and Ann guessed she had no wish to witness her erstwhile husband's grief. Later she told Ann: 'I just needed to know if he *was* alive for the children's sake.'

Gwyn apparently knew nothing more than that Arthur was in the Forest of Weir. So Ann directed him to the tree she had seen lying across the Spinner. She was guessing by now that everyone had taken refuge in the Mansion of Gnomes.

Gwyn flew over the mound, landing outside its entrance, and changed back to himself.

'You two go on in,' Ann said. 'I've just seen something I need to investigate …'

It had been quite by chance that she had spotted the lone figure at the brook's edge. Gwyn seemed not to have noticed, nor Diana. It had so reminded her of another time long, long ago when she had first picked up the White Wand and gone running to meet August with it believing he needed it. He had stood on The Wandle then, waiting for her

Can I still walk on water …? Of course she could. Once a Wych, always a Wych. With a little smile, Ann crossed over the brook and ran lightly up to where he stood waiting on the other side; a tall, silent, unmoving figure. She began singing as she went:

Be thou my Lover, Wand;
Gladness is on me.
Joy's in my heart, Wand;
Bliss in the depths of me.

Gone is my loneliness;
Rapture is on me.
Come with thy wealing Wand;
Love now surrounds me.

Bless with thy healing, Wand;
Wyn me my Wand.

Throwing back his Weird, he met her crossing with open arms. 'Oh, my dearest Ann,' he said, 'It's you!'

'My dearest August,' she said. 'I love you. You have been waiting for me.'

'Ann, you are all I desire. But I haven't changed, my love. I'm still the same witless wizard that you never wanted to see again back then. For the life of me, I couldn't understand why Arthur wanted me to be here. I didn't know who or what I was waiting for. I never thought it could be you ...'

*

The Great Hall looked grey, bare and sombre without the jewelled tapestries that Ann remembered used to twinkle with movement in the flicker of its torch lit walls.

Arthur sat in the Master's chair, with Diana and Gwyn ap Gwyn alongside him, at the huge table around which Omric himself, with Amyas and a number of others were engaged in discussion.

All rose to their feet at Ann and Myrddin's entrance.

'There,' Arthur said to Gwyn. 'Does that answer your question? You have done us great service.'

To Ann's astonishment, Gwyn knelt, making the sign of the cross and bowing his head, to say: 'No more than my duty and my joy, my Liege.'

'I thought – I was given to understand that Gwyn Ap Gwyn–' Ann stopped, the words out before she realised what she was saying.

Gwyn smiled and finished for her: '–would *never* acknowledge Arthur as his sovereign Liege? And true enough that was so – of mortal Arthur. But Immortal Arthur is another kind of King who has saved us all.'

As he rose, Arthur gripped his hand as an equal. Wordless but with eyes alight, Gwyn left the hall.

When the two new arrivals were brought up to date with everything that had happened, Arthur said to Ann: 'Redweird and Stella will leave with the Weirdfolk. I have asked Myrddin to be our Wychy for the rest of our people. But there is something more I have not yet asked him. We have explained a need for a presence here to welcome and restore returning fae–'

Ann surprised herself by interrupting him. She wanted to save him from even having to request it. 'And you're going to ask me if I will be happy to stay with Myrddin to look after them?' she said, and looked aside at her erstwhile Partner, covering his hand with hers. 'We're not going to say no, are we?' she asked.

He shook his head. 'Of course not, Beloved.'

THE END

APPENDICES

Appendix 1:

The Holy Grail: The author originally intended to telescope two Relics into one because not everyone appears to know which is referred to by that broad description. The Grail is a dish supposedly used to catch the blood of Christ; The Chalice is often confused with it. The Grail according to legend is quite lost but not so, according to legend, the Chalice. The following quotation from a small Guide to Glastonbury makes this quite clear: 'CHALICE WELL, situated between the Tor and Chalice Hill is held by a trust in perpetuity and is open to the public by permission of the Trustees. The masonry is said to be pre-Roman and possibly of Druidic origin. Legend says that under the waters of the well, Joseph of Aramathea hid the Chalice of the Last Supper and that thereupon the waters gushed forth red. The first written record of the spring is that of Wm. Of Malmesbury who mentioned that the waters are sometimes blue and sometimes red. There is reason to believe that the first Christian baptism in Britain took place here and that around the Well the wattled huts of Christian anchorites assembled. The spring, which is considered one of the wonders of the world, is chalybeate and its output 25,000 gallons a day. The Well is 8 1/2 feet deep

Appendix 2

Lugh of the Long Hand was gifted with a powerful spear. It's head was tipped in blood, and blood sought blood, once thrown it never missed its mark. It blazed with golden light and when not in use it had to be cooled in cauldron of blood. When it's power would be used wisely, it is the light that drives away the darkness.